VENGEANCE BURNS HOT

by Rick E. George

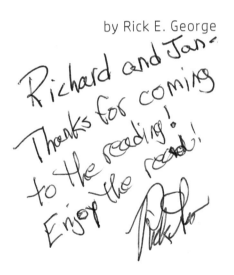

Richard and Jan-
Thanks for coming
to the reading!
Enjoy the read!
[illegible signature]

VENGEANCE BURNS HOT

First Edition Paperback.

Published by Unsolicited Press
www.unsolicitedpress.com

Cover Art: Kathryn Gerhardt
Editor: Saidah Kamaria

For information, contact the publisher at
info@unsolicitedpress.com

Unsolicited Press Books are distributed to the trade by Ingram.
Printed in the United States of America.
Library of Congress Control Number: 2019903407
ISBN: 978-1-947021-91-4

I am grateful for the advice and feedback I received during the writing of this novel, beginning with the members of the White Salmon Valley Library Writers Group, particularly Randi Bacon, Rob Roy Crowley, and Ashley Salisbury. Thanks also belong to Shannon Hassan of the Marsal Lyon Literary Agency and Saidah Kamaria of Unsolicited Press. Finally and most especially, I owe deep gratitude to my wife and chief encourager, April.

VENGEANCE BURNS HOT

by Rick E. George

Chapter One

Lewis

There. Almost hidden among the grapefruit—an old flip cover cell phone. Lewis darted his eyes back at Captain White, who was looking at the list in the grocery cart.

What a dumb place to leave a phone. Was it a plant? A trap?

Lewis backed up a step, reached behind him, probed where he'd seen the phone. He bumped a grapefruit loose, shifted his hand left—there it was. He grabbed it and watched the grapefruit roll toward the captain, bounce off the cart's back wheel. White and that stooge Bailey spun around, but by then Lewis had stuffed it in his back pocket, dropped his arms to his sides, casual, nothing to hide.

"Sorry, Sir," he offered, retrieving the grapefruit.

"Jesus, Lewis," said White. "Make yourself useful and go get eight bags of oranges."

"Yes, Sir." He returned the grapefruit to the stack, accidentally dislodged another one that took aim at White's foot.

"Does this look like a bowling alley?"

"No, Sir."

White picked it up, sent it flying back. Lewis caught it.

When White and Bailey turned toward the refrigerated greens, Lewis slid around the side of the grapefruit display and headed for the oranges. He'd been doing a bajillion pushups every damn day but eight bags of oranges still felt heavy, not like they'd feel to White, his arms thick as firewood, his chest like some comic book hero. Lewis wished he wasn't so damn skinny.

At least his beard matched theirs. Shaggy, springing out at their cheeks and down their chins enough to snag yellowjackets mid-flight. In a week or two—after they struck—the Patriots United Militia of America would all be clean-shaven.

Lewis would give anything not to be there when it happened.

Maybe, just maybe that cell phone would be the means. If he didn't get caught—and didn't get the hell beat out of him, or worse. He set the oranges on the floor, leaned down as though to tie a shoe, quickly transferred the phone to his right front pocket, where it wouldn't be as visible through the fabric.

If he connived some chance to make a call, if the damn phone even worked—to whom? Certainly not 9-1-1. Try telling some jaded dispatcher the long story that put him in this mess.

What's the nature of your emergency, Sir?

How about the loss of his soul? Marinated in anger, drilled to kill.

If he triggered a law enforcement response, many would die. He would likely die.

"Beg your pardon, Captain White," he said when he reached the other two. "I need to use the latrine."

"You can wait until we're done."

Of course. PUMA soldiers went nowhere alone.

"Yes, Sir."

If he couldn't try the cell phone here, he wouldn't be able to use it at all. Especially not at their compound, out of range in the canyons west of Ellensburg.

What if he turned and bolted from the store, sprinted who-knew-where until his guts burst, as long as it was away? But they'd catch him, they'd get the hell out before anyone with a badge could show up, and that would be the end. Not just an escape, but a permanent exit. Bye-bye, cruel world.

The phone was his only hope, although if some crazy-ass ring-tone suddenly blared out next to his crotch, he had no idea how he'd explain it to White. He'd have to hand it over.

They moved through the meats and canned goods. White's slate-gray eyes seemed aware of every direction. If someone lobbed a can of soup at them over the top of the aisle he'd not only see it, he'd catch it, leap above the top of the shelving, and put a dent in someone's skull. They picked up five-pound bags of rice, black beans, kidney beans, split peas, boxes of energy bars—and five bags of disposable razors. In the magazine section, a Rhino .357 pointed off the cover of *Guns and Ammo.* White tossed two of those plus a *Gun Digest* into Bailey's cart.

"For you and the other soldiers—you ought to be reading."

"Yes, Sir. Thank you, Sir."

It would be rotten to drag his father into this mess, but who else? His father knew about combat, always used his head, figured stuff out when everyone else panicked. Not that Lewis heard about any of it from his father. Other soldiers—U.S. Army Special Forces—talked up his father at reunions and parties.

At the register, White rang a little bell to summon the cashier. "Pick yourselves a candy bar."

Lewis put the closest one into Bailey's cart.

"Thank you, Sir."

White paid from a roll of cash.

"The latrine, Sir?"

"What the hell. We'll all go. Long ride back."

In the stall, Lewis grunted a couple of times, added a groan for extra effect, managed to loosen the bowels. Finally, White and Bailey left.

The cell phone was not locked. It did not have one of those tiny keypads. Knowing White would storm back any moment or send Bailey to do the same, Lewis fumbled with the number pad, cursed when he messed up and had to start again. They'd catch him for sure if he tried a voice call. He moved his fingers quickly, didn't bother spelling every word.

His father would get the idea. If he read it.

More likely he'd see the strange incoming phone number and delete the message and that would be that, all this trouble for nothing. Lewis took a breath, cleared his mind, began entering the numbers at the end of the message, the most important part for getting his ass away from the band of idiots he'd gotten himself mixed with.

The bathroom door swung open, banged against the wall.

"What the hell you doing, Kline? Camping out?"

Lewis swung the arm with the cell phone behind him.

Did White see it? A quarter turn and he'd be looking through the crack on the side of the stall door straight at Lewis in all his crap-posture glory. Lewis brought his other hand back, transferred the phone to it, gave a split second look at it down low next to the wall, enough to see and touch the "send" button, then dropped the phone into the toilet.

Like an idiot. He had fucking panicked. He hadn't finished the numbers. No one would find him, not his father, not anybody. Even if White left—which he showed no intention of doing—he couldn't risk the time it would take to retrieve the phone, and imagine if White saw him hunched over with his hand in the toilet as though to swish around his own shit. Funny, yeah.

On the return trip, White exited the freeway and parked the pickup close to a not yet open shopping mall. They sat on a bench in the sun outside the entry, then looked across the acreage of a nearly empty parking lot.

"That it?" asked Bailey.

"Just watch," said White.

Ten minutes later an armored truck entered the little lot in front of the bank, stopped parallel. The driver exited. From a distance they could see he carried a pouch.

"Soldier Kline, see how if you're standing on that island under the hedge maple you can see everything in front of the bank, the whole mall parking lot, to the trees on the south side?"

"Yes, Sir," said Lewis. Which direction could he go, when the time came? North instead of south, perhaps, get his ass in the Burger King at the street corner, mix with the crowd, duck into the bathroom before White came looking, shit, put on a cap and start flipping sausages.

"Soldier Kline, I want you to think of all the ways this mission can go bad," continued White. "What's one?"

"Both guards get out."

"They won't do that. It's not part of their protocol."

"So both guards get out."

White nodded his head.

"That's why you're the trailer, Kline. Make sure you game it."

Back on the freeway, an hour from the bank, over Snoqualmie Pass onto the east side of the Cascade Mountains,

White leaned across the front seat, removed an envelope from the glove compartment, and handed it to Lewis.

"Open that envelope and read what it says. Loud enough so Bailey can hear it, too."

It was addressed to the *Wenatchee World.* Inside, the letter had been typed on a typewriter, including words X'd out. Of course—no computers or electronics at the compound. The feds would find them.

For immediate release

Effective immediately the Patriots United Militia of America, otherwise known as the PUMAs, warn U.S. citizens against doing business with any bank larger than a small community or regional variety.

The PUMAs have declared multinational banking syndicates antithetical to the values of a free people. The days of international corporations controlling governmental agencies to repress citizens worldwide without consequences soon will come to an end. Action will be taken against an unnamed large bank as well as governmental enablers. Because the PUMAs respect innocent and uneducated citizens, we urge all people to withdraw their money from large banks and to cease all commerce with them. Do not be caught in the crossfire. The PUMAs also encourage so-called "elected" representatives to examine their consciences. Ask yourselves if your actions conform to the Constitution and the principles of the Declaration of Independence. Representatives who speak and act against the present tyranny of government will be spared, but those who serve as toadies for corporate and governmental domination will be subject to elimination. The PUMAs hereby warn citizens that it will be extremely dangerous to associate with tyrannous representatives.

Other freedom-loving militias—now is the time to act. Are you mere Keyboard Commandos or are you the real deal? Prove it.

"Wow, Captain White, that's awesome," said Bailey from the back seat. His beard was more brown than red, with a short blonde crew cut atop his head. "How long do you figure 'til it's a full-bore revolution?"

Lewis shook his head. Yeah, sure, tomorrow. Fucking numbskull.

"Hang on, Bailey," said White. "It took years of resistance and small actions before the original American Revolution began, and I expect some years to pass before we reach critical mass this time. That's why we must succeed. I expect us to inspire the local militias who've been waiting for their cue. We're the head of the hammer. Wake up, people! You've been anesthetized. Time to take back our democracy. You ready for that, soldiers?"

"Yes, Sir."

"How soon, sir?" asked Bailey.

"Soon. There's another one in there for the *Seattle Times* and another for the *Spokesman Review.*"

"I'll get them for you, Sir," offered Lewis, and before the captain could object, Lewis had pulled from the compartment a small stack—two letters and a warranty for tires that he put back. A smaller slip of paper fluttered to the floor and reflexively Lewis picked it up, his eyes unable to avoid a glance. A vehicle registration for Henry Baker.

So you're Henry Baker. Captain White Sir.

Whatever that meant. Or the truck belonged to Henry Baker. But White wouldn't be so stupid, driving someone else's truck.

Burning under the glare from White/Baker/whoever-the-hell-he-was, Lewis shoved the registration back in the glovebox.

"They can't say we didn't warn them," said Bailey, oblivious in the back.

"Exactly," agreed White, half-staring at Lewis, half-staring at the road.

"Sorry, Sir," said Lewis.

"I trust you two," said White. "That's why I bring you on these trips."

"Thank you, Sir."

"These hills are crawling with turkeys," he said. "Did you know, Soldier Kline, your dad and I bagged plenty of 'em? Did you know how highly we regarded him in Special Ops?"

"What?" Lewis felt as though the air had been knocked out of him.

"Oh, yes, soldier, believe it. I know your father, know him well. We wanted his helo. Taliban never hit it. He had a sense about the RPGs and the SAMs. We'd scorch through the air and all the sudden he'd drop us like a stone on some lip of land and we'd haul ass and off he'd go, night black as hell, no moon, gone like a phantom."

He caught his breath but felt queasy, dizzy. Was that why White had recruited him so heavily? It had been a year since he'd responded to a blog post White had written. Now none among them had any web presence, no cell phones, nothing. They did not exist.

"You're a talisman, Kline, a piece of your old man. Combat will do that to a man, make him superstitious. You'll find out soon enough."

Chapter Two

Ed

The glimmer of dawn and the *wheee-wheee* of a mountain chickadee woke Ed Kline, and another long dormant sense brought his lips to a smile—the scent and the heat of a woman and the sound of her deep contented sleep.

Nancy Avila, the Snoqualmie Hotshots fire crew superintendent, *in bed with him.*

How would she react if he disturbed her rest with a head stroke and then...well, a little more hanky-panky, eh? It had been seven years. Maybe she'd forgive him for being a little greedy.

She'd been lonely, too. Both their marriages—casualties of their addiction to fire. Sudden departures, absences of unknown duration. And, in his case, Ed reflected, his ex-wife could add his twenty-five years of service to Uncle Sam.

Facing away from him, Nancy breathed in a soft, languid rhythm—her skin a mocha latte, back and arms sinewy and strong, hair black and ruffled across the base of her neck. Although the gray strands hidden in the pale light might suggest a decline, Ed knew otherwise. She could outrun half the men and women she commanded and piston through a quick dozen pull-ups.

He'd be lucky to get his chin above the bar more than

twice. When she woke, she'd see more gray than black in his thinning hair. Nothing but a middle-aged helicopter pilot.

Next to the bed, a large pack of coyotes burst into song, a cacophony of baying and yipping.

The damn ringtone. This time of day, it had to be a dispatch. He and Nancy both rose to a sitting position and he caught a glimpse of her magnificent breasts before he turned away to lift the phone off the nightstand.

"Yeah?" he answered.

It was a dispatch, all right. Thirty minutes to get his ass to the base. The lightning last night—the real kind, not the he-she variety in his home—had ignited a high elevation fire. They'd give him the coordinates when he arrived.

"Of course you're gone and of course it's supposed to be our weekend," she said. "If it hadn't been you it would have been me."

She smiled, her lips unadorned and honest. The whites around her hazel eyes red from smoke and the diagonal scar above her right eye where a rock thunked her head on a fireline years ago reminded him why he allowed himself to fall for her. She understood. She lived the life, too.

"Box Ridge outside Alpine Lakes, so they're going to let us put it out," he said.

"Wonder if they'll call us in."

"We'll get it."

She kissed him on the lips.

Incredible—he could wear that kiss all day, and there would be more of them once the fire gods permitted another rendezvous. And where would that take place—his house or hers? Would they live apart for a while or could they start their lives together right now? But maybe that was too much too soon.

She rolled off the bed on the opposite side, strolled around the foot of it to the living room where she'd left her clothes. Ed walked to his dresser.

"What are we going to tell our crews?" she called.

A two-toned bell cut in before he could answer—doon doon! Doon doon!

"You getting a dispatch, too?" he asked.

"Not my phone."

"Not mine, either."

She leaned her head into the doorway.

"Ever get texts?" she asked.

"No, not really. Maybe it could be my phone."

He walked back to the nightstand. Sure enough, the screen indicated a text, and he pressed the icon.

Holy shit.

He gaped at the screen, his legs riveted to the floor.

"Text?" she called.

"Yeah."

He managed to lift a foot and sat in his underwear at the edge of the bed.

Lewis.

He scanned the message again.

bad thg I wk
i leve i die
cops evryI dies
help L 47033012

"Everything okay?" she called.

"Yeah."

Like hell. What else could the *L* be? Nine months he'd

heard nothing from Lewis, not since his son left a note with all that garbage about how everything was corrupt, shit jobs and shit wages, how he was going to defend himself. Sure, it scared the hell out of him and his mother, who received a similar note. Between the two of them, they contacted everyone they knew who knew Lewis. None of them had a clue about where he'd gone.

But Lewis had never been the kind to do anything off-the-charts crazy. At least that's what they told each other. Give him time. They'd hear from him.

Now this. What the hell could he do with a message like that?

He checked the phone number—a 405 area code, same as Snoqualmie Pass and most of east King County. What if it didn't come from Lewis?

Another number on the phone—current time—caught his attention. Since the dispatch, five minutes had elapsed.

He donned his clothes and his boots, rushed with the phone radiating in his pocket to the living room where Nancy sat fully dressed looking at his *Sports Illustrated.*

"So," she said. "Our crews?"

He strode to the front door and unzipped the large compartment of his fire pack. Freezer bag with food—nuts, figs, granola bars, red vine licorice—right where it was supposed to be.

"Sorry," he said. "Had to think."

"Cool-headed Kline? I don't think so."

"Sorry." He stood and leaned against the little space of wall between the door and an entertainment center. For a moment he felt like reaching over and grabbing from it a photograph of Lewis grinning with a big sockeye salmon nearly the length of his height, back when he was fifteen years old. Last night, Nancy noticed that photo and the one of his daughter. They already knew about each other's children—her sons both in college, Ed's daughter, Sarah, a driver for UPS. About Lewis, Ed had adopted vague language—*don't know what he's up to, haven't heard from him in a while*—and she had the decency not to pry.

"He looks happy," she'd said of the picture.

If he were alone right now, he'd hold that photo close and ask his son some questions.

"The text," he said. "It was weird."

"Might be phone spam."

If only, he thought. But he couldn't tell her.

Oh, hey, by the way, you know how at our age it's a package deal? Sounds like your boys'll have to support us in our old age. I just got a message from my son. He's about to get his ass killed.

She wouldn't say it out loud but she'd probably act it out. She'd flee the hell out of Ed's orbit. It would be easy to decide what they'd tell their crews about their relationship.

Nothing.

Because there'd be nothing, except more loneliness.

"Can we talk later about our crews?" he asked.

A quarter mile from his house he idled his pickup on the road, forested on both sides with Douglas fir and hemlock. An hour could go by before another vehicle approached.

If Lewis sent that message, he might be holding the phone this very moment, might have only this tiny aperture of time for communication. Ed retrieved the phone from his pocket, contemplated it a moment, then hit *send* to the originating number.

Six ringtones. Generic voicemail greeting, nothing personalized.

"Hello, this is Ed Kline..."

i leve i die.

Oh god. If Lewis couldn't leave without risking death, and then wherever he was someone found he had contacted his father...

Ed touched *stop*, repressed a whimper, repressed a shout.

His call could cause Lewis's death.

Thirty minutes later, Ed lifted his Sikorsky S-70A off the asphalt, with first-year helitack Captain Dale Everett at his side and a crew of eight in the back. Dubbed the Firehawk for firefighting purposes, most folks knew its wartime tag, the Black Hawk, the same bird Ed had piloted during the Gulf War, the Balkans, and the first year in Afghanistan before he retired. Discarding both monikers, Ed called her "Bessie." Bessie always brought them home.

Long and lean with a blunt nose and a single main rotor, Bessie danced through the skies dressed in a white underbelly with a thin red stripe. She covered her upper body in cobalt blue, quite the showoff compared to her military cousins garbed army green. Inside, she wasn't much to look at—a standard cockpit with pilot seats on both sides and a bare cabin holding a row of back-to-back jump seats. Oh, but did she know how to move. She could juke and jive, pirouette, climb 20,000 feet, sprint just shy of 200 knots. She could trot, piaffe, rein back, and counter canter, but put her in a different arena, and she'd run a damn good barrel race.

i leve i die

He'd never flown with that thought in his head and he damn well needed to push it out, son or no son, because he had nine souls on board who counted on him to protect their lives. He'd done it before, flown brain-clear despite the horror of dead soldiers or worse in back of his helo, soldiers with legs blown off, with portions of their skulls shot out, their cries and groans blotted by his headset, by the scream of the rotors. Fly bee-line. Fly herky-jerky. Do the hokey-pokey. Whatever it took to get the soldiers back to base.

But none of them had been his own kid.

The phone burned like he'd picked up a hot rock and shoved it in his pocket.

Past Keechelus Ridge, Ed and Everett surveyed the boiling smoke of their adversary, leaning its billows west in twelve-knot winds. They raced toward the gray shroud, cleared Box Ridge, beheld fire two-thirds up the Mineral Creek drainage. Red-orange flames gobbled at a crowd of avalanche brush, shot off the crowns of scattered firs and hemlocks, all of it steep terrain. Upslope, the green tangle thinned until it surrendered to scree, like piles of slate suspended mid-slide, splinters from the mountain's jagged spine.

bad thg I wk

No. Not yet. First, he had a fire to put out.

It took the crew half a minute to disembark, grab their tools, scramble to the front of the helo where Ed could see them. Back in the air, he moved up to the fire, descended along its heel to the creek, scanned for hazards such as wires or rope from long-ago logging operations. Against the smoke, Bessie seemed small as a grasshopper, Ed a mere speck behind its eyes. Larger fires reduced Bessie to a gnat, Ed to a molecule.

He rotated a half-turn to start a flight to Kachess Lake for water, then drew back his head in surprise. Human figures in yellow fire-resistant shirts were cutting indirect line through thick brush *upslope from the fire.*

What the hell was Everett thinking?

He took a deep breath, exhaled some of the tension, told himself to grab the water ASAP. At the lake minutes later, he quietly thanked the ground rangers when he saw they'd evacuated fishermen and boaters. Lowering the Bambi bucket, he did a half-circle before approaching the surface, watching the bucket shadow and the bucket itself converge until it dipped into water. Just as he lifted with 530 gallons of what he liked to call a douching solution, Everett radioed.

"Need you here. Little flare-up."

The exact scenario he feared. He pictured a recent incident report they'd studied—a circle on a map to show where the body had been found.

Back at the fire, the crew clustered at the end of a pathway Carrera continued to cut. They were forty yards in the green, too close to a miniature inferno shooting straight up, with no wind to bend the flames and smoke away from them. It brought to mind what that crew on the incident report must have experienced—the sudden assault of superheated air they'd swallowed when the wind stilled, the jolt of fear, no escape back up the way they came, the brush too damn thick and the footing too treacherous to back away.

Below the helicopter, it didn't look good. Bessie could handle one Roman candle tree, but a half-dozen of them, flames fifty feet above the tops and the heat rocketing even higher? And what would 530 gallons be—a shot glass against a bonfire?

"C'mon, old girl," he cajoled Bessie. He coaxed her where she should never be, and he eased her forward while the water gushed down. When the bucket emptied, he hauled ass away, pivoted, saw that he'd nearly doused the whole shebang, at least that little cluster of trees. The flames should have revived and shot back toward the sky, but they didn't, and the yellow-shirted figures counterattacked, rushing the flames reduced to ground level. Crewmen managed to pry loose enough dirt from the rocky tangle of brush to fling it at the base of the flames and calm them.

"Under control," Everett reported, his voice panting from the exertion.

Yeah, right.

"Copy," said Ed. "Back in fifteen with another drop."

An hour before sundown, Ed ferried the helitack crew back to base but kept three to help transport a ten-person overnight mop-up squad back to the now-contained fire. After setting Bessie down for the last time halfway through dusk, Ed found Everett and the others around a work table inside the warehouse, sharpening their chipped tools.

“Got a second, Everett?” Ed called. Everett left his shovel secured in a vise and they walked outside past the helicopter, where his mechanic, Ted Zweigert, already had illumined portable lighting for inspection and maintenance. They stopped at a chain link fence separating them from the dark, wooded wall of Granite Mountain.

“I’ll get right to the point,” Ed began, his voice tight. “You put your crew in danger.”

In the near night, Everett met Ed’s gaze without a flinch or a flicker.

"How so?"

“We just got done studying the Tuolumne Fire. How long did it take the fire to overrun them when the wind shifted?”

“Not the same scenario. Different fuels. We know the winds around here. They don’t shift that time of day.”

“You didn’t answer my question. How long did it take for the fire to overrun them?”

“It’s a moot question.”

“I’m guessing you designated the fireline as the escape route. How fast do you think your crew would have made it up that steep shit, slipping on a rock or two, 'til they got to the scree? Faster than the flames?"

Everett kicked at the ground.

"Shit, Ed, will you listen? You know the wind patterns around here. If anything, it gets stronger and blows the fire away from us. When it eased off, we backed away. Simple."

"Hold on and listen to yourself. Surprise. The wind dies and all the sudden you're in a hot stove. Suppose Carrera's saw quit. Then what?"

Everett shook his head silently, gave a look that said he saw no profit in continuing the debate. "Nobody was in any danger. All I asked was for you to cool it down."

"What did you gain by anchoring upslope?"

"We had to hotline the heel. Might as well do it on the way down to the creek because that's where we had to go anyway."

"In other words, to save time."

"The conditions were safe. You're overreacting."

"And you're being defensive. Think about it. You made that decision to save time."

Everett sighed. "All right, Ed. If it'll make you happy, I'll think about it."

"You damn well better. The stakes are high, buddy."

Ed extended his hand.

"They told me about you," said Everett, accepting the handshake. "I was starting to think what they said was overblown."

"I've heard it—Cautious Kline and worse. That's fine with me. I don't care how it makes you feel—I *will* be looking over your shoulder."

They began walking back to the warehouse.

"Tell you what, *Cautious Kline*. You do that. Just keep on

doing that."

Ed nodded his head. Maybe Everett would become a competent leader after all.

But Ed drove the point home. "Thirty seconds," he said. "That's all they had, and for one of them, it wasn't enough."

Seated in his pickup, still on base, Ed hesitated. He'd agreed to call Nancy, and he'd bet five dollars she'd want him to see her house this time. But how could he bliss away what was left of the night when, like the prodigal son, Lewis had come home with a plea for help in the guise of that cryptic text?

He could spend time with Nancy, sneak out, stare at the message, pray for an epiphany. He'd never sleep, not with his son facing...death? Nancy would notice the vacant space next to her, and how would he explain it?

But he'd made her no promises beyond the phone call. He could do that, then pace the paths around his own home in the brooding woods, mutter, curse, throw objects, think, think, figure out some kind of plan. And then act. That was the most important part.

He owed it to his son—growing up with a dad who made grand cameo appearances and then, boom, gone, see you in eight months, see you in a year. Something had happened that last deployment, fifteen months. When he came back, the mirror in Lewis's eyes had morphed Ed from hero to intruder. Lewis had ventured into teen-dom. It was to be expected, but…

Ed started the truck, established the end-point coordinates—home. He'd call Nancy. He had to be back at base by 4:30 a.m. so they could retrieve the mop-up crew, replace them with the helitackers if the ground still nurtured smokes. She'd understand, and they could have their rendezvous the next night.

She'd never know he'd never slept.

Chapter Three

Lewis

Lewis sat in the middle of the classroom, same place as always, a dozen PUMAs around him and Captains Green, White, and Red sitting facing them from the front. Like the other soldiers, he was supposed to be copying the daily quote Green had written, but he found his fingers pressing the pencil so tightly that he might squeeze the lead out.

Because next to the quote the daily alert code announced *RED.*

It was too late in the morning to get across the mountains to the bank and for the other PUMA squad, Green Team, to do whatever secret deed they were training to do. So, what did it mean? Tomorrow? He thought he had a week. It would be just like the captains to spring it on them earlier. No way would his dad have time…

What the hell was he thinking?

He'd fucked up the message anyway—didn't get all the numbers down before he panicked and flushed the phone and whatever chance he had of rescue down the toilet. But what if his dad figured it out?

Don't bring the cops, no big show of force, just sneak in on your own, dear old dad, and snatch me away from these maniacs. Sure. Exactly how?

The PUMAs would kill him. He pictured Captain White checking out the dead man's wallet, finding the name *Edward Kline,* glaring at him—Lewis Kline.

Explain this, Soldier Kline.

Maybe his dad would bring along some backup. Showdown time, like what happened to certain other militia idiots around the good ol' U. S. of A. Except the PUMAs had the firepower and the tactics to kill a lot of people. And they were crazy enough to do it.

For the millionth time, Lewis wondered how he'd been stupid enough to get mixed up with these goons. And now he might have dragged his father into it. His dad would know the *L* meant Lewis. He'd go crazy trying to find his son. Even if he figured it out—and he would—it would be hard to find them. The PUMAs occupied a camouflaged dot on a line of what, 250 miles?

Don't find me, Dad. Don't even look.

"Writer's cramp, Soldier Kline? I've got some chin-ups to cure it."

Next to his classroom desk at the front, Captain Green stood tall, his white beard like the hairs on a corn husk. He aimed his brown eyes in their deep sockets directly at Lewis.

"Sorry, Captain Green, Sir."

Holding the pencil between his thumb and hand, he flexed his four fingers several times and finished copying the quote.

"Cherish nothing and no one. Only then will you be free to follow the path of a warrior."

Just so he wouldn't look like some damn disciple staring at the captains and panting to hear the daily wisdom, he scanned the room. Men wearing identical button-down khaki shirts over white tee-shirts, army green cotton canvas trousers, spit-shined black combat boots, beards, haircuts performed a week ago by Doyle, who'd drawn the lowest card after a long day of labor. On plywood walls more warrior quotes plus topo maps and highway maps. A collage of photos of them training, a group photo two months old. Through the doorway across the hall a barracks devoid of dust and debris.

They had already done thirty minutes of exercise, followed by a five-mile run, and although they'd taken showers the night before, the scent of sweat tinged the room still baking from yesterday's heat. They had performed their morning house chores, too, and eaten and cleaned after breakfast.

Green, who had sat down after reprimanding Lewis, rose again and pointed to the words on the whiteboard. Standing on the side of the room, Hernandez raised the camera, its red light indicating "record."

"How's that quote apply to us, gentlemen?" he asked in a high-pitched voice. "Be prepared to answer in twenty seconds."

You're trying to empty us. But Lewis knew he'd better have a different answer than that.

"Soldier Nelson," Green called after time had ticked by.

Nelson stood. "Captain Green, Sir, we have surrendered our old lives. We have given ourselves to a just cause."

"Thank you, Soldier Nelson. Soldier Doyle."

Nelson sat and Doyle rose.

"Captain Green, Sir, we have no contacts beyond our brothers in this room. We are the head of the hammer."

"Thank you, Soldier Doyle. Captain White, you have the floor."

Lewis repressed a sigh. It was time for another "PUMA Profile"—this time Soldier Beckham joined the captains at the front. White paced back and forth, wheeled a sudden quarter turn, stared them all down one man at a time like the glory of God almighty, and then wielded his preacher's voice.

"When I think of Soldier Beckham—how, like all of you, he played the game, was honest, hard-working—and the big two-ton shaft he received for his troubles, it burns my heart with anger, shapes my hands into fists.

"Beckham did well in high school, went to college, went to work for a little lumber mill, was a loyal employee, missed only three days of work in twelve years and then boom! The mill goes bust. He and his wife and their girl had a house, couldn't make the mortgage. The banks repossessed it, and the next thing you know, they're living with his in-laws at their house and not his own. Twelve years of work—for nothing, worse than nothing, because now he had a bad credit rating. The stress robbed him of his wife, robbed him of his daughter, and Beckham found himself alone."

Lewis tuned out the rest of the speech, recalled how two weeks ago he'd stood at the front, facing men who'd taken up arms and prepared to kill. White painted him as the college-kid-with-no-prospects, thanks to politicians in cahoots with multinational corporations. Lewis knew he was a symptom of something bad and maybe White diagnosed the cause.

But Lewis no longer endorsed the cure.

Later, after a stop at the armory, Lewis and the rest of Red Squad stood in an arc at the shaded edge of a Ponderosa Pine forest, squinting at Captain Red, who stood in a clearing with the sun behind him. On the west edge, a false building front with windows and a door. In front of it, an old white Plymouth Voyager.

"Variation B, Soldier Wilhelmson—what is it?" A lump of Red Man chew in the left cheek made Red's face appear lopsided. His light brown beard hung several inches below the chin, pointy and uneven, like a torn rag.

"Law enforcement...Captain Red, Sir...public or private, or fire or paramedic personnel visible within the area, including the mall parking lot."

"Correct. The response?"

"Abort. Sir."

"How?" Red spat a stream of tobacco juice.

"By calling *my wheel's loose,* Sir. Or, if it's Soldier Kline, he'll say *your wheel's loose.*"

"Correct. Be vigilant. Stupidity will get us into a mess, but it won't get us out. Where we're goin', Captain White and I have studied. That time of mornin' you most likely won't have any loose wheels, but you must assume Variation B to be present until you're certain it is not."

"Variation C, Soldier Ferguson—what is it?"

"Captain Red, Sir, guards are down, a man steps out of the bank."

"Correct. Our response?"

"Elimination, Sir."

"Correct, regrettably correct. Why?"

"Could be a plainclothes officer. We cannot take a chance."

"Correct. Reds, remember that Captain White has taken steps to warn people away from multi-national banks. Everyone in that building should know exactly who they're givin' their money to. They've been told it's risky to be doing business with that kinda outfit. Now we understand most folks won't pay no attention to the warning, 'cause nothin's happened yet. That'll change. But most folks have enough sense to stay inside if they hear gunfire. Someone steppin' out into it...that's someone who's either a threat or hopelessly stupid. Chances of Variation C are less than twenty percent. However, we'll game that scenario first."

"Now Soldier Kline, I never thought I'd see so many variations by the guard in the cab. I don't know what you're gonna cook up today, but you keep challenging us. Red Squad, assume your positions." He spat again.

How about the variation where I just walk the hell out of here? Good-bye, loony bin. But then—hello, electronic surveillance perimeter. That was a problem—and it would doom his father, too, if he ever found them.

After lunch, the same routine—The World according to Captain White.

"The federalistas are selling you out with illegal treaties. When the fat boys holler jump, they jump, and when they say crap on your workers they assume the squatting position in due haste, right over the United States Constitution, the Declaration of Independence, the words of our Founding Fathers.

"What kind of government does that to its own people?" White raised his voice. "That's no damn democracy! It makes my blood boil. Someone has got to stand for those 10,000 workers down in Oregon and the thousands more in our own state. Who will stand for them?"

"Pumas!" the men called in well-rehearsed unison. Lewis mouthed the word but gave it no voice.

"Someone's got to stand for the millions whose factories have been shuttered, whose farms have been swallowed. Who will stand for them?"

"Pumas!"

Blah blah blah.

"Soldier Lewis, I asked you a question." Captain White and everyone else in the room was staring at him.

"Beg pardon, Sir. Could you repeat the question?" Damn—White noticed everything.

"I can, soldier, but I don't see why I should. I'll come back to you. Be ready when I do. Soldier Marquez, what have we learned in regard to these treaties that our false representatives have used to cheapen our lives?"

"Sir, only local citizens have the right to establish or agree to treaties or laws that directly affect them."

"A basic truth, Soldier Marquez. And now Soldier Kline, a chance to redeem yourself. What is the legal definition of local?"

"Sir, an area not to exceed fifty square miles."

"Indeed, Soldier Kline." White took several pensive steps toward the left side of the room, then stopped and spoke in a disappointed voice.

"Once again, the federalistas exceeded their authority. And the states went along with it, and the counties, and even if Soldier Beckham's community didn't agree, even if they were most definitely and most profoundly affected, they...did...not...have...a...voice.

"Soldiers, our forefathers had the courage to call out despotism. That's what they did in the Declaration of Independence. 'Governments long established should not be changed for light and transient causes, but when a long train of abuses and usurpations evinces a design to reduce their citizens to absolute despotism, it is the right of the citizens, indeed, it is their duty, to *throw off* such a government and to provide *new guards* for their future security.' I ask you all, who will stand today, though the cost be dear as life itself, to throw off such a government?"

"Pumas!"

Chapter Four

Ed

Sitting in one of the living room rockers, angled slightly away from the bookshelf where both Lewis and his daughter, Sarah, smiled from their photos, he retrieved the text.

bad thg I wk

i leve i die

cops evryI dies

help L 47033012

He'd already called back and like a fool ID'd himself. Maybe something bad had happened already, thanks to his idiocy. He'd better think it through, all the permutations of every possible decision.

He couldn't see any hidden codes in the message's wording, and besides, they hadn't messed around with codes since Lewis's Boy Scout days. The numbers had to mean something. But why would Lewis make them some kind of code when he was already writing in plain words?

If he could find out who owned the phone, then he could Google the name.

Moving to the desk in his bedroom, Ed opened his laptop, searched and learned, as he expected, no simple way existed to identify cell phone owners. Certain companies claimed they could sleuth it for a fee, most likely a scam. He entered the phone number itself as a search item, found the number was associated with Issaquah, population 34,000, that it was issued by US Cellular.

With all the privacy concerns flapping around the Patriot Act, if he did go to the police, they'd probably need a search warrant to get the phone company to cough up a name.

cops everyI dies

So suppose he went to the police, someone agreed the message was threatening enough to request a subpoena, and they queried the phone company. Would Ed have triggered a little wave that ultimately tickled the chin of a depraved badass who'd implement *everyI dies,* including Lewis?

47033012

Too many numbers for a zip code, not enough for a phone number. Suppose it was a code, such as substituting numbers for letters? *D...G...zero? 47 or 70?* No, they weren't letters. He did a web search, *8-digit numbers,* found case numbers for clinical trials, phone numbers in India, speculations about telemarketers or scammers, number games and mathematics sites. He tried a web search using the actual number, found links to chemistry, bio-technology, somebody's Flickr photo, a French Air Show, something about soybeans. The internet was not going to help.

Back to the phone number, even if he *did* take a chance with one of those internet ID companies, and even if doing so yielded a name he could Google, would he have enough information to know what to do next?

Although he'd not smoked in more than seven years, not since the Army days, he wished he had a cigarette. He could feel it in his hands. He'd tap it on the desk, roll it back and forth with his thumb and fingers, light it, draw in the tobacco, feel his nerves loosen.

He paid the twenty bucks to get the kind of report that supposedly provided not only names but also bankruptcies, criminal records, properties, work information, neighbors, hell maybe they'd even tell him when the owner had lost his/her virginity, and with whom.

The name turned out to be Becky Sterling, 59 years old, living in Sammamish, just down the freeway from Issaquah. No criminal record, no bankruptcies or judgments, her place of work, ironically, the phone company. It sure didn't sound like Lewis, but then again, he couldn't see a woman with that kind of profile sending that kind of text, either.

Calling her landline right then and there would be rude with the hour just shy of midnight, but *i leve i die* granted permission to forego social niceties. An answering machine greeted him, this time at least with a name, Bill and Becky, please leave a message.

"Um, hi, my name is...I'm calling because I received a text message from a cell phone in your name. If you're trying to reach me I want to reply, but if it's...well, my name is Ed, and please feel welcome...no please *do* call me so I'll know if it's...well, just to put my mind at ease."

Hell, he never knew what to say even if it was a buddy's voice mail. He hoped he hadn't put Lewis in danger. While he sat listening to an owl hoot outside his window, he gazed at the phone, wondering if it had become an instrument to harm Lewis, and then it rang.

"This is Bill Sterling, Becky's husband." It was an older-sounding voice, hard-edged.

"Oh, yes, I just called you."

"Becky's phone was stolen this morning. She left it in a grocery store. Who sent the text?"

"I don't know. There wasn't a name."

"You're not trying to protect someone, are you? Because

we can find out."

"How can you find out? Because that's what I'd like to find out."

"I...oh, hell. You said there was no name?"

"That's right. No name. I've been trying to find out."

"When did you get it?"

"This morning."

"Had to be, because we cancelled that phone this afternoon."

"Can you track it? Find its location?"

"You sure seem interested for someone who doesn't know us and supposedly doesn't know who sent the text."

"It was...a disturbing message."

"How so?"

"I can't say."

"Well, no, to answer your question. We can't track it. It wasn't one of those fancy phones. Listen, it's late. Obviously, we can't help you. We don't know who sent the message and wherever it is, the phone's useless now."

"Yeah, yeah, you're right. Sorry to bother you. Goodbye."

At least that answered one question. Calling the owner of the phone had not endangered Lewis.

Stolen. Lewis had his issues, but thievery? Never. One time, in a shopping center parking lot, Lewis found a small tool kit and insisted the whole family bring it to the service desk. At a parent conference his eighth-grade year, the history teacher told how Lewis had brought him a dollar he'd found on the floor between classes. He pictured Lewis at the conference, looking away with embarrassment, his curled brown hair sticking out a hundred places and little pimples dotting his jawline.

Lewis never strategized about values. If a bully picked on someone, he'd react, even if it meant getting his own ass kicked. That happened twice his freshman year in high school. Ed hadn't been there, because he'd been dashing Special Ops in and out of ravines, grill-hot summer, ice-pond winter.

If he had been home then, would any of this be happening now?

He opened a drawer from the desk, withdrew a letter, Lewis's last known communication, almost verbatim what he'd written his mother.

I'm sorry, Dad, but I can't be part of this corruption. They're taking all the money, leaving shit jobs and shit wages. Taking away the only way we have to defend ourselves. Distracting us with false enemies. I'm going to resist, and I hope you'll understand. You're a hero, but the country you fought for doesn't exist. It's nothing but a syndicate of bankers and CEO's and government stooges. Don't know when you'll hear from me again. I love you. Lewis.

Before that October letter, it had been April, more than 14 months ago, since he'd seen Lewis, a Dad-Son trip fishing California's drought-drained Whiskeytown Lake on a rented boat, the third straight year they'd connected there. Guess they could call it a ritual now, Ed had said, a pre-fire season ritual.

Just by way of small-talk, the old Lewis would have said something like "guess so," but the new Lewis didn't. Almost a year after he'd earned his Range Management degree, Lewis lived with his mother and clerked at a big sporting goods store. "Bait and bullets," Lewis called it, disappointment in his voice.

They argued. You carry a gun? Lewis wanted to know, and Ed said not since the Army, where he'd seen enough guns and the outcomes of guns to last a lifetime.

"Everybody needs a gun," Lewis said.

"And why's that?" He quashed the impulse to joke.

For one, said Lewis, the good guys needed firepower

because so many crazies already had it. For two, he said, the government doesn't want us owning guns and that's reason enough right there to have one, and he quoted something that supposedly George Washington said on the same topic. They went back and forth on the wisdom of arming every soul, on the menace to liberty the government represented, and then they decided the best thing to do would be to just fish and drop the whole subject.

They'd talked by phone several times during last year's fire season, both of them polite enough to avoid contention, and then at the end of the season, the letter came and Lewis was gone. Until now, maybe, if the text came from him.

He bolted from the desk, strode through the living room. Shame prevented him from glancing at the photo of Lewis and his salmon. He stepped out the front door, stood on the little porch in a chorus of crickets and tree frogs in a theater of cool dark air.

Why hadn't he listened? All that gun talk. The evil government.

He'd offered a token rebuttal, opted for temporary harmony, fled to his precious Bessie. He abandoned Lewis to stew in his...what was it?

Anger. Like a lover betrayed, his son was raging.

Ed had made the same calculation he had always made—facing fires and bullets was less complicated than fixing family.

But no—that was too harsh.

Sorry, Ed addressed all the men and women who'd ever served, spoke the words aloud toward the night forest across the road. *This one's on me. It's not about you.*

After midnight, Ed pretended to himself he'd sleep a few hours until 3:30 so he'd get to the base on time. *He's asking you for help,* he repeatedly reminded himself in the room lit only by the red numbers of an old clock-radio and a tiny blue bulb on his computer. How would he answer that call? What could he do that he hadn't done? Like emergency flashers, the text words and number pulsated in his brain, but there was nothing, nothing at all to answer the challenge.

He must have fallen asleep, because he remembered seeing 2:17 a.m. on the clock and now here it was playing classic rock, the time 3:34, so already four minutes had gone by and he needed to get his ass to the base.

Pings.

Maybe he'd dreamed it in that short hour because now he remembered reading about an old couple marooned in a car on some snowbound road they should never have taken four or five years ago. A family member noticed their absence, and authorities got permission to ping the cell phone. That's how they found them, frozen and dead. They could ping the phone, even if it wasn't a fancy one, but at the moment Ed didn't have time to set in motion that kind of search. He had to convince himself he was wide awake, one hour of sleep had been enough, a con game he'd played on his body frequently, although that same body, now that it had seen more than five decades, was apt to call the ruse bullshit and then they'd duke it out, his will versus his body.

He could not permit himself to strategize the tracking of pings because now, especially without sleep—no, he'd had an hour and it was enough—his mind would drift and he'd be picturing cell phones or the old frozen couple when he needed to watch where he was flying Bessie. The pings would still be pinging when his shift ended, and he could take a little nap to refresh his brain, but no, he wouldn't need a nap, he was fine. He was wide awake.

Despite the overnight mop up crew's claim to have extinguished every spark, Ed flew the helitack crew back to what they now called the Box Fire. From the air it looked like a black gash amid miles of mountains garbed green with brush and timber and topped with gray-scale scree. Puffs of ash lifted with the breeze. Two wispy vines of gray suggested spots the mop up crew had missed. Ed and Bessie waited three hours on a rocky flat thirty yards wide while the helitackers systematically combed the area, squeezing through burned and unburned brush, snuffing sparsely spread cinders.

Three hours while his son's predicament screamed inside his head. A hundred eighty minutes for implications to churn in his stomach. Should he share the text with his ex? Why alarm her when it might be nothing? What if someone else wrote it and misdialed? If Lewis ended up dead, would they ever know about it?

What kind of hell-shit group had he gotten mixed up with?

With so little time left of their weekend, after the mop up inspection, most of the crew opted to stay on base and retrieve lost hours of sleep. Equipped with a cup of strong coffee, Ed went straight for his computer when he reached his house. Cell phone companies, he learned, would ping a phone's location, but only with permission by the cell phone's owner.

What the hell, he thought. So what if he pissed off a certain Mr. Sterling from Sammamish?

Mrs. Sterling answered the phone.

"Wait a minute," she said. Then Mr. Sterling came on the line.

"Mr. Sterling, there might be a way we can find your…"

"Never mind. It's found."

"Really?"

"Store called this morning. Turns out their toilet was

clogged. They had a plumber over. Turns out it was the phone clogging it. I told 'em thanks but they can keep it."

"I see."

"Whoever took it, first he crapped on you with whatever that message said, and then he crapped on the phone. What's to worry about? Let it go."

"Yeah, thanks."

Ed lay back on his bed, one closed eyelid from sleep, then sat abruptly. The store. Wouldn't it have video surveillance? He redialed Mr. Sterling.

"Sorry, Mr. Sterling, but…"

"Enough already! Case closed!"

"Don't hang up. One last question. The name of the store."

"Red Apple. Good-bye, Mr. Kline."

Yes, the store manager said they did have videotape. But no, he wasn't going to show it to Ed, not for a cell phone that the footage probably wouldn't capture anyway. And no, he wasn't going to look at it himself because he didn't have time to do it. He was busy, he was sorry about the disturbing message, but that was the end of it, the store couldn't afford to go showing its video surveillance every time someone thought they might see something interesting. If it was something bad or against the law, Ed could contact the police and maybe they could subpoena the video but it would take a lot more than a cell phone to get the police to bother the courts.

As soon as he hung up, Nancy called.

"Your phone's been busy," she said.

"I had to make some calls."

"We've been dispatched to the Gifford-Pinchot, northwest of Mt. Adams."

He forced a half-chuckle.

"You know how it is," she said. "Most likely there won't be cell phone reception."

How long would she be gone? he thought after hanging up. Could be days, could be weeks.

bd thg I wk

And what would happen while she was gone?

After two hours of dead sleep, Ed woke in a half-conscious haze. Only by checking the clock-radio did he perceive it to be early evening, not the next morning. With both hands he wiped his face and when that didn't work he splashed himself with water from the bathroom sink. In the living room he eased himself onto the white-padded rocker chair facing the entertainment center with the television and his children's photos, opened the phone book, and looked up the sheriff's number. It was time to do something.

bad thg I wk

He was done sitting on his ass sifting through the swirl in his brain like some Sherlock wannabe. It was his son, damn it, and his life was in danger. Maybe they were cops, but hell, everyone couldn't die. There were nine million people in Washington State alone. Try killing all of them, huh?

Fucking pricks. Try threatening my son.

He wouldn't sit around waiting. Whoever they were, they had Ed Kline to contend with.

What would he say?

Hello, I'm calling to report a possible "bad thing" in less than one week.

Crap.

Hello, I recently received a text on my phone and whoever

wrote it said if he leaves he'll die. And he said if the cops get involved lots of people will die. Leaves from what? Um, I don't know. From where? Don't know that, either.

He put his phone on the coffee table.

Way to go, Mr. Action Man.

Later that night he woke at 2:09 a.m. realizing he hadn't investigated Homeland Security. They dealt with threats.

"To report suspicious activity, contact your local law enforcement agency," directed the Homeland Security website, "or go to the *National SAR Initiative.*" Local law enforcement—cops. He'd already vetoed that option, sure to be fruitless flaying.

He took a breath, clicked the link. *SAR—Suspicious Activity Reporting.* No phone number, no contact name, no address, just a form to fill out and submit.

"If this is an emergency, call 9-1-1," advised this latest web page. Cops again.

Ed positioned the cursor and began composing.

"Four days ago, on July 26, I received a disturbing text…"

He told the story, the bit about the stolen phone, how *L* could mean his son. He entered the required contact information and sent the vague crackpot missive into cyberspace. And since he knew he wouldn't be able to sleep despite the hours remaining before his shift, he did a bit of math.

If on any given day one out of every 10,000 people had something suspicious to report, limiting the reporting group to only the U.S. population, not allowing the possibility that anyone overseas would have the same notion, that would mean Homeland Security would receive three thousand e-mails. If it were only one out of every 100,000 people—three hundred e-mails. His particular contribution:

bad thg I wk

Sure, that one would go straight to the top of the priority list.

Chapter Five

Lewis

Captain White stood staring out the briefing room's solitary window into the still-dark compound while an unspoken question hovered over every soldier's head. Why had they skipped PTs and chores, substituted MRIs for breakfast? The most likely answer to that question quickened Lewis's heart.

But lately they'd been doing unannounced defense drills. Two days ago, Green interrupted one of White's speeches, suddenly barked GRADE drill—Ground Assault Defense and Evacuation—and they grabbed their M-16s and fragmentation grenades, dashed to Sector 1, leaped into dugout fortifications in the woods north of the compound entrance. Twice more during the day, including the middle of dinner, they repeated the drill.

That same night, lights snapped on at 2 a.m. and there was Green standing in the aisle between the bunks, his voice like a militant goat, AIR-D drill, AIR-D drill, move it move it! Bailey, prone to deep sleep, sprang his butt out his sleeping bag before Green could move his head-smacking hand one step his direction. Everyone cleared out wearing untied boots and skivvies, packs on their backs, in probably less than thirty seconds, Lewis guessed. He and Bailey hurried to the armory where White handed out Russian-made RPG launchers. They trotted to the road lit only by stars then north to the open field to confront a hypothetical air assault, positioning themselves near a camouflaged weapons cache containing a half-dozen grenades with timed self-destruct mechanisms.

Half a year ago when bitterness piled inside him like the snow blanketing their compound, he and Bailey carried armed launchers, and all the PUMAs hiked east cross-country out of the trees into the open hills. White had them angle the tube-like launcher thirty degrees into the ice blue sky, had them fire at the same time, a thundering BOOM as the rockets launched with flaming tails and concussions of blue-white smoke, and they pierced the frigid air jet-speed climbing in a straight diagonal line until simultaneous explosions flashed a thousand feet above the ground, followed in a split second by another boom as the sound waves reached them. Fireworks on steroids. They whooped and howled like coyotes. It was fun and uplifting to wield such crazy power. If anyone ever messed with them, especially the federalistas, they knew they had an answer, they could buy time, they could escape. It was as though his spirits launched with the rocket, the sudden detonations of flame and smoke obliterating the betrayals he felt.

Where all their weapons originated none of the soldiers knew, but everyone's speculation centered on White, who talked of his years contracting security for Gibraltar Defense Services. He divulged more hint than detail, dark operations beyond the reach of government or at least beyond what it wanted to know, parallel universes among desert yardangs and equatorial rainforests.

Now, from the side of the room, White studied the men, his gray eyes turning turbines, the rest of his body impassive. A solitary cricket fiddled its tune outside in the void of pre-light dawn. White nodded toward the doorway, prompting

Hernandez to switch on the camera.

"It was cold, bitter cold," he began, "when General George Washington addressed his soldiers, December 1776. Ice chunks filled the rivers, and the roads were rutted mud, some of it frozen, some of it like wet cement. They'd been getting their asses kicked, forced to retreat, hungry, ill-provisioned. The idea that their little band could prevail against a mighty empire seemed ludicrous. Sensible men and sensible armies took the winters off, licked their wounds and strategized spring campaigns. But not General Washington and the forefathers of our freedom.

"'*These are the times that try men's souls,*' Washington challenged his men, quoting the words of another soldier, a man by the name of Thomas Paine. '*But he that stands it now deserves the love and thanks of man and woman. Tyranny, like hell, is not easily conquered; yet we have this consolation with us, that the harder the conflict the more glorious the triumph.*'"

White recited the lines without a glance at his clipboard, then strode to the front and turned to the men. His eyes animated the room, saturated the musty heat with adrenalin. Lewis felt his back push upright against the chair, his arms tense and springy, and he detested how his body and spirit were sucked in the spell that White cast.

"Back to your high school history classes, soldiers. What happened next?"

Several hands rose.

"Soldier Gallahan."

"Captain White, Sir, isn't that when they crossed the Delaware and ambushed the British?"

"Quite right, Soldier Gallahan, except they attacked Hessians, a mercenary German army. Citizens like us gathered from throughout the colonies to fight them. They mustered on Christmas Day, marched through the night, endured hours of bitter cold until they crossed the river at 4 a.m. December 26. They snuck up on the enemy, attacked, and won. Winter could not defeat them nor could the British and their flunkeys, not when freedom was their cause.

"Gentlemen, more than 200 years later we've lost *almost* everything they fought for. I say *almost* because, despite the campaign to piss on the constitution, the Bill of Rights, and the Declaration of Independence, despite all the lies and propaganda, one thing we have not lost is the thirst to be free.

"'I thank God that I fear not,' Paine wrote, though he faced the gallows if he were captured. *'I see no real cause for fear. By perseverance and fortitude, we have the prospect of a glorious victory. By cowardice and submission, the sad choice of a variety of evils.'*

"Gentlemen, you know well the variety of evils besetting our nation. *These are the times that try men's souls.* That was true in 1776, and sadly it's true again today. I'm proud to stand with men like you, men of the militia. We give ourselves to the cause of freedom. We've spent many months preparing for battle."

At this moment, Captain White paused, his eyes afire, then proclaimed, "and *today* is the day we begin our fight."

Captains Red and Green shot to their feet.

"Who will stand for liberty?"

Soldiers Bailey and Gallahan sprang up, inspiring the others from their seats, leaving Lewis to wonder if he was the only one who stood so that others would not notice him sitting.

"Pumas!"

"Who stands for the people?"

"Pumas!"

"Green Team! You will report to the armory."

"Red Team! You will report to barracks."

"Go!"

Having drilled every detail, including this step, Lewis knew they'd better be lined up within ten minutes. Nine minutes later they stood at attention as Red examined them one at a time, checking off details on his clipboard. Lewis wondered if the thumping hearts of his fellow soldiers drowned for them the warbling song of the sparrows wakening outside in the dim dawn, wondered if the day would arrive when men understood the earth provided enough for all, a day when killing would cease. God, how he wished he'd understood before White riled him into rebellion.

In his role as Trailer, Lewis would arrive on scene wearing khaki pants and a powder blue dress shirt, beneath which he wore green cargo shorts and a chartreuse polo shirt. Beneath all that he wore a concealed holster.

Red marched them to the armory, issued each a Beretta automatic with three clips, one to insert immediately, the other two to pocket in the cargo shorts. Weapon in hand, Lewis hardened himself to end this first mission right now, the way he'd visualized it, including the part where he would die.

He'd get Red first, then pivot and shoot until one of them took him out. If he were crazy lucky, he'd hit them all before anyone had the wits to elude and respond. He put his finger on the trigger, a half second to flip the safety, to stop the insanity.

But he froze.

"Soldier Kline!"

"Captain Red, Sir," he mouthed by habit.

"Holster your weapon."

"Yes, Sir."

These are the times that try men's souls.

Lewis Kline was the Trailer. For the Pumas, he would kill

whomever was necessary to kill. He didn't have the guts to do anything else.

Maybe on the way there, in the rig. Blam blam. Red would be driving, would get the first bullet, and if Lewis timed it right they'd plow through a guardrail and roll down a cliff.

But Lewis knew deep down he wouldn't do it. Couldn't do it.

Chapter Six

Ed

He arrived on base groggy. Waiting on her pad, Bessie looked like an old sepia photograph. What had it been—he bit down a yawn and added the numbers—four hours of sleep the last two nights? And the night before that, less rest than usual with Nancy.

But that was for a good reason. Thank God she was off battling a fire because he was a damn mess. For an instant he pictured her sitting in bed two mornings ago, then saw himself next to her, wrecked with worry and exhaustion.

When a dispatch came within the hour, he pumped his fist and hollered with more gusto than usual. Action. Time to con the body once again—we're wide awake, he told it. Coordinates 47°13'30" by 120°51'00"—he knew exactly where that would send them, Cle Elum Ridge above the Teanaway River, drier there, Ponderosa pines, white oak, sagebrush, parched grass and wind.

They hit it hard, not just the helitack crew but two Forest Service engines, three DNR engines, and local fire district volunteers. In just over three hours he dipped his bucket 24 times in a pond on a small field still dotted with recently cut hay bales. The smoke and smelter-hot flames churning among the mixed vegetation meant more than spectacle to the crowd of people gawking behind a barbed wire fence next to the field. This was their home country.

Focusing on wind direction and speed, he positioned Bessie to dump cooling baths on flaming snags. He felt that fire blessed him, for against it he could take tangible action, play a role in sending civilians home with stories to exaggerate on social media. But as soon as he set Bessie down back at base, Lewis shouldered his way to the front of his mind, gazed at him, waited for him to act, and instead of striding strong steps toward the helitack office, Ed felt himself slump, trudging as though time had gnawed his vitality.

Normality tipped askew at the sight of Zweigert sitting without word or motion at his battered metal desk. Ed couldn't think of a single instance when Zweigert wasn't already standing with a pack full of tools next to the pad as Ed set Bessie onto the big white "H." The next blink of discontinuity slithered forward via the absence of country music, replaced instead by a radio broadcaster's voice in mid-report. Zweigert held up a hand, and, as though facing a crossing guard, Ed halted at the doorway, the dread that had been seething in his heart pushing harder against his chest. Pressing his flight helmet hard against his side, he directed his mind to the words punching out a radio atop the file cabinet behind Zweigert's desk.

Words describing two very "bad thgs."

Chapter Seven

Lewis

"The baker's one block west," reported Tonkavitch, seated out of sight on a bus-stop bench.

Lewis looked at his watch—9:22 a.m., right on time. A Starbucks latte in his left hand and a cell phone in his right, he stood atop bark dust beneath a hedge maple, a miniature island bordering the small Wells Fargo parking lot and overlooking the almost-empty asphalt field behind the shopping mall to his right.

All he had to do was turn, step out from beneath the shade, and walk away. When the terrible thing happened, he would not be there.

"Blue check." White's voice, wherever he was. He watched from somewhere—maybe the grocery store, or seated by a window at the Krispy Kreme, or sitting in his rig over by the Jiffy Lube.

"Clear," Lewis responded.

"Clear," echoed Tonkavitch from the street and Bailey from the larger lot, he and Hernandez tic-tacking skateboards, nothing complicated, easy moves.

If he walked away now, "abort" would replace "clear."

Get Kline, would be the next words. That fucker's trying

to bail. They'd redirect their firepower, make certain Kline's exit was permanent, return to base, deploy another day, another place.

Not yet, he told himself. Later. Stay with the program.

He brought the cell phone to his ear. It was a fake—no battery.

"Hi, honey," he said. Bailey and Hernandez carved to slow their boards near the sidewalk separating the two lots. In an old green Cherokee, Ferguson and Wilhelmson drove into the lot, paused before the drive-through window lane.

"Are you sure? Why change the date?" Lewis asked. During rehearsal he'd pictured Scarlett Johansson on the other phone, the way she lured those men in *Under the Skin.* But not now. What was coming extinguished imagination, demanded be-here-now on the opposite side of nirvana.

"We haven't made reservations. It might be doable." For the past month every Tuesday, Thursday, and Friday, Red had them wear the shoulder holster so they'd know the feel of it, had them grab the pistol, so they'd know the feel of that, too, all in addition to the rehearsals. Despite the repetition, this morning the gun weighed like a bag of lead, burned like a branding iron beneath his two shirts.

"I'll check Priceline while I'm at the office. Keep your fingers crossed."

A white Loomis armored truck with two guards turned into the lot, stopped sideways across the parking stripes in front of the bank. Bailey and Hernandez crouched, ollie-popped their boards out of the air. Showoffs. They began strolling, crossing the sidewalk, angling behind the truck as though heading toward the street.

"Blue check."

"Clear."

"Clear."

"Clear."

"Do it."

"I'll call you during lunch. I should have reservations by then." Lewis pantomimed screen touches.

Bailey and Hernandez broke left, disappeared between the side of the armored truck and the bank.

The gunshots were loud. The world would hear them, thought Lewis, even if the victim didn't.

Bailey and Hernandez re-emerged, sprinting east toward the line of Douglas firs, Hernandez clutching a pouch. The driver's door burst open and a uniformed man leaped to the pavement, one movement short of pointing his pistol at the fleeing duo. But behind him, wearing latex gloves, Ferguson had simultaneously stepped out the Cherokee, the guard less than thirty feet away. Shots snapped the air, slammed the guard onto the pavement in a headfirst crack of skull, the momentum of it twisting his body so that even fifty feet away his white eyes and open mouth implicated Lewis, the only PUMA left. Ferguson and Wilhelmson, sprinting full-speed, had already closed half the distance to the trees.

"When you hit those trees, you stop and walk out the other side like you're strolling to church," Red had emphasized late at night two weeks ago when they'd done a walk-through. Past the firs they had stepped onto a neighborhood cul-de-sac where Marquez waited behind the wheel of an old blue Voyager van, and Tonkavitch would already be riding shotgun. Lewis's mind flashed the subsequent steps—the four-block drive to another Voyager, this one burgundy, the five-block drive to the edge of a forested greenbelt. Sixty yards in, they'd shed their outer clothing, use wire-cutters to open the pouch—likely equipped with a GPS device—and take the money. Two hundred yards after that they'd walk out on a different street to another

Voyager, this one white, the actual getaway vehicle to take them back to their compound.

What would they do when they noticed Lewis was not with them?

Because Lewis had left his little island, was crossing the universe of asphalt separating him from the Burger King open for breakfast at the corner of the lot, gambling that with everything in motion, he'd make it before White, wherever he was, could catch him. Without a wallet or identification or a single coin, if he made it through the door he'd be free.

He wouldn't say a damn thing, wouldn't rat them out. Responding to his flight, the PUMAs would vanish. Only the captains knew where they'd go. They'd drilled the evacuation scenario a half-dozen times—in twenty minutes they could empty the armory and collect intelligence files and gear. They'd survive. If word ever spilled out—PUMA defector confesses to authorities—White would retaliate, and that meant Lewis's family.

Another fifty yards. It looked like business as usual through the windows of the Burger King, the pavement distance and the little island of maple trees enough to keep customers clueless to the robbery and—call it what it was—murders.

He'd disappear. He'd pawn the Beretta or sell it on the street. He'd beg near Pike Place, he'd hang with the day laborers, he'd hold an empty gas can at a freeway rest stop...somehow, he'd get some money and go north, maybe find a fishing boat, he didn't know, *something,* something that didn't require killing.

From behind him on his right side, a vehicle approached. Feigning nonchalance, he kept moving toward the Burger King, an ordinary man with nothing to hide.

But there was Captain White in the driver's seat and Captain Red in the back of the king cab, pointing a

Beretta. Aimed at him, the pistol looked large as a canon.

Red unlatched the door, slid back, kicked it open, the pistol's line never wavering from Lewis's chest.

"Get in!"

In his mind, Lewis had gamed this scenario, too. He'd fight them. He'd either prevail, or he'd never get to the fishing boat, never grip the rails of a tossing trawler or smell the frigid salt waves. Neither would he have killed an innocent man.

But his body countermanded his mind, threw him off script, crumbled his legs, dilated and fixed his pupils upon the gaping metal barrel. He did what he was told to do.

While White drove slowly past the Burger King onto a side street, police sirens belted piercing arias. White proceeded away from the thoroughfare, pulled to a curb. With the engine idling, he turned toward Lewis, lifted a gun to the top of the backrest.

"Captain Red," he said. "Remove Soldier Kline's pistol."

Chapter Eight

Ed

"Witnesses heard between four and eight shots in rapid succession, and both the State Senate Majority and Minority Leaders fell immediately. The two shooters, both with large beards and wearing dress slacks and shirts, whirled and ran, leaped up and hurled themselves over a concrete wall…"

"Been goin' on nonstop since ten o'clock this mornin'," said Zweigert.

Ed felt his legs buckle. He grasped the door frame to keep from falling.

Zweigert gave him a curious look. "Damn right it's fucked. Robbed a bank, too. Killed two guards."

Eight steps to his desk seemed too far. He sat on the visitor's chair nearest the door.

"...police chiefs from Seattle and Issaquah as well as the King County Sheriff's department said they planned to coordinate investigations into both the assassinations and the armored truck robbery and murders. Seattle PD spokesperson Connie Muzano cautioned that no concrete proof as yet linked the two crimes, but she noted the common elements of stunning speed, multiple assailants, and…."

"You okay, Ed? I mean, you don't got a brother working at a bank, do ya?"

"I'm fine. Just...yeah, it's fucked."

"I was gonna say, we're due to service the landing gear, including the shock struts."

"They catch anyone?"

"Nope. I figure I'll hit it tonight, have you ready by sunup. I'll get out there now. You bring her back in one piece?" Zweigert picked up the maintenance logbook.

"You mind canning the radio?"

"Yeah, yeah, sure." Except for a square-box floor fan, the room turned quiet. A sweat droplet trickled the length of Ed's nose, stopping at the tip. He withheld a shout, for an instant envisioned springing from the chair, grabbing it, hurling it across the room at the radio, imagined the satisfying clatter and destruction. He looked at his watch, wondered how he'd survive three more hours on shift.

"I'll go out there with you," he said.

At home that evening, from the high shelf in the cupboard over the sink, Ed took the bottle of Courvoisier that Nancy brought with her only a few nights ago in what now seemed like an entirely different life.

"Been sitting in my cupboard since Christmas," she had said, taking it along with a Jiffy Pop popcorn and a DVD from a brown shopping bag. They never did finish watching the movie.

After settling on one of the living room chairs, he took a large sip. The liquid burned down his throat and warmed his gut. He'd already looked at the *bad thg* text on his phone when he'd reached his pickup cab at the end of his shift. It didn't offer anything new then, and it wouldn't now. The cops might find it interesting but the only place it led was an old lady's phone in a toilet full of crap.

He looked to the photograph on the bookshelf and set the bottle on the floor.

"I fucked up, son," he said aloud.

He'd have just a few more sips, and then he'd put it away and think about what to do next. He retrieved the photo, brought it back with him to the chair, and took another swig.

The first time he ever saw his son, after a nine-month assignment on the Horn of Africa, Lewis was five months old with brown and gleaming eyes, a perfectly round head, a toothless smile. He took another swig and remembered that same smile with teeth, a curly-haired four-year old tearing down the sidewalk on a Big Wheel. Another time swinging and missing and swinging again at the ball perched on a tee in their backyard. No matter how many times he missed, Lewis exuded delight with every swing, and soon he turned into a damn good first baseman. Home-and-away years, Cub Scouts and Boy Scouts and merit badges—including "Signs, Signals, and Codes." But nothing in the telephone text worked as a code.

"I tried," he said to the smiling young man with the salmon.

A small reading lamp on an end table next to his chair offered itself.

"Excuse me." Ed placed the photo upright between the cushion and the chair's padded frame. He maneuvered his arm behind the chair to unplug the cord, looped it to fit in his palm, grasped the neck of the lamp. In one motion he twisted left and hurled the lamp across the room at the wall next to the window. With a thud and a clang, the metal shade battered the wall and bounced to the floor.

He took another swig.

"Tough guy, aren't I?"

He lifted the photo.

"You see that, son? Haha, yeah, that about sums it up, don't you think? How come you couldn't give me another clue?"

Lewis wouldn't answer.

"Fuck it." He set down the photo and the bottle, procured from the kitchen a box of pretzels and a one-pound chunk of cheddar cheese. If he ate something he could drink a little more, so he alternated bites of Bavarian pretzels and cheddar, chewing the two together.

"It's like a sandwich," he explained to Lewis, washing it down with another swig.

Already the chair felt as though it were swirling. He raised the bottle to eye-level. Another swallow and it would be half empty.

"You won't mind, will ya?" he addressed Nancy, wherever the hell she was. If she knew, she'd understand. The next swig he swished from cheek to cheek until it peppered his mouth.

"This ain't me, you know. Ain't me at all. So I'm hopin' you'll stay with me. I'll get through this." He decided he'd drunk enough, and besides, the Mariners were on television.

Ninety minutes later, the Mariners flailing inning after inning without a run, two-thirds of the bottle was gone.

"Fuckin' Seattle," he yelled after the Mariners left a runner on third with nobody out in the eighth inning. "Ev'ry fuckin' year you can't score shit!"

He'd get another bottle of Courvoisier tomorrow, and Nancy would never know how much he'd drunk.

"Good thing yer not here now!" he told Nancy. "Ha ha! You coulda been a secr'tery home ev'ry night, but you hadda be a firefighter. Thas cool."

Oh, she'd toss him in the trash for sure if she saw him then.

Christ, what was he going to do? He could either tell her or not tell her, nothing in between.

Why did Lewis have to go run off with a bunch of crazies? When he could be sitting right now in the chair next to him, pissed at the Mariners, sharing the fancy brandy, the two of them nothing more than a couple of half-drunk dudes watching a ballgame? That was about as good as it got.

The Mariners showed themselves capable of surprise, scratching out a run in the top of the ninth then adding two more on a home run.

"What the fuck you doin'? You never score in th' ninth! You never come from b'hind! You jus' wanna break my fuckin' heart, like y'always do."

Three outs later, the Mariners vindicated Ed's suspicion, losing 4-3, and there were no other games to watch. Again, Ed picked up the photo.

"What you doin', son? You with 'em? Wazzat you?" He looked a circle around the swaying house, saw the windows framing woods not quite dark. "Les go fer a walk." Unable to fit the photo in his pocket, he clasped it in his left hand and lurched out the door across a small yard of patchy grass and onto the road, no headlights ahead or taillights behind, night darkening the firs on his left into pale columns hoisting dim boughs uphill. Not twenty steps from his home, the photo slipped and the glass smacked the road.

Ed stumbled forward, his boot crunching a larger shard. He picked up the frame and eyed the paper photograph exposed by diagonal gaps from what had been a 5-by-7 plate, but Lewis kept smiling anyway, his hold on the salmon no less firm.

"Dropped ya again," Ed said to the print. "Never meant ta drop ya, son."

A bit farther away, his stomach turned stormy, a gale of

churning waves, rivulets of saliva tinny-tasting in his mouth, forcing him off the roadway.

"Think I'm gonna be sick. Don't look." He turned the photo in its broken frame away from him so that Lewis showed off his sockeye to the empty road while Ed upchucked waves of cheese-tinged vomit through his mouth and nose, his eyes watering from the violence of it. Afterward, he stayed hunched over to catch his breath, his stomach grateful for the eradication of too much, the foul drip of it lingering around his nose and lips. He used his shirt to wipe his face before letting his feet feel their way back to the road. Keeping Lewis's eyes pointed away, he reeled back to the house, replaced the photo on the shelf and plopped into the chair to study his son by lamplight.

"I'll get those fuckers. You hear that? I'll get those fuckers.

"But I gotta know: wazzat you today? I'll still love ya but ya gotta tell me." Several minutes later the brandy shut down his body, sweeping a blanket of sleep over his nightmare.

Chapter Nine

Lewis

Six foot by six foot, maximum. On the concrete floor, Lewis used his body to measure the storage closet adjoining the kitchen—his cell, dark except the half-inch line of daylight glimmering beneath the door. Empty except the plastic water bottle they'd left, and scents of ammonia, detergent, and dust sequestered by concrete walls. He'd always wondered why there was a hasp on the outside part of the closet door.

Naked and padlocked inside, now he knew the answer. Had anyone else ever been cocooned in this particular dormitory?

He would know if someone had been locked in here. He'd been a PUMA from its genesis.

What's wrong with America? asked a Facebook "You May Also Like" link eighteen months ago. Anger gyrated in his mind back then. He lived with his mother and her new husband and subsided on minimum wage as a sporting goods clerk. All he had to show for his forestry degree was student loan debt with a final payment fifteen years down the road. Everyone knew corporations benefitted by keeping workers in servitude, a setup that bloated the guts of CEOs and Wall Street insiders with billions in cash. But how did they do it? How'd they twist the meaning of America so that an honest man with an honest job couldn't support even himself, never mind a family? His grandfather Frank bought a house and sent Lewis's aunts through college and what was he? A truck driver.

And so Lewis clicked the link.

He studied the internet, found websites offering answers. Oath Keepers. Constitution Party. Get Out of Our House. He studied the Virginia Ratifying Convention of 1788, examined the enumerated grievances of the Declaration of Independence, and pored through the John Locke essays that influenced Thomas Jefferson and Samuel Adams. He found himself agreeing: generation after generation, paid-for politicians skewed the Constitution's meaning until the Founding Fathers would not recognize, let alone approve, the power structures determining people's fate. Corporations the equivalent of human beings. Government agencies pilfering control from local towns and neighborhoods. Sham elections. Empty slogans.

Unemployment checks, shit jobs and shit wages.

"Angry enough?" challenged another homepage. "Enough to resist? Enough to act? If you're not, leave this site." The challenge grabbed Lewis by his shirt, yanked him deeper. The same day Lewis posted a comment, Captain White responded.

"Lone wolves cannot win the people's sympathy nor bring down the federalistas," White wrote. "Many prove to be undisciplined kooks animated by senseless hate."

"I don't hate anyone," Lewis wrote back. "You don't know me."

"Granted," returned White. "Tell me about yourself. No names or addresses. Simply this: why did you come to this website?"

Why? How could he have been such a damn fool?

He guessed it had to be 90 degrees on the concrete floor, and it seemed he was breathing in his own exhalations from the confined air. But a shiver intruded and he wrapped his arms across his chest, wondering how his teeth could chatter in such heat. With nothing but time and foreboding, Lewis recalled the chats that both mocked and lured.

Was it a seduction?

This is about all the people, not just yourself, White replied after Lewis bared his grievances.

I know it, Lewis said. Didn't you read what I wrote?

You've been studying.

Yes.

Words never bring change. Action does. All those websites: self-indulgent rants, fake feel-goods because I-told-you-so's. Gutless weasels hiding behind faux sophistication. Don't bother me if you're not serious.

Of course I'm serious.

Enough to risk? To serve a greater cause?

What do you mean?

Something very different than internet chatter.

Lewis stopped the conversation right there. But he bookmarked the website. Nobody but White could explain the events of the time with such clarity and insight. And White ended every blog with an admonition not to respond unless committed and serious, and, although he never posted Lewis's comments or anyone else's, he did reply.

It doesn't matter if you're right, he'd say. *What are you going to do about it?*

Maybe you're too comfortable. Wouldn't want to risk that, would you?

How much do you really care?

I know what you're hinting, Lewis wrote once.

And yet you still reply, said White.

I agree elections have become a farce.

Few people have the courage.

I don't want to hurt anyone.

Nor do I. But we must be prepared. Someone must be ready to protect the people.

Lewis never thought the government would actually attack, but he also didn't see the harm in being prepared. And he sure as hell didn't have anything better to do.

At the first meetup, a closed room in a Portland Chinese restaurant, all three captains wore surgical masks, sunglasses, and colored stocking caps according to their names—white, red, and green. He felt like turning around right then, but he didn't want to look like a chicken shit. If he hadn't read all the internet posts, he would have pegged them as a bunch of clowns.

Two others, Hernandez and Nelson, had also made the trek from Northern California. White demanded they consent to a search for hidden microphones.

Why are you here? said White. If you think this is some kind of glory trip you'd best turn around and walk out. If you think we're joking, hasta la vista. Want to blame the Mexicans or the Muslims or some other group trying to get by the same as you and me? We especially don't want you. If you're not willing to press your body and soul into changing America to what it actually means, we don't need you. This movement has no room for freeloaders or haters or kooks.

Why are you here, Kline? Boom. Just like that in front of everyone. It reminded him of a time when he was a kid on a stayover with a friend and they went to a Baptist Church the next morning. Raise your hand if you're saved. Come forward if you're willing to be saved.

We're talking about a militia, White said later that evening. But strictly for defense. God willing, they would never have to act, but if the government did something crazy, like declare martial law, they would defend themselves. What was the harm in that?

Within a month they'd moved to Wenatchee, weekdays working construction projects for the captains, weekends drilling with weapons in the woods.

"You've seen the trajectory of power, the rise of tyranny," White said. "Soon the jaws of despotism will snap upon your spirits. They will plunder your last ounce of freedom and dignity—unless you're prepared to resist. It will be a time to test our souls." Anybody else mouthing those words would look pompous, but White spoke and moved like a prophet who'd lifted a lot of weights.

Lewis surprised himself by how much he relished the feel of an M16, the surge that rocketed through his veins every time he demolished a target. It was like being a kid again, except the sense of awe sprang from firepower beyond BB guns and make-believe. He was having fun, a hell of a lot more than he had wasting away at his mother's home. His new buddies had balls, a big change from the weenies back home.

White created scenarios and obstacles, fed their egos, deepened the spell.

One day after an especially powerful talk, White convinced them to sign up for a three-year enlistment. Lewis wrote his dad and mom, and then, with the others, relocated to a hidden compound, built multiple layers of defense, and drilled a variety of scenarios. He belonged to something bigger than himself.

During those times if he wondered what the hell he was doing, he figured he could leave anytime. The enlistment was just a piece of paper. It wasn't like the militia was a real army.

Early in March, the captains woke them at three in the morning, gathered them in the classroom, and announced the federal government had formally declared war against citizen militias. The captains had hoped their preparations would turn out to be overdramatic; it was tragic but not unexpected that war had finally come. Lewis looked around the room and saw the other soldiers swallow it. A couple of them pumped a fist, prompting others to do the same.

White informed them that all militias, declaring a state of emergency, had mobilized. They would find out which groups had the guts to resist and which were merely keyboard commandos. As for the PUMAs, all leaves were suspended, their base electronic perimeter activated and under permanent guard, and no one was allowed to go from point to point by himself.

They would take small but bold actions: protect the innocent, speak truth, inspire an awakening. The government must never prevail against its citizens.

At a nod from White, all three captains shouted a by-then familiar challenge:

"Who will defend the people?"

For an instant, Lewis held back his voice and watched the men; he recoiled when they responded without hesitation.

"Pumas!"

That was the day Lewis decided he had to escape.

Hours passed, the sunlit strip of floor faded from concrete gray to just about dark. No lunch. No dinner. Water bottle half-empty. A drain in the center of the closet served as Lewis's urinal. He lay on his side, aimed carefully, but despite his care piss now added its signature to the cleaning supply aromas.

Images of his death and how it would come blinkered in his mind—a pistol barrel touching his temple, a view of rifles while tied to a tree, the first slice of a knife to the throat. He thought of all the times he could have run. Better to have risked it in those early days after White announced the advent of war. They would have known right away. They'd have known exactly where he'd breached the perimeter and so his start would have been small, but it would have surpassed the predicament he faced now.

"When the hunt begins, I am the one to fear."

The walls blunted Lewis's laughter. One of the captains' favorite warrior sayings, in the dark cell those words drooped impotently, tasted like rancid soup.

At some point they had to open the door. They could leave him there a week, let his body shrivel from lack of water and food, await the cessation of his heart, but Lewis doubted they'd resolve his fate that way, despite the irony—act as though he no longer existed until he no longer existed. No, Captain White liked a show. Ritual served to indoctrinate, and Lewis felt certain he would become a cautionary tale woven into the militia's lore. The only variable was the length of time between the drama White distilled from his defection to the inevitable end.

But they wouldn't just leave him to die. The door would open. It opened out. He'd stay awake, all night, all the next day. He'd listen, hear the key turn in the padlock, the twist of the knob. He'd coil like a snake, rocketing toward the door, barreling to the ground whoever was out there, dashing past the captains' quarters out the back door. With his mind he'd numb his naked feet, sprint into the woods and keep going, keep going, keep going.

Bright light burst into the room, burst into his sleep.

In a single movement, Lewis sprang from the floor, hunched low on his toes, blinked his light-blinded eyes. A rocket. He was going to be a rocket.

White stepped in, a fucking stone gate of a man and behind him, fuzzy in the glare, two others, Nelson and Doyle, all clean-shaven now.

Lewis launched himself—backward. His head banged against the wall.

Nelson laughed.

"Shut up, Soldier Nelson," said White. "Bring me a chair."

Sure, a rocket. The kind that fizzled on the launch pad, collapsed on its side, self-imploded. Escape? What a joke. He was a weenie with no balls.

Stop it, he told himself. He had to think.

"I'm sorry, Captain White, Sir." It was a whine, a snivel. *Damnit, speak like a man.*

"That makes two of us," replied White, accepting the chair that Nelson brought. The captain motioned for Lewis to sit and so Lewis sat, leaning his back against the wall. "We've invested a lot of time, a lot of training in you. Desertion is a serious crime. Militias frown on it. In war, commanders shoot deserters on the spot. Doing so accomplishes the desired effect upon the soldiers who remain. Thus, no matter how grim and hopeless their situation may be, soldiers keep to their posts, living or dying with honor. It's a horrible price for walking off the job, but do you see the purpose of it?"

"Yes, Sir." *There. That's the voice. Show no fear.* "With all due respect, Sir, I did not desert my post. I stayed there through the whole thing. I...lost my head. I evacuated the wrong direction."

"I personally do not condone summary executions. I subscribe to lawfully conducted court martials, after which the penalty must be paid. The militia movement will grow, Mr. Kline. Our cause is just. PUMAS bear a great responsibility. Apparently, the others have responded to the government's declaration of war by going into hiding. They're waiting to act. The fate of our nation depends on our success. We cannot forgive desertion."

Captain White turned his head toward the door. "Soldier Nelson, bring Mr. Kline his bowl of food."

Oatmeal. Whatever they'd eaten, for Lewis they boiled oatmeal. But his body thanked him for the sustenance as he slowly chewed.

"I promise you a speedy trial, Mr. Kline. One way or another this matter will be resolved within forty-eight hours. We cannot afford distractions when we have another mission to rehearse."

"Captain White, please believe me."

Damn. He was whining again.

Empty water bottle, mouth dry, lips cracked, nose clogged, calf muscles cramped. Long darkness, time devolved to a guess. Daylight's half-inch gave the only clue.

Then, as before, sudden bright light but this time no strength to pretend, only an eye-flick across the gleam.

White again.

"Stand up!" A boot kick then pain barking from his bare ass. He wobbled upright, exposed, puny, quivering before White's position a foot in front of his face. Past White's shoulders, Nelson and Doyle stood watch outside the doorway. Perhaps it was noon.

"You're disgusting, Mr. Kline. How you've reduced yourself is pathetic. How could you possibly prove your worth as a soldier?" Lewis felt White's eyes like hand drills twisting into his brain. "Mr. Kline, that was a question."

"I messed up, Sir."

"That's right. You can start by admitting the truth. You were less than a minute from the Burger King door. Had you made it that far, what was next?"

"I was confused, Sir. I was looking for the van, but I turned the wrong way."

White swung an open hand hard against Lewis's head. Pain thrashed his ear drum. A siren pealed in his skull. The blow spun him sideways, and he sank to his hands and knees against the wall.

"Bullshit!" White turned away, ran a hand across the top of his head, sighed, turned back toward Lewis.

"Get up."

Leaning on the wall, Lewis complied.

"Look at me."

The eyes softer.

"I regret that, Mr. Kline. But do not play me for a fool. Once again: had you reached the Burger King door, what was next?"

"I was confused. I don't know, Sir."

White's hand thrust forward. Lewis flinched, but instead of striking, the hand found a soft spot beneath his throat, lifted his chin, elevated him toward the ceiling. The other hand patted Lewis's cheek twice and the eyes grew questioning, like those of a lover.

"But you *do* know. Tell me."

"I'm...confused..."

"You're afraid." The hand that had patted his cheek formed a fist. While the first hand lifted Lewis by the underside of his chin, the fist drove forward to the mouth, smashing the back of his head against the wall, spinning the room dark.

Urine squirted from his penis, splatted White's khakis. The fist turned again to a hand, patted him on the cheek, while the other hand released its grip and Lewis slumped to the floor.

"You're afraid, Mr. Kline. I'll be back."

Bootsteps exited, a door closed, light fled. He remained on his hands and knees, a sonic boom throbbing in his head. The ringing in his ear dimmed the sound of his sobs. His tongue curled around a dislodged tooth, while the tip probed a loose gap of gum, tasted blood. He spat the tooth, let his upper body fall, his cheek against the floor, his breaths echoing like someone else's breathing, someone in a movie on the other side of pain. He smelled blood and urine.

Lights again, an open door, boots.

"Get up."

He did not believe himself capable of movement.

"Get up or I'll pull you up by your hair."

He opened his hand to the floor, straightened an elbow, rose off the concrete, strained his trunk upright, moved his legs, tottered against the wall, his sight focused upon the textured cement floor, dribbled with urine and blood, a solitary incisor tooth inches from the shiny black boots.

"Soldier Nelson, bring us a warm mop."

"Yes, Sir."

The sound of a faucet, clatter, footsteps. A mop handle against his chest.

"Mr. Kline, clean up your mess."

A weak grip, the motion of mopping, the scrape of tooth on concrete like writing a line with stone. The mop a prop to hold him up.

"Soldier, come get the mop."

"Yes, Sir."

"Look at me, Mr. Kline."

Above the boots, a fresh pair of blue jeans, thick chest behind a black tee-shirt, beardless face revealing wrinkles etched downward from the nose.

The eyes compassionate. One fist holding iodine, the other cotton balls.

"You're wounded, Mr. Kline."

"Yes, Sir."

"Look at me."

Gently, the hands administered stinging saturated cotton around his mouth. The eyes regarded him sympathetically.

"Let's try again. You were less than a minute from the Burger King door. You were walking a straight line. Once inside, what was next?"

CHAPTER TEN

Ed

Daylight strobed through his eyelids. The hell? Still in his chair?

A demolition crew blasted inside his skull. He had broken his vow. Seven years ago after Sharon pronounced them finished, he'd downed near-poisonous quantities three times that first month before promising himself never to binge again. Well, here he was, and the next day didn't feel any better than the next-days all those years ago. The sledgehammer rearranging his brain and the cauldron bubbling in his gut did not bury the heart-pain, only heightened it.

He twisted in his chair, gazed the blurry space across to the clock on his kitchen wall.

Shit. Another reason not to do this anymore. Twelve minutes to get his butt out the door and on the way to work. He clasped the armrests, pushed himself up.

And there on the bookshelf right in Ed's face, Lewis smiled through a gap in the glass. He freed his son and placed him in a different 5-by-7 frame that held a group shot of the last Rangers squadron he'd shuttled from one hell to another. Was it a murderer he'd restored behind uncracked glass in the place of that crew?

Ed looked at the faces of the Rangers who'd been there

that day for the group shot. Suppose one of them wanted out? No, he'd be stuck in that photo, wouldn't be able to walk away exposed in a war zone. Hell, they'd have arrested anyone who tried.

I leve I die.

"Where are you?" he spoke aloud.

At the base, Everett announced he'd haul the helitack crew to the back side of Mt. Catherine to clear brush, and Zweigert said they should do a helo wash and collect oil samples.

He and Zweigert also rolled out the equipment they needed to run a computer check. They found Bessie to be in top condition and rewarded her with a warm soapy wash. They scrubbed dead bugs from the stabilizers, the tail rotor, and the windshield, and examined screws and rivets and pitch change links. While they let her sun-dry, they collected oil samples, then finished her with a full-body spray of RV wax/cleaner.

An hour into the ministrations, Ed opened a granola bar, chewed it thoroughly. He'd been forcing down sips of water, continued to do so throughout the morning. By lunch, he'd nearly accomplished his own internal wash. What remained in his body was low-grade torpor supplemented with dread.

In the office, Ed took a second granola bar and a handful of crackers from his desk.

"You see this bullshit?" asked Zweigert between bites of burrito, viewing his computer.

"What?"

"Fuckin' idiots."

Ed walked to Zweigert's desk.

Militia demands negotiations to end attacks read a headline from the *Seattle Times.*

A militia group claiming responsibility for yesterday's political assassinations and armed guard murders announced a "cease-fire" and demanded negotiations with U.S. government representatives, according to a document left at the Seattle Times *office yesterday.*

Referring to themselves as PUMAs—Patriots United Militia of America—the group's lengthy document included what it called a "Modern Renewal" Declaration of Independence containing enumerated grievances, in addition to a separate list of demands. It threatened to "resume operations against representatives of federal and state governments and of international financial and corporate syndicates" if its demands were not met.

Ed put his hand on the corner of Zweigert's desk, steadied himself, stepped back to his desk and turned on his computer.

Syndicate.

Lewis used that word in the letter he sent.

As for the text, now six days old—the word *die* did not overstate the stakes. They had already killed.

The attacks dominated the *Seattle Times* front page.

State Patriot representatives repudiate violent tactics
Shock, defiance, fear among legislators

Ed clicked on the article Zweigert had been reading.

"...Complicit political parties have joined the international syndicate of corporatists and bankers to tyrannize American citizens," claims the letter, which later threatens to "show no

mercy for any such representatives or their property." Among the group's demands: the convening of a new Constitutional Convention. (To read the text of the entire document, click here.)

Syndicate. Again.

Ed skipped the rest of the article, clicked the link to the document. From his peripheral vision, he noticed Zweigert no longer looked at his own screen but instead stared at Ed.

"This shit's unnerving," said Ed.

"No kidding. I never seen you so....I don't know…"

"I'm okay. What's the world coming to, Zweigy?"

Zweigert put a potato chip in his mouth, shook his head, brought his eyes back to his screen. On his computer, Ed saw that the *Times* had created a JPG of a document that looked as though it had been written with an old typewriter.

Declaration of Independence: A Modern Renewal

Except for a tiny number of wealthy individuals, the people of this great nation experience increased hardship, bankruptcies and oppression. Some have given up and survive on public dole. But most work harder than ever yet cannot own a home or afford an education for their children. What has happened to what we once called a "government of, for, and by the people"?

Just as conditions escalated to the intolerable oppression of our forefathers, so today's federalist/corporatist colossus suppresses our citizens to such a degree that our contemporary station can be regarded only as tyranny. Although much suffering shall ensue as the people reassert their rights, we take inspiration from our eighteenth-century founders who acted resolutely to smash the shackles of tyranny so that we, their progeny, would enjoy liberty. As they felt compelled to enumerate the grievances that comprised their bondage, so the PUMAs herein document the oppression that characterizes our contemporary status:

The President, Congress, and the Supreme Court have far overreached the authority granted them by the U.S. Constitution, smothering the voices of self-determination at the local level;

Federal and state governments illegally have entered the nation into a web of international agreements, disingenuously justifying the arrangement as the inevitable outcome of globalism, the result of which has been the surrendering of national sovereignty in the service of an international syndicate of corporatists and bankers whose sole aim is to hoard wealth;

The federal branches have confiscated over 600 million acres of land that rightfully belong to the people who occupy those lands, dictating what local populations can and cannot do with their own resources;

Federal and state governments have imposed restrictions on how local populations may or may not utilize the remaining 1.7 billion acres that comprise our great nation;

Federal and state governments confiscate earned income and wealth from its citizens, imprisoning anyone who objects;

Federal and state governments have mandated all people must adhere to dictated definitions of marriage and personhood, thwarting the free will of individuals to exercise their relationships according to their church and their God;

Elected and unelected officials have collaborated with representatives of international corporations, financial institutions, and labor unions to limit who has a legitimate opportunity to obtain office and to limit the scope of issues and dialogue conducted prior to the vote of the people;

Governmental representatives have conspired to destroy Second Amendment Rights and thus citizens' capacity to resist tyranny.

Ed paused, noticed the crackers on a napkin and the granola bar, and decided he didn't want them. Had Lewis fallen for this load of crap? Had Ed ever mouthed that kind of conspiracy stuff?

No, he hadn't, not that he could remember, not even joking. If he'd been home more while Lewis was younger, he could have more deeply exemplified a level, sensible mind. And then that whole episode at Whiskeytown Lake—he failed Lewis then, too.

Stop it, he scolded himself. He looked again at the document.

The Declaration of Independence and the Constitution respect the sensible truth that the farther away from people that power is exercised, the farther away from freedom and liberty will those people reside. Ninety-six percent of the power wielded by federal and state governments rightfully belongs to people at the county and more localized levels.

To remedy this perversion of power we demand the following:

Federal and state governments cease and desist enforcement of all laws except ordinances directly related to matters of war and peace, treason, piracy, and counterfeiting;

Federal and state agencies will cease and desist collecting income, estate, business, and wealth taxes; the only lawful revenue that may be collected shall be duties from interstate and international commerce;

A new constitutional convention must take place within one year, the purpose of which will be to restore local sovereignty to the county level or smaller entities not to exceed a population of 100,000 individuals or 100 square miles;

Each state by a vote of its people shall elect five delegates to the convention; in order to negate the capacity of wealthy elites, unions, corporations, and bankers to purchase votes, candidates may receive contributions, not to exceed $500, from individual citizens only.

Because we seek first a peaceful resolution, we are prepared to enter negotiations with existing governmental officials, despite their complicity in abrogating the Constitution. We await overtures in order to implement a cease-fire. Until such time, inspired by the ideals that drove our forebears to rebel against the tyranny of their times and to compose the great documents which ought to guide our nation, Patriots United Militia of America vows to fight. We request that for their own safety, citizens avoid proximity with all officials of federal and state governmental agencies as well as executives and guardians of international corporate and financial syndicates.

Ed had fought wars against other thugs who tried to justify mass killing with fancy words. Men and women he regarded as friends had paid with their lives. How could his own son fall for that kind of rhetoric?

He force-fed himself the rest of the crackers and the granola bar, then turned off the computer and stood.

"Zwiegy, I'm going to use some personal leave to run an errand. Might last the whole afternoon, I don't know for sure. But my cell will be on, and I'll know if we get a dispatch."

"Yeah sure, Kline. Whatever it is, you take care of it. Seems like somethin's eatin' at you."

"Everything's fine. No worries."

Chapter Eleven

Lewis

Iodine.

Why give a condemned man iodine?

Some thirty minutes or an hour after White left, the antiseptic benefits of iodine squeezed into the rubble of reflections about what the captain had revealed and what he'd concealed. Certain he would die perhaps this very day, Lewis marveled at how his brain parsed every question White asked, every answer he'd provided, as though the words he chose could impact his fate. Most likely White sought a semblance of confession as spice for a ceremony. He'd exploit a sunset or a midnight, hurl Lewis's words at the men, obliterate anyone's tendency toward pity or pardon.

Iodine? Nothing but a prop. Compassionate eyes, nothing but a ruse. Face it, Lewis told himself: *you're dead.*

The padlock's clatter announced another arrival. From inside the light assailing his isolation, Captain Red threw a bundle of clothes onto the floor.

"You got some pissed-off brothers out there," he announced. "You best at least have your clothes on."

So would that be the means? Rile the men to blows of boots and fists, pain before numbness and, finally, nothingness?

Red, with Marquez and Beckham, escorted Lewis to the classroom where beardless soldiers sat in desks as though awaiting their daily briefing, except their eyes fixed upon him. Red motioned to a single chair in front of the room before joining the other two captains in chairs that from the side of the room faced Lewis, as though they comprised a three-man jury. And maybe they did. Seated cross-legged on the floor directly in front of him, Hernandez recorded Lewis and his swollen lip.

Minutes passed. Men clearing their throats and the buzz of flies provided the only motion and sound. Lewis probed the gap among his front teeth, willed a steady gaze in the direction of the men. Only his hand fidgeted, his fingernails tapping the metal seat. White rose, positioned himself behind and to Lewis's left, spoke past his ringing ears toward the men.

"We all know why we have no computers or cell phones. We shall not be found by electronic means. But had we such access, we would hear how the manipulated press and stooge politicians are reacting toward our mission yesterday. Because their rhetoric is so tired and predictable, we don't need access to know what they're parroting today, and that is this: *We shall find them. We shall hunt them down and bring them to justice.* And so forth, as though they have earned the right to define justice."

White's boots treaded left to right behind Lewis, who felt the back of his neck turn prickly.

"Why this matters," said White, "is why we're sitting here this afternoon, when we should be savoring a triumph. Instead we are contemplating one of our own, Mister Lewis Kline, who yesterday was only steps away from a betrayal."

No, Lewis pretended to decide with gallows humor, those were not looks of affection from the audience.

"Let me remind you that Captains Red, Green, and myself

have sworn an oath that if one of us tries to leave, the other two shall kill him. Although your enlistments will last three years, ours will endure until the day we die. None of us doubt that long before then America will be transformed, restored to her original glory and promise. When citizens wake and rise to reclaim our nation, we will return from exile. There will be time for us to live free, to marry and work and raise a family.

"But until that day, we three are pledged to fight."

White stepped past Lewis, moved to the side of the room where he faced the men as well as the remaining captains. Hernandez kept the camcorder on Lewis only. Was this recording meant for distribution, so that only Lewis's face would be shown and the others remain hidden?

"I cannot leave because away from the PUMAs I am nothing but an information device."

White ambled to the third row, pointed one at a time to Gallahan, Beckham, Marquez, repeating for each: "And so are you...and you...and you..." He moved up the rows, pointing and repeating, until at the front he turned and aimed his finger at Lewis.

"And so, Mr. Kline, are you. An information device, having recorded our location, our personnel, our methods, our defense, our security."

White stepped aside, providing a direct view between the rest of the PUMAs and Lewis.

"Mr. Kline, tell the men what you told me earlier today about your actions and your goals as Operation Redistribution reached its withdrawal stage. You understand perfectly well what I mean. Should you pretend not to understand, the two of us shall return to your current accommodations to discuss the matter further."

Iodine. White had administered iodine. Strange, Lewis thought, that his mind would retrieve and cling to that gesture.

"I guess I panicked…"

"No excuses, Mr. Kline. You were not asked to analyze your character when under fire. What were your actions and what were your goals?"

"I walked away. The wrong way."

"Mr. Kline…" A hint of menace in the voice.

"I meant to. I saw a Burger King, and I wanted to go there. I wanted to get away. My whole goal was to disappear. I wouldn't have told anyone. I swear that's true. If I did, they'd have put me in jail, too."

"Mister Kline, if I were to attempt to do the same—to leave—what would happen to me?"

"I guess…"

"No guess. Certainty."

"Captains Red and Green…they'd kill you."

"We are called to meet a very high standard. Each one of us: an information device, a danger to our brothers. As much as we might fantasize silence, we would be found. The enforcers for the corporate-financial syndicate have effective methods. In the end we would talk.

"Mister Kline, look at me." A pause. "We are all equal, none of us more privileged than another. Therefore, Mister Kline, what is the penalty for your action yesterday?"

"Die."

"Louder, so all may hear."

The heat-pressed room began a slow spin, the buzz of flies louder, the faces of men dissolving to generic blurs.

"Die. I fuckin' die."

Chapter Twelve

Ed

"Tell you what, Ed," Sheriff Darrin Stewart said at the Cle Elum station after examining Lewis's recent text and year-old letter. A thick gray horseshoe moustache hid his upper lip and curled down both sides of his mouth. "Let's call the big boys."

While they waited for those big boys to drive up and across the mountains, Sheriff Stewart dropped what he had on his afternoon task list. He insisted Ed accept his offer to go to a grocery store Starbucks for coffee, where he shared parenting stories and probed Ed for the same.

Now, squeezed against a conference table beneath fluorescent lights in a narrow room, the sheriff and Ed sat to the right of FBI Agent David Thomas and King County Sheriff's Detective Leticia Rosario as those two took turns moving their eyes from the letter, to the text, to the PUMA document the *Seattle Times* had posted. An air conditioning unit hummed quietly while failing its skirmish against sweat.

Thomas and Rosario exchanged a glance and then they turned toward Ed.

"Thank you for sharing these two communications," said Thomas, who wore a white business shirt and blue tie. "Is there anything else that could link your son to the PUMAs?"

Ed exhaled a long breath. "Last time I saw him we were

fishing Whiskeytown Lake more than a year ago. He talked about losing our liberty, blamed the government and corporations. We argued about whether everyone needs to be armed. After that, we both avoided the topic. Fire season hit, we talked by phone a couple of times, nothing serious, then comes that letter at the tail end of the season."

"And no communication since then?"

"None. Except maybe that text."

"Do you know anyone else who's heard from him?"

"No. He didn't show for Christmas, hasn't spoken to his mother or his sister."

Thomas picked up Lewis's letter. "I see the word *syndicate* and I'm assuming that's something you noticed, too. His disappearance, the sudden text, the homicides. On the other hand, there are hundreds of websites and Facebook pages with the same kind of language. These people parrot each other's rhetoric. It's not easy to distinguish one particular style or phraseology."

"How many websites in Washington?"

"Quite a few. Patriot Guard Riders. United Patriots. American Patriot Party. We the People, just to mention a few—we've checked them and haven't found any direct connection to the PUMAs."

"I've had letters and phone calls," cut in the sheriff. "They don't care if I know who they are. Expect me to put up armed resistance when the feds come to take their guns and haul 'em off to a FEMA camp. They don't think you can be a patriot unless you've got an assault rifle."

"Same thing in King County," added Rosario, a short woman in a neatly pressed uniform. "Oath Keepers. Mommy Patriots. Had a group at Joint Base Lewis McChord. Collected guns, recruited snipers, manufactured bombs. Thought they'd blow up a dam, poison the apple crop, figured they'd restore the nation by the year 2031. Then they started killing each other."

"That's what usually happens," said Thomas. "At least so far, it looks like the PUMAs are different."

"What's your gut tell you?" asked Stewart.

"Pardon?"

"The text. The letter. Ed's son."

"I've learned not to trust my gut. My gut follows my brain, and my brain has little stories I want to believe or disbelieve."

"Can't tell you how many times my gut's given me the answer."

"What I *want* to believe," continued Thomas, "is that it's all connected. Might be coincidence, might not be, but we'd be negligent to not follow this strand as far as we can. Sheriff, could you summon a deputy tomorrow at nine to accompany me on a visit to the owners of the phone? By the way, Mr. Kline, you did well to track them down."

"All it took was ten bucks." Ed pitied the old couple. Leave a cell phone in a store, and the next thing you know the FBI's on your doorstep.

"As for the numbers on the text, doing that online search was a start. I don't think they're random."

"Agent Thomas, don't you have people who specialize in that sort of thing? Encryption?" asked Detective Rosario.

"We do. I'll give all this to the experts."

Both investigators took photos of the letter and the text. Ed agreed to give Thomas the letter. They wrote their cell phone numbers on business cards and gave one each to Ed and Stewart, who watched from the outside doorway as they left in an unmarked black Taurus. Stewart retrieved a tin of Copenhagen from his pocket, tapped it against his leg, and took a pinch.

"You on that fire they had above the Teanaway River?"

"Yeah. Right about the time all this other shit happened."

"We must've had a hundred 9-1-1 calls. There oughta be a law against having a fire that close to an interstate." He spat on the pavement below the steps. "Let's you and me let those numbers in that text percolate in our noggins. It's all we've got to go on. Usually these sorts of things are starin' you right in the face. You figure it out, and it was obvious. Wish I could find out what other moms and dads got a letter like you got. Good chance they're all within a 200-mile radius."

"That's my guess."

"Text out of Sammamish, armored truck in Issaquah, hits on the senators in Bellevue. Even though they're active on the west side, my money's on the PUMAs being holed up somewhere my side of the mountains. I got college kids, rednecks, farmers and farmworkers, mountains, desert, firs and pines and sagebrush. Might as well have a militia, too. Sure sorry about your kid. I'll say a prayer he's not mixed up in this. If it is him, he wanted out and rang the alarm."

He took a faded green bandanna from his trousers, wiped it across the top of his nearly bald head. "Got to go in and get my hat or I'll turn red as a stop sign."

"What would you do, Sheriff?"

"What would I do? If what?"

"If it were your kid. Or you thought it was."

Stewart spat to the side, pondered a moment.

"Like I said. I'll say a prayer."

"Thanks for all you're doing," said Ed, reaching his hand out for Stewart to shake. "How can I find out if you or the others are making progress?"

"I'll tell you straight. In the middle of an investigation we can't share a damn thing. Generalities is all."

Ed nodded his head and walked down the steps. When he had nearly reached his pickup across the small parking lot, Stewart called out to him.

"Hey, Ed. You done all you could."

Ed got in the truck. Maybe today he'd done all he could. But what about the other twenty-three years? He hesitated before putting key to ignition, his body heavy, his stomach unsettled. A breeze inched through the cab, slow-danced the conifers outside.

They'd fished around here, too, Lewis and he, although at the time neither could have guessed Sharon was a month away from dismissing Ed from her life. Several miles west on the Yakima River, they caught cutthroat and rainbows. They followed a creek up a draw, thought they'd bushwhack diagonally back to the truck and ended up using the GPS to make sure they were moving the right direction. That was a long time ago, a hot day of hauling fish and gear through thorny brush, learning the hard way that direct lines don't necessarily save time.

Ed started his truck and drove slowly to the parking lot exit, the long-ago day still playing in his mind. They'd brought their scratched legs to a pizza parlor, left their fish under ice in a cooler beneath some shade. Lewis wanted shrimp on his pizza, same as always, and—

Bingo.

It didn't make total sense. The numbers weren't all there, but maybe, just maybe...

In the rearview mirror, Stewart still stood hatless on the top step. Ed put the truck in reverse and swung a half-loop until he backed into the parking space. His heart quickening, he hurried to the expressionless sheriff.

"Coordinates," he said.

Stewart's eyes flickered comprehension.

"Might be," he replied. "Let's go in."

"Let's call those other two back."

Twenty minutes later, Thomas and Rosario joined Ed and the sheriff studying topo maps arrayed in a line on the conference room table.

"47-03-30 runs straight through my neighborhood," said Stewart. "If it's a coordinate, a 1-2 longitude could be anywhere from halfway across the Pacific to damn near Moses Lake."

Stewart placed his forefinger above Gray's Harbor on the Pacific Ocean, moved it east. The line of latitude climbed up and down mountainous miles of isolated Olympic Peninsula timberland, dropped down through Olympia, Fort Lewis, pastures and farms, before climbing again into the Cascades north of Mount Rainier through alternating sections of wilderness and private land, descending the east slopes through isolated and increasingly sparse forest until reaching sagebrush in the Columbia Basin, passing six miles north of Ellensburg. Off the east bank of the Columbia River, longitudinal lines decreased into the 119s.

Ed felt sure Lewis was somewhere on that line. *Let's go,* he wanted to say. *Let's look. Let's get him the hell out of there.*

"Why would someone leave out the rest of the coordinates?" asked Rosario.

"Look at the text," said Ed. "He's scared, he's asking for help. Maybe he couldn't finish it. They found the phone in a toilet, remember?"

They stared at the map as though waiting for the squiggly lines and mountain peaks to provide an answer.

Ed felt like jumping onto the table and giving a speech. *Let's go. Call the cavalry, launch the drones. Parachute the smokejumpers. Scrape winos off the sidewalks, put them on the team, too. Let's go.*

"If they're anywhere close to Ellensburg I'd put my money west," said Stewart. "A man could hide out and never be found. Logging outfits have a hard time keepin' their lands patrolled. Gang of crazies—sorry, Ed—could buy a piece of land out there and pretend they've got their own little republic."

"We could read every license plate on every vehicle, photograph every structure," said Thomas.

"Yeh, but could you smoke out the right bunch of crazies, assuming it's the outfit we're lookin' for? 'Cause I can tell you, those hills are crawling with wackos. Every five miles of logging road there's some landing with cans and buckets and pumpkins and old jeeps blasted to smithereens. They're all squawkin' about running out of ammo. And how long would it take you to get all those pictures and do anything with them?"

"Depends."

"Yeh. Always does."

"I expect they'd give this high priority," said Rosario. "These guys just took out our top two legislators. They're not shooting at beer bottles."

"We could have operative intel within a week," said Thomas.

"How about right now?"

All three turned toward Ed. "I've got a bird that can fly a straight line."

Nobody replied.

Ed walked away from the group, stopped at the wall on the right side of the room, strode to the opposite side of the table. He placed both hands on the table, leaned toward the others.

"There are all kinds of reasons for a helicopter to buzz

by—logging, fires, pot gardens. We don't need to wait for all the desk jockeys to sign off on an e-mail."

Thomas broke the silence.

"When can we leave?" he asked.

Chapter Thirteen

Lewis

On cement in ammonia darkness, Lewis lay on his back, clothed this time, hands clasped behind his head. Although the time of his death remained uncertain, a collage of people and places popped into his mind.

Vance Elliott, a kid he rode bikes with in second grade. Stephanie, the cheerleader who sat in front of him in U.S. History—her beauty so unnerved him that he never had the guts to say so much as "hi" to her. The day he and Martin unloaded pallets of life jackets at the sporting goods store—yeah, like that was a truly significant life event. His brain had gone weird. He reached for a different kind of memory.

Camille—the first one, a petite Filipina he met at Shasta College…almond skin, dark espresso eyes, thick black hair, legs explosive as a cheetah's, turning, twisting, clutching. Oh, Camille…it was all play to her. If he had meant something to her, where would he be now? Tara was next, wide hazel eyes and an intense voice, jumping into his life during an internship in Yosemite National Park. Oh, those lunch breaks in her blue dome tent! They had kept in touch two years, a crazy hot rendezvous every few months, until she met a guy in Bakersfield. If Lewis had only asked, he felt sure she'd have settled with him, and then where would he be now?

For one, he'd still have all his teeth and his left ear wouldn't be ringing like a siren and he wouldn't be lying on cement where darkness sucked away the measuring of time. He wouldn't be waiting like a horse thief on a platform behind the hangman's noose.

He felt sorry he let anger lure him into the whole PUMAs thing, sorry he hadn't chosen a better time to escape, sorry he'd never get to find out what his life could have been. If he had another chance he'd pretend to be a full-bore rabid PUMA and the first chance that presented itself he'd run, no subtlety to it, just flat-ass haul. But he'd never get the chance. As soon as White lured him into pronouncing his own death sentence he ended the session, directed Marquez and Beckham to escort him back to the cell.

Nothing fancy for a last meal, either. Cold oatmeal. They must have made a big pot just for him.

When light suddenly glared out the single overhead bulb and the padlock rattled, Lewis raised his head, slid backward to the wall, waited. The door opened and Red stepped in, Marquez and Beckham behind him.

"Hands behind your back," he said. With a white rope the two soldiers bound his hands.

A right turn out the kitchen, down the passage past the classroom and barracks, outside into early dusk, bright and vivid to his hibernating eyes, across the dirt clearing, the pines and scrub oak mutely observing. Another right turn around the workshop building and there stood all the bare-faced PUMAs in army khakis, button-down camouflage shirts, and black PUMA caps, but no guns, no noose. Marquez and Beckham looped the rope several times around his chest and a cottonwood tree trunk. As soon as they stepped away, Hernandez started the camcorder.

Captain Green held up a machete.

"There are many uses for a machete, Mr. Kline." White had noticed Lewis's glance. "How we'll use this one depends upon you."

A breeze rustled the cottonwood leaves, escorted fuzzy seed clusters across the clearing. He tried to interpret the moods of the men staring at him. Hatred. Fear. Confusion.

"For the record, answer the following questions. On the morning of July 30—that is yesterday—did you report to your assigned post for Operation Redistribution?"

"Yes, Sir."

"While your fellow soldiers accomplished their mission and vacated the site, what was your job?"

"Provide cover, Sir."

"And then how were you supposed to withdraw?"

"Follow my teammates, Sir."

"We have already established what you did instead. What did you do?"

A fucking machete. He didn't have to answer—what difference would it make?

"Soldier Kline."

"Sir?"

"What did you do?"

Someone in the group cleared his throat. In the woods behind him, a lone cricket rubbed harsh notes.

"Walked away, Sir."

"In other words, you abandoned your post and you abandoned the mission. Is that correct?"

"Yes, Sir."

"We have established the penalty for desertion, haven't we, Soldier Kline?"

"Yes, Sir."

"What is the penalty?"

He wouldn't give White the satisfaction of saying it this time.

"Soldier Kline…."

"Soldier Kline, to pay the penalty is to declare the gravity of the crime, a sad but necessary example to those who remain. No militia can succeed if its soldiers can decide to leave in the heat of battle. When a coward flees, his brothers die.

"But despite your betrayal, Mr. Kline, we have decided to present you one final choice."

What now? The means of execution? The duration of pain?

"Mr. Kline, if you had the opportunity to redeem yourself, to prove your loyalty to your brothers, would you take it?"

Another day? Another handful of hours? Surely he'd have to pay, have to perform some abomination. But the first chance he had, he'd run. It couldn't be worse than now.

No sobbing—put metal in the voice.

"Yes, sir, I would."

"Do you recall, Mister Kline, I told you this matter would be resolved within forty-eight hours?"

"Yes, sir."

"Twenty of those hours have passed. The remaining time is short. Are you prepared to fulfill a mission, no matter how lethal?"

"I'll do it, sir."

Like hell. But a bullet in the back would beat a slice to the throat.

"Captain Green."

Keeping the machete raised, Green stepped toward Lewis. A couple of the men sucked in loud breaths.

Lewis heard himself swallow. *Dear God, let it be the rope and not the neck.*

Green stopped in front of Lewis. With his free hand, he

grabbed and gripped Lewis by the beard. Lewis's eyes went wide when he saw the machete move toward his throat. Despite his determination to show no fear, a muffled cry pushed out his mouth.

The machete caught the hair between Green's fist and Lewis's chin, sliced a portion of beard.

Chapter Fourteen

Ed

"You mean you can hop on that helicopter, take a little run whenever and wherever you feel like it?" asked Rosario.

They had exited their vehicles at the helitack base and followed Ed into his office where he gathered headsets for each of them.

Hell, thought Ed. She was right. Two thousand bucks per operating hour said he couldn't do that.

"Seems like we've got business enough," said Stewart, who'd remembered his hat, a spotless cream-colored Stetson.

"Maybe you two can do that, but I sure can't," said Rosario. "I'd better get clearance."

"How many links up the chain before you get an answer?" asked Stewart.

"One. I'll bother my sheriff directly on this one. What would you say if one of your detectives or deputies asked permission for this?"

"I give them latitude. Latitude—there's a line for you."

"I'll see how amused my sheriff is." She turned toward Ed. "How long you figure this will take? I'd better have an answer. Plus, I've been planning….Hell, I don't know what this sounds like in the scheme of things, but my girl's birthday is tomorrow and I'm meaning to bake cupcakes tonight instead of buying store-bought."

"Let's say an hour, maybe ninety minutes," said Ed. "You don't have to go if you don't want to, but I'd like to have someone with me, extra sets of eyes. Otherwise it's just some wacko helitack pilot whose word you'd have to take."

"Howdy, Ed." Although his shift had ended a half hour ago, Zweigert stepped inside. Now Zweigert would know. He'd know anyway, the next time he viewed the printout and saw additional flight time. The ones who stayed on base in barracks would hear Bessie leave, but they wouldn't think it particularly unusual. Ed took her out from time to time, tested systems, scouted water sources.

"Hey, Zweigy. Got a few law enforcement folks with me. They want to take a look-see south of here."

Zweigert turned his chin one degree left, combining the move with a long look that needed no words to interpret. Why didn't they use their own damn helicopter?

"So I volunteered Bessie," Ed continued. "We take her up anyway after maintenance. We'll just have some guests this time."

Zweigert nodded. "She's ready." He walked to his desk, gathered a daypack and coffee cup, and left.

"Test flight, huh?" said Rosario.

"You bet," said Ed. Cautious Kline—they'd faint from shock if they could see him now. But all the way driving back from the Cle Elum substation, Ed heard his son calling from somewhere in the forests south of the freeway.

I'm down here, Dad. Help me.

Not that they could simply land and pick him up. But if they found something, they'd have a head start. The feds would do what they do, a siege or something, try to wait them out, minimize casualties. Maybe sweep in during the dead of night, the way they did in the war.

And bring Lewis home alive. A noncombatant held against his will, a text message to prove his innocence.

Twenty minutes later with Thomas up front and Stewart and Rosario in the back, Ed lifted Bessie off the concrete pad. He pointed them diagonally southwest toward the line of latitude. Below them, green fir cloaks blotched with clearcuts rose thickly toward mountain summits, while ahead Mount Rainier towered its rounded crown of ice. In a split-second gap of trees, the White River churned with glacier melt. Although they flew 400 feet above the land and the sun settled toward the western horizon, the day's heat still seeped into the helo.

"We're on the line," said Ed.

"Lotta road between here and Ellensburg and none of it straight," said Stewart.

"Nearest grocery store would be Enumclaw," observed Rosario.

"Now we go east. Fifty knots work for you, Agent Thomas?"

"Fine. Just don't change speed. We don't want to spook anyone, in case there's anyone to spook. Keep north of any structures so I can get a good shot."

While Thomas took a camcorder from a black pouch, Ed picked up a topo map from the collection he had tucked next to the center console, examined the circles he'd drawn at every spot a road crossed. They passed two logging roads, State Highway 410 on its southern sweep toward Rainier, Dalles Ridge, two tiny lakes tucked beneath cliffs. Douglas firs continued domination, admitting a few Black Cottonwoods within their canopy, occasional clusters of Western Larch, and clear patches where hikers parked their rigs. At 400 feet they were low enough to spot the colors backpackers wore where the trails revealed them in open areas strewn with rocks.

"Yahoo country ahead," said Stewart after they left wilderness, a dirt road along the Little Naches River just to the south. After crossing a paved road, they encountered more isolation, rolling mountains, narrow canyons, brush-choked drainages.

And then a sudden gouge among the trees, solar panels on green metal roofs, a scurry of figures, narrow dirt path disappearing south into forest, gone, behind them now.

"Not on my map," said Stewart.

"How old's your map?" asked Thomas.

"Needs updating, that's for sure. Don't suppose they're Boy Scouts. They'd have gotten a building permit."

Easy, Ed cautioned himself. It might mean nothing.

Firs ceded turf to pines, oaks, then yellowed grassland tumbling to a plain, irrigated alfalfa, homes, Interstate 90 and Ellensburg southeast in the distance. Above a hillside of sage and a dozen uplooking steers, Ed paused the ship.

Less than twenty-four hours ago he'd been drunk, dropped Lewis's picture, vomited. Pathetic. But now...

We're coming, son.

"Can you do ten knots slower and a couple hundred feet higher on the return trip?" asked Thomas.

"Should we have a return trip?" asked Rosario. "I thought we didn't want to spook them."

"Let's let a little time go by," agreed Ed. "But it makes sense if we're on a flight path that we'd return the same way we came."

"No building permit," added Stewart. "Hell, that's reason enough to jump 'em. Just drop in out of the sky, here comes the sheriff. That'd teach 'em not to mess with the planning department."

Chapter Fifteen

Lewis

Green opened his hand, dropped a fistful of beard to the ground.

Lewis decided he liked his neck very much—solid, unopened.

"Mister Kline." White stood among the other soldiers, who stared wide-eyed at Lewis, their shudders almost visible. "You shall be escorted to your temporary accommodations, where you shall remain until we're ready for you to perform your mission. You must perform. The PUMAs have no use for men who cannot fulfill their duties. Soldiers Marquez and Beckham, untie Mr. Kline, return him to his quarters, and lock the door."

Untied yet still unfree, Lewis moved away from the cottonwood. In the distance from the west, a slowly approaching noise chopped the air, a sound that always accelerated their heartbeats. Lewis slowed his pace as much as Marquez and Beckham would allow.

A helicopter.

Could be loggers, or government weed busters, or a rich schmuck on his way to Spokane.

Just don't let it be his father. Not now.

"PUMAs, return to barracks. Your duties are done this evening. If we are fortunate, we will soon have a certain Soldier Kline back within our ranks."

The hum of an engine aloft and a rapid thwump-thwump grew louder as the helicopter neared. Men moving toward the path to the barracks paused.

No. Not this way.

Rotor blades, still hidden west somewhere behind the trees, hacked at the sky, moving closer, until a white underbelly with black numbers 212 sped overhead. His father's helo. More than once, Lewis had visited the base. He remembered the numbers, the blue top, the thin red stripe in the middle. All the PUMAs gazed upward at the exhalation of its passing, and then it was gone, its sound chopping quieter.

White spun a half-circle, charged Lewis, stopped six inches from his face, glared fire, his mouth twisted and tight. Marquez and Beckham bounced back.

"Your fuckin' daddy!" he roared.

"No!"

"Your fuckin' daddy! We were pals, remember? I know his fucking bird."

Later no longer existed. The time was now.

He ducked and whirled, sprang toward the trees. Sprint. Escape or bullets. He dashed past the cottonwood, rocketed his feet across the needle duff, pumped his arms to gain speed, leaped a downed log, picked a gap in the trees now ten feet away. He'd reach the woods, dodge among the darkening trunks, let the hope of freedom push him faster and farther.

Heavy iron arms wrapped his waist, threw him hard to the ground. Knees thrust a kidney-blow to his back.

"Where you going?" snarled White, breathing rapidly.

Lewis awaited the bullet, the blade, whatever came next.

"Captain Red!" White shouted while his knees pinned Lewis. "Order number one—AIR-D! If that bastard returns, bring him down, and then get your soldiers here within two minutes. Captain Green! Order number two—begin evacuation load-up immediately and then await further orders."

Red and Green barked commands behind him.

"You know AIR-D, Traitor Kline," White said. "That's when you shoot down enemy aircraft."

White pivoted from one of the knees on Lewis's back. A hand grasped the back of his shirt collar, yanked upward, forced him to his knees and then his feet, twirled him a half-turn to bring them face to face.

"A flight path directly over our base. What's next, Traitor Kline?"

What was next? Terror locked his jaw, froze his tongue.

White glared, awaiting an answer Lewis could not provide, and then he shot his arm hurricane speed and a fist smashed Lewis below his lip to the left of his chin. His head snapped back and he heard his jaw rupture, felt the movement of bone, and the pain of it shot to the top of his skull, withered his legs. He crumbled, but White grabbed a fistful of shirt before he hit the ground, spun him toward the buildings, kicked him hard in the ass. He sprawled face-first to the ground, groaned involuntarily, his entire head a vortex of pain. White grasped the back of his shirt collar, twisted it tight against his throat, yanked up his head then lifted the weight of his body until his feet touched the ground. He pushed Lewis forward while squeezing the collar, constricting air.

"If your daddy comes back," White was breathing hard, "I want you to hear what happens, so you can feel proud of yourself. If he doesn't come back it won't matter for you. We're finished with you, Traitor Kline."

Chapter Sixteen

Ed

Below Copter 212, rows of irrigation pipes marked dusk like chameleons, silver gleam fading to muted gray. Alfalfa leaned east with the breeze while metallic blue sky tinted the northern horizon. Ed swung a wide 180-degree arc, backtracked past trotting Herefords, hovered above native wheatgrasses and sage beyond the green edge of farmland.

An image lodged itself in Ed's mind, a five-second snippet of flight among the dashing conifers and meadows and undulating land—the sudden green roofs and gawking humans. Dread lay like a chunk of wood in his gut. If later tonight or tomorrow Thomas and Stewart and Rosario gathered a posse and raided the place, and somehow his son survived…which Lewis would they find?

A Lewis who killed or abetted killing? A Lewis who wanted to escape? Both?

Perhaps he had already escaped.

"No electricity, no cell phones, no internet," said Stewart. "But it's ATV central and if that was them they'd be hidin' in plain sight. Couple months ago down that direction, one of my deputies hauled out a 16-year-old girl. Pitched herself headfirst out a four-wheeler and the four-wheeler on top of her. And she wasn't even drinkin'. Suppose those are the

PUMAs and they're shooting a thousand rounds a day. They'd fit right in. We got places where bullet casings outnumber the rocks."

"You say it's common for helicopters to double back the way they came?" asked Thomas.

"Same flight path, you bet," said Ed.

"Let's do it," said Thomas.

Ahead of them, desert foothills lay in repose after the intensity of sun and heat. They traversed back across the rising, desiccated land, crossed canyons an eye-blink wide already night-black at the bottom where summer had dried the creeks. Vegetation passed in reverse order—oaks, pines, firs, from isolated specimens among the withered grass, to clusters, to a thick mass cloaking the ground.

"Any moment now," said Stewart.

The feds would surround them and negotiate, wait them out, avoid a shooting match. That's how they did it these days. It might take months, but there was a good chance Lewis would emerge alive.

Ed pictured a jury scene—would there be sympathy for his son? *He wanted out and he rang the alarm.* Even Stewart, a lawman, recognized Lewis was innocent. Lured and then forced to stay, death if he tried to leave. Perhaps he would not face charges at all. Lewis could be seen as a hero—risking his life to give away their location, to stop these monsters. Maybe Lewis would be home soon.

They'd go fishing then, oh yes. Do one of those charter boat trips and if it were fire season, fuck it, he'd take a leave. Someone else could have Bessie for a couple of weeks.

Thomas leaned forward, angled the camcorder down.

A cut in the trees, green roofs but humans absent, starboard to give Thomas a good view, then gone, behind them.

Two puffs of smoke popped up from the edge of a meadow. Flame flashed in the center of each puff.

Ed's rational brain—not here, not now—lost out to his Afghan veteran reptilian brain.

Impact in one second.

He let Bessie drop while thrusting her hard to port, felt the torque yank his guts. In the next instant a fiery luminescence lit the dusk-dim sky behind them. A deafening bang burst through the clamor of the engine and knocked them with a roundhouse punch twenty degrees starboard. There was a split second of silence, replaced by the blare of the ENG OUT signal blinking on the front console.

No power.

They were strapped inside fifteen thousand pounds of dead weight seven hundred feet in the air.

Ed's feet tap-danced the pedals, kept them level. "Hold on!" he shouted while lowering the collective, idling the throttle, easing them down so that air flowed up through the rotor blades, kept them spinning, propelling Bessie into autorotation. The front console showed six hundred feet Above Ground Level. If he did it right, they'd meet Earth in 25 seconds. If he made a mistake, they'd drop like a Fiat and the impact of ground would be their last living memory. He had performed the maneuver in training but never with lives at stake.

Adjusting to maintain rotor RPM, Ed flicked his eyes from the console monitors to the landscape, finding nowhere to set Bessie down except the meadow directly below.

They'd be sitting ducks.

"Copter 212 mayday mayday!" he radioed, doubtful that among the mountains and canyons his voice would find air traffic control.

Twenty seconds, 400 feet AGL.

"We'll land fine," he said for the others. "Get ready to haul ass." They were quiet, frozen, fearful. But he didn't have a slot in his conscious for them, had to focus on Bessie. Spinning blades reassured with a loud high pitch. Without the roar of the engine, Ed descended, circled the outside perimeter of the clearing that hurried toward them.

Ten seconds, 150 feet AGL, airspeed 50 knots. Ed rolled the throttle, flared Bessie, reduced speed, hovered.

Spiderweb holes peppered the windows. Thomas dropped the camcorder, slumped in the harness.

Thirty feet AGL. Ten feet. Apply the collective, level the ship, windshield holes multiplying, a surge forward, a jolt. On the ground.

"Get out!" Ed yelled. He yanked loose his harness, flung aside his headset.

Automatic rifle fire smacked chings and pings against the helo. Ed thrust open the door, landed hunched, jittered back, opened the cabin door.

It looked as though they were sleeping. Shaking them flopped their heads, failed to rouse. A red sting hammered his hand as though from a ten-pound honeybee and another smashed his upper arm. Pain buckled his knees, tottered him forward. Instinct dropped him to the ground, kicked him scrambling down the fuselage, around the tail, a hunched sprint into the woods, his right arm hanging useless. His foot struck a downed log, and he sprawled forward into pointy-twigged brush. He popped up, whirled around the tangle, reached a maze of tree trunks, zig-zagged left and right.

He forced himself to stop, to ignore pain, to slow panting breath, to listen.

Two-second bursts of automatic weapon fire tattered the air, gained volume. He willed himself to stay put. He could run again if he heard them enter the woods.

"Three of them!" shouted a voice. Through the trees it was difficult to determine distance—fifty yards away?

"Good marksmanship, soldiers."

"Thank you, Sir."

"What about the other one?"

"Our orders are to switch to evac mode. They've found us and they'll come back. You three sweep ten yards apart twenty yards into the woods. If you find him finish him. You've got thirty seconds. Beckham, count off the tens."

Bootsteps swished through grass, closed into the duff, crunched old needles and cones. How far in had he gone? Ed straightened and squeezed against the pine, willed himself invisible behind the furrowed bark.

"Ten," called a nearby voice. They would walk past him, see him peripherally or when they turned to go back. Each touch of foot sounded louder, the twigs and the needles more defined but the intervals slow and deliberate. Breaths panted while modulating from their sprint to the helicopter.

"Twenty."

When they reached his tree, he'd jump at the nearest one, hope to hell he'd make contact before they'd fire. If he were between two shooters, maybe they'd hold off from fear of friendly fire. Either way, he wasn't going to wait. He'd go down fighting.

The near sound of another step prickled his neck. A man cleared his throat, close enough so that Ed could whirl around the tree and connect with a single punch. He tensed his muscles, ready to spring.

"Thirty."

"We're done, soldiers," called the leader from near Bessie. "Spray a few rounds and then get back here."

Gunfire burst, percussions warping the air. Like a dog or a horse in wild panic, his legs said run. His brain overruled them, pushed him harder against the tree.

The ringing in his ears muffled the sounds of retreating steps.

"Beckham, cover our rear. Gallahan—finish them, a bullet each."

Three shots followed, seconds apart, each one evoking from Ed a quiet cry of anguish and guilt and animal rage.

Chapter Seventeen

Lewis

Dual thunder blasts boomed ground level a hundred yards away. Lewis recognized the explosive percussion of an RPG launcher. One second, maybe two seconds followed, no whoosh like the movies or the video games, only a jab of helicopter sound, then two more explosions from the sky reverberating down into the twin ventricles of Lewis's heart. Trees blocked the view, but after the secondary explosions the sky no longer carried the sound of a helicopter engine. Lewis awaited the sound of a third explosion to punctuate the meeting of helicopter and ground. No such noise came, but the rat-a-tats of automatic weapons tore into the dusk.

"You would have your brothers killed, or, worse, captured," said White, still behind Lewis. They had both paused when the RPG launchers fired. "For that, I detest you. But I pity you, too. Your father was a good man."

When White loosened his grip, Lewis slumped to the ground. He felt his heart spasm, an agonizing concussion sweeping over the damage to his jaw, his mouth, his nose. Hatred flooded his being, and he turned his battered body to confront the source of all the pain. White unholstered his Beretta, pointed it at Lewis's head, and Lewis found he did not care.

"Whatever you did to fetch your heroic father, you summoned him to an early death. You knew what would happen."

"You bastard. You killed him."

"No, Traitor Kline. *You* killed him. He was my friend. Now you'll die with that knowledge."

"Shoot your fucking gun."

"My friend."

"Shoot…the…fucking…gun!"

White lowered the Beretta, re-holstered it.

"No, I will not execute you in this manner. I don't understand you, Traitor Kline, but that's irrelevant right now. We shall dispose of you lawfully. You shall serve an instructive purpose."

Men rushed by them on both sides, carrying crates and boxes one way and returning empty handed for more equipment. Captain Red hustled in from the pathway that led from the meadow.

"Captain White, we took it down."

"But you missed."

"He took evasive action. We knocked out the engine."

"How hard did it land?"

"RPG's went off right above the tail rotor. Looked like it hit a little bump, then it circled the field and landed like a feather."

"It's called autorotation. What about the occupants?"

"We shot it up good. Killed three. One got away."

Please, God, let it be Dad.

"Was it by chance the pilot?"

I'd run if I could. Imagine us finding each other in the woods.

"Might've been. He came out the front. There was another

in the front we killed."

"We must leave now. You and Captain Green have the men retrieve their packs and report to their rigs. Do a head count. Take my pack while I escort this prisoner to the truck."

"Why bother? If it's his papa that got out, let him find a corpse if he comes snoopin' around here."

"I recognize the contingencies of war, Captain Red, but if we are to restore a nation governed by laws, we must set the example ourselves."

"I'll shoot the sunovabitch myself."

"Perhaps. But not yet. Please remember my pack."

White bent to Lewis, pulled him upright by the shirt, marched him to a pickup, shoved him against the side.

"Odds are fifty-fifty your father's still kicking. A lot better than your odds, Traitor Kline."

Chapter Eighteen

Ed

He stood as straight as the Ponderosa Pine behind whose trunk he hid, fighting to silence his breath despite the knife-gouge pain shouting from his arm and hand. The call to leave, to let him escape, had to be a ruse. Someone waited for him to reveal himself. Minutes ticked by while he listened for the crunch of a footstep among the downed needles and twigs.

An owl hooted and crickets chirped in full chorus. Bats darted overhead.

Images hammered his skull—Thomas holding the camcorder, Stewart in his cowboy hat, Rosario in a kitchen, frosting cupcakes for her daughter. His mind supplied a photo for Rosario's birthday child—Sarah, his own girl, her pre-kindergarten face glowing behind a birthday cake. Now all his passengers were dead, dead because of the only rash action he'd ever instigated his entire life.

And what about Lewis—had he endangered him, too? Why else would they shoot him down? They'd be crazy to shoot down a random helo just for the hell of it or out of paranoia. It didn't match the cold-blooded execution of their other crimes.

On the other hand—what if Lewis had fired the RPG or one of the assault rifles?

What would Nancy do when she found out? Because the truth would emerge. This would be national news, juicy especially because of the foolish pilot hoping to extricate his son from a band of terrorists. He'd flown good people to their deaths. He'd become poison—a son gone lunatic and murderous and as a result, Ed himself addle-brained, defying procedural rules, causing death.

The oncoming night carried a chill. His legs began to shake and then his chest, his jaw, his teeth. With his good hand he gripped the pine's furrowed bark, leaned to hold himself upright. He moved a quarter turn, rested his back against the tree, freed his good hand to touch the wounded one, a spot that turned out to be an actual hole, blood-damp, coagulating. He twisted his neck to study the dark damp oval marking the other bullet's pathway into his arm. Something about that particular pain suggested splintered bone. His flight suit was moist with sweat.

A small clearing in his head reminded Ed that wounds, physical and otherwise, brought shock, turned the world chill. The night was probably still warm.

What was he going to do—call 9-1-1? Not out here. He slowly unzipped his flight suit, listening for a reaction to the noise. Nothing. With his left hand he reached across his chest to retrieve the cellphone from the right front pocket of his jeans. Placing the screen against his body to hide the glow, he lifted it up, lowered his head for a brief look.

No reception.

Did someone in the area see the RPGs explode behind his helo? Maybe yes, maybe no. Even so, such a someone would have to drive to get help, or, disastrously, fancy himself a hero and speed toward the scene.

Who would notice Bessie's absence from her pad at Snoqualmie Pass? A helitack crewman might think nothing was amiss. Come morning, Bessie's vacant cement bed would grab Zwiegy's attention right away, but he would have no idea where to look for her.

Even if the Mayday had been heard, rugged terrain might muffle Bessie's emergency transponder. Thomas wasn't married, but Rosario and Stewart were—fear would gradually nestle into their spouses as night hours crept by without them. They'd leave messages, eventually would call dispatchers. They'd gather a search team, but where would they look?

Search and rescue—deputies, paramedics, volunteers, Forest Service folks befuddled by what the hell the helicopter was doing in this remote region without prior communication—they'd ride into an ambush. Maybe this nutcase militia harbored martyr fantasies, a warehouse of armaments to blast away before death transported them to some "patriot" variant of a thousand virgins.

Three murder victims gnawed his conscious—and more might already be in route.

Still shivering, Ed brought his mind back to the woods where he hid. Exactly where was he? Meadow to his left—that was north of the PUMAs, so PUMAs to his right. Somewhere behind him a logging road cut through the trees. In front of him lay many miles of rugged canyons progressively more dry, eventually rolling into hills of sage and yellowed grass. Twenty miles north, a campground huddled beside a creek whose name he couldn't remember.

He lowered himself enough to pick up a pinecone, tossed it twenty feet. Crickets paused then resumed their courtship. Hunched low, he stepped out, did a test-dash to a different tree, dove for the ground.

Sudden thrashing shook the brush next to him. His face pressed to decaying needles, he recognized the rhythmic gambol of a retreating deer.

No bullets had fired. No footsteps stormed his direction.

They were gone.

Heart thumping, he raised himself, sat on the ground, his throbbing arm and hand admonishing him. What was he going to do? Rush the camp, tackle multiple armed men, subdue them all like a Hollywood banshee? He took a long breath, cleared his mind, calmed his nerves. Shivering, his empty stomach queasy, pain waves now a uniform ache, he decided to remain near Bessie. When the rescue sounds approached, skyward or by land, he'd dash to visibility, warn them by voice, by waving his good arm. Perhaps an ensuing spree of PUMA bullets would finish him, but they would also serve to emphasize the danger and to mitigate his guilt.

Somewhere toward the PUMA camp a diesel engine pierced the night's stillness. Two other vehicles stirred. Gears engaged and engines moved like a distant mechanical stream carving a pathway his direction, yet no headlights reflected off trees or cast beams toward the stars. He hurried toward the road, found it closer than he thought. Panting human breaths and steady footfalls sounded as the engines neared. From around a corner two moonlit men emerged, followed closely by four shadowy vehicles, three vans and a pickup, soon in front of Ed then past him, gone.

So they were fleeing. Was Lewis in one of those vehicles?

For a moment Ed thought about trailing them, jogging through the dust clouds they'd stirred, tracking them to wherever they were going. But he wasn't a young man anymore. He couldn't run like Nancy.

The vehicles hadn't come far before they'd passed by. That meant the compound, too, was closer than he thought. The rescuers would be safe—unless the PUMAs left some individuals behind.

Weaving back and forth from the woods to the road, he

crept south among the trees, pausing many times to listen. Half an hour later a large gap among the moon-lit treetops announced a ground-level clearing just ahead. He settled at the edge near a building with one door and a single window on both sides. Rabbits shared a patch of grass with a doe and two spotted fawns. Tree frogs, crickets, and a pair of owls sang a soft chorale. The night air carried a warm evergreen scent but he could also smell his own body beneath the flight suit, old sweat, dust, fear, grief, guilt.

He forced himself to wait, to listen and observe an additional thirty minutes. He imagined himself trying to explain: to Nancy, to his ex-wife, to his daughter Sarah, Forest Service supervisors, law enforcement people, executives of Pacific Aviation Services, the grieving relatives of his murdered passengers. And to the passengers themselves, staring specter-like in his brain. To Lewis.

He was sorry. God, he was sorry. Would God forgive him, if there were a god? He wished he could believe.

He moved from the woods into the open, found the door unlocked, and stepped into a darker world than the one outside. His eyes already adjusted to the night, he spied a coverless light-switch box against a wooden post, considered a moment, decided against lighting the room. He turned on his phone's flashlight.

To his right, an opening led to a small room with three beds and three empty portable wardrobes. To his left, an office contained three desks, bare at the top, all missing the big lower drawers where files would be kept. Past these two rooms he found a latrine and shower room to the left, a kitchen and dining area to the right. A walk-in pantry contained enough canned vegetables and fruit, packaged pastas, grains, beans, and flour to feed many people a long time. Farther ahead, another door at the end of the central passageway had tacked to it a facsimile of the Declaration of Independence. Plywood extended from post to post. Nowhere did he find a painted surface or sheetrock.

Doorless entries led to a classroom on the left, a barracks on the right. In the fourth locker of the barracks, permanent black marker on the inside waistband of green camo-trousers identified the owner:

KLINE

This locker contained much more clothing than the first three, as well as a small duffle pack, a sleeping bag, deodorant, a toothbrush and toothpaste, soap. He looked through eight more lockers. None had sleeping bags, packs, or personal items.

Why?

In the classroom, a large USGS topo map caught Ed's attention. On it someone had drawn a small, neat circle to mark the location where he now stood, explaining exactly how Lewis had known the geographic coordinates. Elsewhere a dozen signs printed boldfaced on 8 ½ X 11 sheets of paper exhorted the abandoned room:

A warrior lives not by his contemplations but by his acts.

A drink from the cup of freedom harbors the taste of blood.

The defense of America depends on the edge of a sword and the soldier who wields it.

It reminded him of one of the colonels who had rotated through his base long ago in the Balkans—corny stuff, but his soldiers bought into it.

He returned to the kitchen, found iodine in a cupboard beneath the sink, poured it directly on his hand, sucked in his breath as white foam formed inside and around the hole. With a knife he cut a slit in the upper sleeve of his flight suit and shirt, ripped away fabric, and through the opening poured iodine on his arm wound, gritted his teeth. The sink yielded hot water. Awkwardly using only his left hand, he wrapped his right hand and upper arm with clean strips of a white dish towel.

Outside through the front door, Ed noted another building twenty yards to his left. Thirty yards straight ahead down a pathway stood large sheds on both sides. Past them, shadowy beneath the half-moon sky, a little road angled toward another structure partially visible through the trees. Before Ed could take more than a few steps, another faint engine noise brought him to a stop. It approached from southeast, opposite the direction the militia had left.

He dashed back into the barracks room, grabbed Lewis's trousers, then hurried through the veil of woods to the road where he hid behind a bramble of vine maple. Headlights waved across the dark and the engine noise split into multiple vehicles. The first rig rounded a corner, spotlighted tree trunks, glared eye-blinding light. As it passed, Ed identified a "Sheriff" logo. He squeezed through the willow limbs, stepped onto the road, shielded his face from the lights as the second rig came into view. It stopped, fixed him in its lights, waited.

"Ed? That you?"

A man stepped from the passenger side of the vehicle.

"Yeah, it's me," he answered through half-chattering teeth. "Zweigy, that you?"

"Christ, what happened? Where's Bessie?" asked Zweigert. The driver stepped out—it was Jack Henderson, the district ranger. Two sheriff deputies approached from the first rig, and two men stepped out a third vehicle parked behind Zweigert and Henderson.

"PUMAs shot us down. Bessie's up ahead in a field."

"Where are the others?" asked one of the deputies.

"In the helicopter. They're...they're dead."

"Get the hell off this road," said the second deputy. "All of us."

"It's okay. They're gone."

"Into the woods. Now."

The second deputy placed a hand on Ed to herd him to the other side of the road, connecting directly with the arm wound. Pain gyrated to his legs, dizzied his head. For a moment he hoped the pain would absolve him like a priest with his hand on his head, but it did nothing except hurt. He staggered off the road to where the others gathered. He checked to see if he still held his son's trousers, felt ridiculous clutching them, would fight anyone who tried to take them.

From a vehicle Ed hadn't seen, two paramedics joined them in a small clear spot among the snarl of undergrowth and trees thirty feet off the road. Drivers returned to their vehicles to switch off the engines and communicate with their dispatchers and afterward the second deputy, who went by the name of Olivera, designated Zweigert, the other deputy, an FBI agent, and a paramedic to establish a perimeter. Olivera said they'd stay put until backup arrived. It was like the Afghan war on the ground that Ed never saw from the air, except it was happening right here in his own nation.

The paramedics examined his wounds, applied antibiotics and competent dressings, cloaked him with a blanket.

"How do you know we're dealing with the PUMAs?" asked Olivera.

Ed recounted what had occurred, including the text message that put them on the hunt.

"I think we need to reconnect with our people, Detective Olivera," said the FBI agent, whose name was Suzuki.

“My thoughts exactly. We need a SWAT team, forensics, coroner, federal aviation, hell, the whole damn show.”

Olivera returned with a blanket, draping it around the one Ed already wore.

"If I hadn’t played superspy, none of this would have happened,” said Ed. He caught himself hoping for consolation, censored himself for this additional weakness. His rashness caused death, and now he wanted pity?

“Don’t go blaming yourself,” said Olivera. “That’s my boss on your helicopter, and I’m not going to blame you. How could you know?”

“Most garden-variety domestic terrorists don’t have RPGs or SAMs or whatever they used,” said Suzuki. “I’m guessing you didn’t have to use force to get everyone on the helicopter.”

He knew the counterarguments. Didn’t matter whether he knew or not. He wasn’t supposed to make that flight, did it without authorization because he knew he’d never get the okay. It was his fault and it would always be his fault no matter how many nice things people said to make him feel better. They knew it, too, but they were too polite to say so.

“I don’t think they’re here,” he said. “I watched them all leave. I was walking around their compound until I heard you coming.”

“Lucky you didn’t hit some kind of trip wire or laser beam and set off an explosion,” said Olivera. “They could have an ambush set up, expecting the cavalry to come for a rescue. These guys are capable of surprise.”

“How’d you find me? How’d you know?”

“Had some calls when your passengers didn’t get home. Backtracked to your meeting at the Cle Elum substation, found out from Mr. Zweigert you’d left. Your bird chirped at us. Emergency radio beacon.”

"I put out a mayday."

"Apparently that didn't go through. You're still shivering."

"I'm okay."

"Ought to put you in my rig."

"Shiver there or shiver here. Don't think it matters."

"It does matter, Ed," said one of the paramedics. "Gets you out of the cool air."

"I'll bet it's still 70 degrees. I'm a veteran. I can deal with this."

"Called in a bio on you before we got off the freeway," Suzuki said. "You gave Uncle Sam twenty-five years, twenty-two of them Rangers."

"Always brought my soldiers home. Until now."

CHAPTER NINETEEN

Lewis

They'd kill him now. If God was real and merciful and allowed just one prayer—for he was not entitled, he had not prayed, he had not believed, he was not sure if he believed even at this moment—Lewis prayed his father was on the good side of 50-50. That would mean the death of someone else on the helicopter, a grief for others to suffer.

Lewis knew he'd be dead before he found out. The miasma of guilt that choked his chest grew darker, heavier.

The pickup bounced into a chuckhole, cranked up the pain volume from his jaw, caromed off the top of his skull. Night forest crept by as White used only his parking lights. Bailey, who'd been running, sat next to him, breathing hard, spilling sweat. Nobody spoke.

As though the main road were not bad enough, White made a turn and gave the shock absorbers a greater test. Shrub and fir branches whacked the sides of the truck as they bounced in the dark until they stopped at a warehouse. Moonlight glinted on chain-link fencing topped by strands of barbed wire. Someone unlocked a gate. Quickly the men unloaded their pickup and the cargo van, transferred all the boxes and gear to four vans in the warehouse. They half-dragged him on his jelly legs to a white Econovan where most of them waited while four men drove their original rigs through the night woods beyond the warehouse. After what Lewis guessed to be fifteen minutes, the men returned on foot and boarded the replacement rigs. They all bounced back out onto the main gravel road, and the convoy resumed.

At some point they reached pavement, and White switched on headlights. Around a curve, a multitude of racing lights marked the interstate, a procession they joined, simple travelers amidst the horde. Fast food and gas stations passed glowing in the night.

In the darkness of the van, Lewis tapped his thumb against the upholstery, counting the beats. Again and again, he rehearsed the cadence.

It just might work, he thought.

CHAPTER TWENTY

Ed

"Your hand won't be so simple," said Doctor Cisneros, a woman perhaps ten years younger than he with curly dark hair that draped her shoulders. Assisted by a stocky nurse with a strong chin and sympathetic brown eyes, the doctor worked on him without chitchat for over four hours, starting almost as soon as Agent Suzuki walked him through the doors of the Kittitas Valley Community Hospital in Ellensburg. He'd rather have driven himself, but at least he hadn't arrived sprawled on a gurney in the back of some damned ambulance.

One bullet had clipped the humerus, torn through biceps and triceps muscles. It would hurt, but with therapy, it would heal, she said.

"As for your hand, a bullet shattered the metacarpal bones beneath your first and second fingers. That will require retrieving bone fragments, some of which we might be able to use. Very likely you also have tendon and nerve damage. Let me show you the X-rays."

"Looks like someone cut a little circle out the middle of my palm," he said. "You think maybe it was a bullet?"

She smiled. "We can fix it. That's the first priority, ensuring skeletal stability. At the same time, work needs to be done to reconstruct tendons and nerves, and likely a bit of skin grafting. It's most effective when done as soon as possible. Sometimes it can be done in one surgery, sometimes two or three."

"Did they tell you, doctor? I'm responsible for the deaths of three people."

She set the X-ray on a desk, looked him in the eyes, started to say something, then stopped herself.

"No. No, you're not," said the nurse, who stood near the foot of the examination table. "You didn't run a car off the road. You didn't smack a guy in the back of the head with a backhoe. You didn't peg someone out hunting for deer. You were shot down."

"At a place where I delivered them," said Ed. "It was my idea to go there. That hurts more than my hand or my arm. Don't suppose there's any surgery for that."

"If there were, a lot of doctors would line up for it," said Dr. Cisneros. "People in our care also die. All we've got is right now, this moment and the next one and the next one after that. The rest of our lives, a million *right nows.* We can't be good for anyone if we spend all those moments agonizing over something that went wrong."

He raised himself onto his elbows, gazed down the table at the hospital socks covering his feet. Three people had no more *nows.* He'd taken *now* away from them.

"Mr. Kline, look at me."

He looked past her head to the dark blue curtain separating them from whatever was happening in the next room.

"Somebody else shot down your helicopter. You didn't do that. Somebody else killed your three passengers. You didn't do that. You could not see into the future. You could not know what would happen."

There it was again. Trying to make him feel better.

"I'm sorry," he said.

"No need for sorry." She typed something on a laptop. "We're going to transfer you to Yakima Regional Medical Center. Unfortunately, they have more experience dealing with bullet wounds. You have a nine o'clock appointment tomorrow at surgical services and they want you there at 8:30 for check-in. Do you have a way to get there?"

"I can drive, can't I?"

"You need someone to bring you for surgery and to bring you home when everything's finished. You'll be on medication. It's not only a matter of driving with one arm."

Who did he have?

Nancy. But she was down south on a fire, which was just as well because he didn't know how to face her. He'd fucked up in a way for which there was no forgiveness. Sarah, maybe, but she was working. God, what was she seeing on the news? He'd need to call her and his ex-wife, too. And the people at the firebase, but how could he face them? Sure, they'd care about him, but they'd be pissed—no dispatches without a helicopter, and once again the finger pointed at him.

Not counting Nancy, his best friend had been Bessie, and it would be a long time before she could take anyone to Yakima.

"I can get there. Can you find out if that Agent Suzuki guy is here?"

"Oh, he's here."

"Can he come in?"

A minute later, Suzuki, his thick black hair disheveled and the wrinkles around his eyes sagging with fatigue or boredom, returned with the doctor.

"Still stuck with me, huh, Suzuki? Bet you'd rather be tracking down the militia than watching out for a dumbass pilot."

"True enough, I won't lie—except for the *dumbass* part," said Suzuki, looking him over as though he were a doctor, too, or a psychiatrist.

"So that part you'll lie about."

"If those nut cases had my kid, I'd want to track them down, too."

"Think you could give me a ride to the Snoqualmie Pass Firebase? It's on your way to Seattle."

They exited through a hallway of patient rooms.

"Veteran helitack pilot Edward Kline, the sole survivor, is currently hospitalized..."

He glanced through one of the doorways up at a television monitor mounted high on a wall, saw his own mugshot in the upper corner of an image showing Bessie in a small meadow surrounded by trees.

"...authorities said the perpetrators fled the scene...."

"Let's get the hell out of here," he said.

"That's why we're going this way," said Suzuki as they resumed walking. "I'm afraid the media's waiting in the lobby."

"Fabulous."

"We've coordinated with hospital administration to hold a press conference at 1 p.m. to share information about your condition. By then you will have been gone for an hour."

"Clever. Thank you. I suppose they're camped at my house, too."

They reached the exit.

"Wait a minute," said Ed. "I forgot something in the room."

He hurried back, found a nurse cleaning the area but no doctor, and picked up Lewis's trousers from the chair where he'd left them.

"The cargo pants," Suzuki said when he returned. "That's actually one of my questions. I don't suppose you grabbed them off the helicopter."

"No."

"But you had them out on the road where we found you."

"Yes."

"So?"

"I don't suppose you'd believe I borrowed them from a bear."

Suzuki waited. Ed told him how he found the trousers.

"Mr. Kline, that's… I can see why you took them, but… there's no way to sugarcoat it. You removed evidence from a crime scene."

"Pants? Evidence? What the hell?"

He handed the trousers to Suzuki.

"Don't know why the hell I grabbed them anyway. They don't fit me. He's got a bunch of other stuff still there in his locker, but all the other lockers are cleaned out. I'd like to think...well, either way it's not good."

Into a morning already hot and a wind beginning to increase according to the usual pattern, they left the building. Suzuki hadn't driven two blocks before Ed's pain pill multiplied the torpor of no sleep. They ordered a drive-through McDonald's meal, the first thing he'd eaten since the granola bar and crackers yesterday. Coffee helped his resolve to stay awake.

Suzuki said he'd be at the hospital in Yakima after the surgery. They'd give him some time to recover and then he and a couple of other people wanted to interview him to learn more about everything he knew and didn't know. Time mattered. At the firebase, Suzuki started to leave the parking lot, stopped, backed to where Ed stood waiting.

"You sure you have a ride home?" he asked.

"You bet."

"How about a ride to Yakima tomorrow?"

"I'm good."

"Please take this business card in case you change your mind or anything you think might be relevant pops into your head. I've written my cell phone number on it."

"Thanks."

Suzuki left and Ed, with his arm in a sling, walked to his pickup. He stopped at a gas station for another cup of coffee and left for home.

Rounding the curve before the road straightened, he saw Nancy's black pickup parked beneath the trees across from his house.

She was back home from the fire—and why couldn't he summon joy? A red feeling bubbled in his stomach, heated his face, urged him to run, but he couldn't swing a U-turn or drive past his own house with her there looking for him.

She stood from the porch steps when he turned into the driveway, still wearing her green Nomex pants. When he reached the porch, she embraced him long and tight, smelling of smoke and old sweat, her hair gritty and clumped.

At least there were no reporters.

"They demobilized us before dawn, soon as we woke to get ready for the next shift. Didn't surprise me, though. Only mopup left to do."

"Well."

"Quick as we hit civilization and our cell phones worked, we saw the news."

He opened the front door, recoiled at the empty Courvoisier bottle and the empty bag of pretzels.

"I didn't know you'd be here," he said.

"Didn't even stop at home. Came straight here."

He left her at the threshold and walked across the living room to the window at the side of his house, looking out at the forest and the empty scrap of road beyond his truck. He reminded himself he was holding a half-cup of coffee.

"Ed?"

"Hmm?"

"Okay if I'm here?"

A chartreuse hummingbird flitted at the window, considered the human standing on the other side, darted away. Ed recognized the downshift of a logging truck before it appeared, watched it pass by.

Answer her.

"I can come back later."

"It's just...I've got some phone calls to make."

"Can I call you?"

"Yes."

"Tonight or tomorrow?"

The same hummingbird reappeared, pecked tat-a-tat at the window, shot away.

"I. . .I've got surgery in Yakima tomorrow."

"Let me take you."

Yes. Be with me. Forgive me. Love me.

"I can get there," he said. "You've got your crew."

"My crew. They'll be fine."

"I'll be fine, too."

"I can't know what you feel. It must be horrible. But you let me in your life and I let you in mine. Not only for good times. Times like this, too."

Come back, little hummingbird.

"Am I wrong about that?" she asked.

"No."

"Do you want me to stay or leave?"

"I don't know."

"Let me take you to Yakima."

"And wait around for God knows how many hours? I'll be fine."

He turned and faced her. Her eyes were moist.

"I'm sorry I'm like this. This isn't me."

"I know."

"I'm sorry about the Courvoisier. That isn't me, either."

"I don't give a shit about the Courvoisier. The pretzels, though—that makes me worry."

He felt a smile inside, one that could not push to the surface.

"I just need some time."

"All right. But I'm worried about you."

"I'll be fine."

She studied him, like the doctor had done, like Suzuki, except their eyes hadn't glistened.

"No one expects you to be fine. I wouldn't be fine. Don't say you're fine."

"I'm fine."

"Christ." She sighed.

"I'm sorry."

"It's okay."

He wanted to turn back to the window. How did he look to her? He felt pathetic.

"This trip to Yakima—I want to be there. I'll bring a book to read."

"You've got to work. It's only my hand. It'll heal."

"You stubborn bastard."

"I know. Guilty as charged."

"I'm going to call you tomorrow night. You damn well better answer."

"I will."

She pressed her lips together.

"I thought I lost you, Ed. Shot down, the others dead, you in the hospital, no reports about your condition and then all the sudden the radio says you're released. I was on my way to Ellensburg."

The others dead. His ship. But by God he wasn't going to ask her pity, he wasn't going to replay the whiny half-hidden pleas. He created his burden and he needed to bear it.

"I'm sorry," he said.

"For what?"

"I…for how I am. I should be better for you."

She forced a smile, shook her head.

"You crazy man. You dear, crazy man."

She embraced him again. Warm. A surge of living. And she backed away.

"You're sure you're okay?"

"Yeah, sure."

The forced smile again, the shaking of her head.

"No you're not," she said. "You'd better answer the phone when I call tomorrow. Promise me."

"I promise."

"'Cause I'll come over and I won't leave."

"I'll answer."

After she left, he walked out the house and down the road, a mile, two miles, his arm throbbing, his hand excruciating. Stubborn. It was true. He'd left the Oxycontin in a bag on the kitchen table. Enough time had gone by so he could take another of the pain pills, but he had been stubborn about that, too. His whole right appendage burned shoulder to fingertip and it seemed right and proper that it did.

Back at his house he turned on the phone, prioritized the messages, planned the return calls—first to Sarah, then his ex-wife Sharon, his brother Tony in San Jose, several other relatives. His parents had both died. He'd call them if he could. One call he couldn't return came from Nancy, who had left her message before he'd returned home and sent her away.

"I love you, Ed," she had said.

He loved her back, but he hadn't told her. He hadn't told himself until then.

How could he tell her the text he'd received that wonderful morning after they'd been together had changed his entire life? He was no longer the man she'd slept with. He was a man whose son's association with homegrown terrorist killers had led directly to his own piss-ass judgment, a fatal miscalculation.

What woman would commit herself to a relationship with a man carrying that kind of baggage?

"You can't make me not be there," Sarah insisted.

"But I don't need any help. I'm by myself right now. I've still got one good arm and hand. I can open the fridge and pour some milk." He looked down at his untied shoes. "I don't want you taking time off work on my account."

"Oh my god, Dad. I never thought...I used to worry about you in Afghanistan. And I still do on fires. And it's that PUMA group?"

"Has to be."

"And Lewis, he's... There's no way."

He told her about the text. Everyone would find out anyway. She might as well hear it from him.

"So he's trying to get out. It's too horrible. And you. They tried to kill you."

"I'm still here, honey."

"It's like war. Only it's here. And it's our own people. Lewis would never do that."

"That's what I think."

"Anyway, I'm coming over. I'm going to finish my shift, and then I'm coming over."

"Sarah, I told you…"

"I'll be there. There'll probably be hordes of traffic but once I get across the lake...let's say about nine tonight. And I'm taking you to Yakima tomorrow."

"No, you're not."

"Doesn't make sense for us to drive there in separate vehicles."

"Honey, it's going to be all day. Surgeries, and then I have to talk to law enforcement people."

"Yakima's cool. I'll walk the river trail."

"Sarah."

"You're my dad, damn it. What, all the sudden you don't want me around? Quit that shit. I'll see you at nine."

Before he called Sharon, his conscience yammered at him:

If you'd been home more you'd never be making this call.

But he had given all he had to both Lewis and Sarah every time he was home. Entire years went by without Uncle Sam sending him overseas. Baseball. Soccer. Camping. Teacher conferences. Little vacations. Both kids loved Wild Waves. Just this past winter he'd taken Sarah steelhead fishing on the Nooksack River.

If you'd been home more you'd never be making this call.

"He was mad, Ed," Sharon told him after he assured her he would survive. "I don't know if you know, but he was mad. At the government. At CEOs. Talking about conspiracies."

"But he wanted out."

He told Sharon about the text. "That's why I was flying there. Because of Lewis."

"When'd you get the text, Ed?"

"About a week ago." He took a breath, knew what was next.

"Why didn't you call me?"

"I didn't know for sure it was from him."

"Bullshit."

"With just an *L*? No details? Why get you worried for nothing?"

"You should have called me and you know it. What if he's...oh God."

He pictured her choking back a sob, felt his own chest heave while moisture stormed the ducts of his eyes. For a moment he couldn't speak. Anything he voiced would be pain.

"They'll kill him, won't they? They must have known it was you. Why else would they shoot you down?"

Tears forced themselves free, gravity pulling them down his cheeks. "I was trying. I was trying so hard. He's our boy." He pictured Sharon's face equally wet. After all these years, once again he was the one who caused it.

Chapter Twenty-one

Lewis

For a man with a busted-out tooth and a broken jaw, whose executioners were formalizing his death, Lewis felt calm, so he had to conjure the panic and terror they expected him to display.

"...Your motivation is irrelevant," said White. "Answer the charges."

God, the man liked a show. Now playing: Trial—The Sequel. Different day, different setting, same fucking cast—including Hernandez with the camcorder.

"I partially communicated my location." He rubbed his hands together, scratched his nose, blinked his eyes, twisted in his seat.

"Eyes up here, Traitor Kline. The location matches that of your colleagues, correct?"

"Yes."

"Then you plead guilty or innocent?"

He clutched the top of his head, rocked forward and back, blinked.

"I plead stupid."

"Let the court take note that the accused is refusing to plead and thereby avoiding the answering of charges. On behalf of the accused…"

Go ahead, Captain. Pontificate. It's what you do. He bit a finger, wrapped an arm around his front.

He tapped his arm, counted the beats and pauses.

"...exposing us to military ambush…"

"Stupid for getting sucked in! Stupid for…"

"Soldier!"

"Stupid for sending codes!"

"Ah! Sending codes. Was that how you betrayed us?"

"At the store. Remember? The rolling grapefruit?"

"Quit wasting our time."

"I found a phone in the grapefruit. Used it to text our geographical coordinates."

"Tantamount to a guilty plea. Thank you, Traitor Kline."

"Got any iodine, Sir?"

"Keep showing us how weak your character is, Traitor Kline. It makes it easier to carry out the sentence. The Court will take note…"

Lewis made his voice a sing-song annoyance. "I plead stupid! I plead stupid!"

"Traitor Kline, you are in contempt. Soldiers Bailey and Gallahan, subdue this prisoner. I want him bound and gagged."

Ten minutes later, with his right foot, Lewis repeated the taps. After all, he was nervous.

CHAPTER TWENTY-TWO

Ed

When she arrived that night, Sarah held him in a long embrace. His little black-haired girl in a young woman's body. It felt strange to be the receiver rather than the giver of comfort, but he realized Sarah, too, gained reassurance in holding a living father when all the others on Bessie had been killed.

If you hadn't been so stupid, they'd still be alive, too.

The next day they put him under anesthesia for a five-hour operation, let him sleep it off, freed him for a mid-afternoon lunch with Sarah, and now here he was, in a small room with a long cherrywood table, plush white chairs, and four men in suits. Painkillers deadened sensations—pins and wires inside his palm where bones had been obliterated, dead and damaged tissue debrided, replaced by muscle they'd cut from his abdomen.

"Do you mind if we turn on a tape recorder, Mr. Kline?"

"Not a problem."

"So the tape recorder's okay?"

"Yes."

The speaker, a man his own age but heavy-set with thick black hair undoubtedly not his own, took a pocket recorder from his shirt, set it on the table, pressed a button.

"Special Agent Steven Vento speaking, August second, at the Yakima Regional Medical Center to interview Edward Kline. With me is Agent Craig Suzuki, also from the Federal Bureau of Investigation, Joseph Fiora from the FBI, and Detective Dean Barrett from the King County Sheriff's Department. Mr. Kline, are you still certain that you do not wish to have an attorney present?"

"Like I said, what the hell for?"

"And as I said, you are under no suspicion of any kind. We hope only that you can help us understand what happened on the night of July 31 and provide us with information to help us apprehend the perpetrators who shot down your helicopter and killed the law enforcement officers who were on board."

"That tops my to-do list."

Vento smiled a half-smile, a smile that told Ed he'd done this a thousand times, humor the interviewee, begin to build trust.

"It may strike you as odd, but before we talk about the incident I want to ask you some personal questions. You don't have to answer any question that makes you uncomfortable. We simply want to know about you as a person."

"What makes the dude tick, huh?"

"Maybe. We do this routinely. Most of the time it ends up being extraneous information. Where were you born, Mr. Kline?"

"Don't get me wrong. I'm on your side, totally and completely. You can look that up. You probably already know."

"You're right. We always begin with some standard questions, even if we already know. But I won't know most of what I ask. We haven't been asking around about you. We have no reason to do so. We do have your military files, which I've reviewed. You served with honor—commendation medals, meritorious service, campaign medals. In fact, before we go any farther, I need to thank you for your service to our country."

"Appreciate that."

"So I'm sorry if some of the questions seem frivolous. We've been doing this for a long time. There's a whole science behind how and why we ask questions this way. A substantial amount of training."

"Okay, I was born in Stockton, California. Oldest of two boys. Grew up with both parents mostly in Modesto, graduated 1979, ROTC when it wasn't very popular, mean sunovabitch offensive tackle..."

"Whoa, Mr. Kline."

"Knocked a lot of boys on their keister. We had a running back, Carl Harris. He ran for over 2,000 yards. I'll shut up now."

Vento smiled a real smile.

"I should tell you that your type of response often indicates a subject with a great deal of anxiety."

"Helluva science you've got there."

This induced a smile from the other three.

"Touché."

"I mean, other than getting shot down and having my passengers killed, it's been pretty routine these past couple of days."

"We can do this later today, tomorrow at the latest."

"Naw, hell, let's do it now."

Prompted by Vento's questions, Ed told of his active but unremarkable childhood, his decision early in high school to join the army during a time when most classmates loathed the military. At a coffee shop near Fort Lewis in Washington State, the first base he'd been assigned after earning his pilot's wings, he met the woman he'd end up marrying. She was loyal, uncomplaining, and a devoted mother to their daughter and son for all those years he was gone many long months, particularly during Operation Enduring Freedom.

"Best woman I've ever known," he said. "I think she just got tired of me being gone. She must've thought it would be different after I retired from the military, but then I had to go off and do this helitack gig. You can't keep me grounded. Never got through my thick head how much it bothered her, but I've got to admit she tried to tell me."

"What was your relationship like with your son?"

"We fished. We hunted. He was a good kid. Only got in trouble when he was defending someone. Had no respect for a bully, no matter how big or old he was. Yeah, we got along fine. I give credit to my ex-wife. She raised him right. I just tried to go with the program all the times I was home."

"Her name is Sharon?"

"Yeah."

"After you and Sharon...broke up...were you able to spend much time with Lewis?"

"He'd started his junior year in high school. Spent a lot of time with him when it wasn't fire season. Next thing I knew he was off to college. How much time does any parent get with his kid after that? Home for holidays, trying to split time between his mother and me. His mother moved to California and I moved out in the sticks where I live now. But we snuck time together. Fishing mostly."

"How was his college experience?"

"Far as I know, pretty good. Got a forestry degree from Washington State."

"And after that?"

"No jobs. Qualified as hell and no jobs. That's when the whole economy went into the tank."

"How did Lewis respond to the lack of jobs?"

"Don't really know. He didn't talk about it much. Well, I guess not so good, seeing how he got lured into that militia."

"Did he ever talk about that?"

"Not about militias. Sharon and I get along fine, and she never said anything to me about that."

"That's what she says."

"When did you talk to her?"

"I haven't. But we had a team with her this morning, and I've had a chance to review the transcript."

"I'll be damned. You guys don't waste time."

"She said he seemed disillusioned. That was her word. Talked about how a few rich families have all the money and power."

"Well, that's true."

"Meaning…?"

"Well, I mean that's true about the rich having all the money. Lots of people say that. That doesn't mean a guy's going to run off with some nutcase militia."

"She said he was pretty angry sometimes. Said banks had more money than they knew what to do with, same for some big companies, said they wouldn't invest in their own country."

"He did rattle off some of that talk the last time we fished together, April before last. Never said anything about militias. Nothing about being violent. Thought everyone needed a gun. Tell you the truth, we avoided the topic after that. Then last October he sends me a letter. You know what I'm talking about?"

"I think so. Agent Thomas e-mailed a PDF copy to his station before he took that trip with you to look for the militia. Is that the one?"

"Yeah. But are you sure he never talked to Sharon about

the militia?"

Vento paused for a moment. "Well, no, I don't remember reading anything about that in the transcript. And our team asked her, too. Am I forgetting anything?" He looked at the other three, who quietly shook their heads.

"Okay," continued Vento. "So it appears he never said anything about the militia. What about the whole patriot thing? The Constitution and the Declaration of Independence?"

"Oh, yeah. Back on that fishing trip."

"The right to bear arms?"

"Yeah. Same fishing trip. Funny thing is, he quit hunting with me when he was sixteen. Said he didn't want to do it anymore. I don't know if he even had a gun. It was just talk, or I thought it was."

Vento asked at least a dozen more questions about Lewis—did he travel, what kinds of magazines did Ed see him reading, and on and on, all the same questions Ed had asked himself after receiving the letter when Lewis disappeared.

They took a ten-minute break and when they returned, Suzuki did the interviewing and it was all about everything Ed had done in response to the text leading ultimately to the helicopter trip.

"What's crazy in all this is I've got a reputation that I go by the book. Don't take chances. I piss people off that way. You've got my records. You can look it up. Then the one time I didn't, the only time…."

Ed sighed, lowered his head, swallowed audibly. "I'll never get over this. Think I'd have rather died with them than live with their deaths on my head."

Chapter Twenty-three

Lewis

When they unchained him from inside the barn and shoved him, with his hands roped behind him, into the back of the king cab, he did not know where they were taking him. But he did know he would not be coming back. Every time his brain imagined an alternative—maybe they'd drop him along the side of a freeway, maybe White knew a guy who could give him an injection to wipe out his memory, maybe the damn truck would get in a rollover accident and he'd escape—he refused to let the fantasy play out, told himself he was going to die but that he should be proud.

Though the sun had set, heat radiated from the ground and into the pickup. Dusk muted the yellows and dull greens that colored the semi-arid hills. Aromas of sage and dust tinged the air. Every tiny leaf on every scrub of brush constituted a miracle. By itself, mother Earth offered enough.

It was a shame that it had to end, that his own stupidity had cut it short, but he'd made it all the way through growing up when not everyone had that chance. He'd known the love of family and the love of a lover. He had walked and breathed on an incredibly rare planet.

Odd, this surprise surge of gratitude—it was the last emotion he expected to feel in this last hour of his life.

The Captain and all the others—they were misguided, they didn't understand about life, and he felt sorry for them for what they didn't know. He did not blame them for what they were about to do.

They dropped off a plateau and switch-backed down a canyon without trees, stopped short of the bottom on a small flat, walked across the road around the bend where two hills almost met. It was isolated, suitable for the task. The coyotes would find him.

He regretted the camcorder Hernandez kept pointed at him. He didn't mind the filming during what passed for a trial when he could send a spoken and an unspoken message to...well, he didn't know exactly. He hoped it would find its way to someone who could stop this militia, someone clever enough to understand and decipher his last contribution to a flawed world.

But here. At this moment. Like the ISIS terrorists who bragged on film before severing heads. If there were a God and Lewis had a final wish, he wished his mother and all the people who loved him would never have to see this, and his father, too, if he were on the good side of 50-50.

"By the time the Patriots United Militia of America releases this video, the news media will have trumpeted how the federalistas found our headquarters," began Captain White. "Learn from this. At some point they will find you. When they do, you must already know how to escape and how to reassemble. Not one of our soldiers has been captured or killed."

Dressed in their cargo pants and black PUMA tee-shirts, Captain White, Captain Red, Marquez, Bailey, Doyle, Beckham, and the rest of the militia stood facing him. None exhibited fear or misgivings. It was just a job that had to be done. They'd spent many months together horsing around and yakking about what was wrong with the country and how to fix it, and now here they were about to apply another fix. They'd walked willingly into their own twisted dreams and been swallowed, and even if they were to awaken, it was too late, and they were in too deep. For weeks he had hated them but now he didn't.

"As we have documented at his trial, Soldier Kline is guilty of betraying the location of our previous headquarters by stealthily contacting his father with a stolen cellphone. Be prepared, fellow patriots—we shot down the helicopter that found our base. You will encounter treachery. The enemy even now may have agents planted among you, like parasites worming into your blood. Or one of your soldiers might turn squeamish in the face of danger. The price of restoring freedom from tyranny is high. The soldier before you was not always a traitor, but he turned out to be weak. No single individual is more important than the welfare of the militia. Without the militia, there exists no pathway to freedom. Freedom will not be given to you. The acquisition of it will hurt. We once had great affection for this man. He kept our spirits…"

White could not finish the sentence.

"Steel your hearts to do what you must do," he said.

"Soldier. Zoom the camera onto Traitor Kline's head."

Two snaps. A black blunt-nosed Beretta unholstered, two quick steps, the barrel an inch away.

Chapter Twenty-Four

Ed

She called that night, like she said she would.
He let it ring, hating what he was doing to his future.

The next morning Jim Andrews, CEO of Pacific Aviation Services and Ed's boss, called from SeaTac International Airport, where he'd flown from company headquarters in Fresno. He wanted a face-to-face sit-down.

"What the fuck," he said three hours later in Ed's kitchen, noting the bandaged hand and arm. "Get your ass shot at all over the world and the only time anyone gets you is right here in our own country."

Andrews felt sorry, expressed condolences for the others, all the things he was supposed to say, and Ed knew he genuinely meant it. Wearing a short-sleeved pastel green shirt with a darker green necktie, Andrews looked as always in excellent physical condition. Like Ed, he knew combat, having flown missions in Central America during the 1980s and Operation Desert Shield, and also like Ed, he embraced the blunt appraisals U.S. military officers imposed upon themselves.

"You've always taken excellent care of our helicopters," he said.

But...Ed anticipated that word, the whole reason why Andrews was present in person at his home.

"You've followed every protocol."

Ed waited.

"I'm not about to believe all the bullshit the cable news stations are pumping out."

More silence.

"They're saying you took those law enforcement officers because you had some sort of idea where to find those PUMA fuckheads. They're saying it's because your son's with them and participated in those terror attacks a few days ago. What they're not saying is that you failed to contact your supervisors before taking to the air. You didn't have clearance.

"What I need is to hear your side of this whole thing. How did you happen to be flying one of our helicopters with three law enforcement officers over the PUMA compound?"

After Ed recounted the progression of events, Andrews rose from the table and slowly walked across the living room, stopped at a window on the side of the house, the same spot where Ed had stood the day before with Nancy there. In a moment, Andrews turned and walked to the invisible line separating kitchen from living room.

"What do the doctors say about your ability to fly?"

"Truth is, I didn't ask them."

Andrews returned to his chair at the table.

"Tell you what we're going to do, Ed. We're going to put you on medical leave with full base pay, of course, for the remainder of the season. In order to come back on active duty, you'll need a doctor's written permission. While you're out, we'll bring up another Firehawk and another pilot so we can fulfill our contract with the Forest Service and the helitack crew. When you're ready to return, we'll see if we've got any other openings on any other bird we've got on fire duty. If we don't, we'll still pay you through the end of your contract."

"So let's just say I'm grounded. What about next season?"

"You can apply like anyone else."

"So no contract renewal."

"Not at this time. But I'm not saying the door is closed."

For a moment, neither man spoke.

"Well, Jim, I can't say I didn't expect this. I had a little hope that flying twenty-five years for Uncle Sam, plus six and a half seasons with your outfit might have counted for something."

"It does count. I have tremendous respect for you, Ed. You're straight up, no bullshit. Fuckin' lawyers, fuckin' risk management, they run the show now. We all have people we have to answer to, myself included." Andrews stood again.

"We'll have all the legal paperwork prepared within two days. Somebody from my office will contact you to arrange signing, including provisions to make sure you get paid even if we don't have any openings after you get yourself healed. More than any of this, Ed, I'm glad you're still here, glad they didn't get you, too."

"If I were you I'd fire me, too. Mighty decent of you to fly up here instead of doing it over the phone."

"You're not done yet."

"Technically, I guess you can say that."

"You make sure you land on your feet."

"Appreciate that."

After Andrews left, the walls of his little house squeezed him like a carnivorous flower digesting its prey. He had to get out, had to walk. He strode for a nearby logging road, one that wound up and up the ridge behind his house, traversing a patchwork of mature forest, clear-cuts, and all the stages in-between. He ascended past a bramble of hardwoods and fifteen-foot conifers, a quarter-mile stretch they'd cut and replanted before he bought his home. Beyond this stretch, yellow weeds, St. John's wort, thistles, and knapweed clogged a hundred recently-logged acres, obscuring the seedlings planted last November as well as scattered branches, burn pile remnants, and chunks of bark left from the old forest. The seedlings closest to the road could have been mistaken for mere sticks pointing out the ground, tufted at the top with a few brown needles. They looked certain to be casualties of the heat and lack of rain, a wasted investment by the timber companies, omens pronouncing nothing more than a scrubland future. But Ed had seen saplings just like these burst out green needles the following spring, brought back from death.

Every year a single individual in a monster machine, like a backhoe with steel mandibles, took out another section of forest. The cutter claws grasped an entire tree trunk, unsheathed a steel saw, sliced through the diameter, lifted and set the tree on the ground. Where were the sawyers who used to do the cutting? How many were home, popping opioids not to dull the pain of a life spent hoisting chainsaws, but from the lack of opportunity to earn those aches?

Past the new and near-new cuts where the sun flung down its heat uninhibited, he entered a wooded section. White firs and Douglas firs provided shade, a forest nearly mature but not enough to have sprouted red ribbon flagging with the words "Timber Harvest Boundary." In the autumn before the snows, while crews replanted the newest clear-cuts, he sleuthed among these woods for yellow-hued chanterelle mushrooms hiding among the fallen leaves of willows and vine maple and dogwoods, brought home cauliflower-sized chunks, cut them, sautéed them for pasta. If his life hadn't changed this past week, when the rains hit, he'd have been sleuthing the chanterelles for a meal that would have included Nancy.

Ed walked through all these forest stages to the top of the ridge. Four years ago, all anyone could see at the top before the road dipped down the other side was a lovely dark forest, but a cutter bit and lifted and plopped its quarry to the ground and cleared it all out. Now to the west, Overland and Summit Chief pushed up their jagged peaks, clutched their shrinking glaciers. If they had a spirit, as the Native Americans believed, they'd be grieving the loss of the ice blankets under which they'd snuggled for millennia. Although the heat beat down, he stood there a long time. He had thought the sight of those peaks this late morning might bring consolation, but they stood mutely bearing their own grievances.

Reluctantly he turned. He'd lost Bessie, lost whatever might replace her, lost the pilot's seat, the cyclic stick and the collective, the little mountain ledges where he'd set his helo down, the adrenalin of hovering over a burning snag with its uprush of heated air.

As he neared the end of his walk, among the debris of a clear-cut and under the assault of the sun, he wanted to cry; but he wasn't a man to cry, not for himself. He knew he was a good man who tried to live his life the right way, but by God, look where it got him.

Why bother? he wondered.

Because his son might be alive—that was why. Lewis would need him because even living would be a trial after he got away from the PUMAs. The law would want to put him in prison. Had he fired any shots? Had he abetted the firing of shots?

How could he prove he had not? Why hadn't he escaped? Lewis would need him through the trials to come, and while Ed could never rationalize the atrocities the PUMAs committed. he could see through the evil to the caring man he knew his son to be. If Lewis had to go to prison, so be it; but he could use a visitor who still loved him.

So Ed vowed to endure, even if he didn't know how.

Everything he stood for seemed cut down, a bare scar of debris exposed to the world. When or how or who would show up one rainy day in his autumn and give him the grace of planting a few new trees?

He stepped onto the paved county road, turned toward his home, and noticed a shiny gray Audi and a faded blue Ford sedan parked across his home. A woman and a man in business attire were standing on his porch and another man sat inside the Ford. Christ, what did they want?

They turned out to be reporters.

"It's an important story," said the woman from KIRO television after he declined to answer her questions. The thirty-something man with her pointed a camcorder and Ed thought about how bad it looked when someone lost his temper and bashed a camera to the ground.

"I've been advised by legal counsel to withhold comments," he lied. "We'll advise the media when we're prepared to release a statement."

He took their business card and the card from the *Yakima Herald-Republic* reporter, and closed the door on all three, waiting for them to leave. With no idea where he was going or how long he'd be gone or if he'd ever come back, he collected random items of clothing into a duffle bag, carried it to the truck, and left.

Chapter Twenty-five

Before, when it appeared the *Crescent Moon* edged from its mooring, the motion had been a mirage, a trick concocted by the waves and Ed's own movement back and forth along the harbor. But this time a bobbing yellow buoy appeared to inch along the length of the oil tanker's red and black hull, confirming the behemoth had lifted anchor.

Waves rolled soft slaps around the pilings of a wooden deck where Ed paused and leaned on a rail. Beneath gray marine clouds, brine and mist saturated the ocean air. His truck had steered him west, as though it also needed respite from inland heat. It deposited Ed in Port Angeles on the southern edge of the Strait of Juan de Fuca, leaving him to pace the harbor while moisture bathed its windshield.

He took his eyes off the *Crescent Moon,* peered down at the seawater sloshing below him, and tried to make sense out of what had happened.

Either the PUMAs shot his ass down in an act of random paranoia, or they did it because they knew he was Lewis's father and he was looking for them.

If the PUMAs already knew, the only way they'd know would be through Lewis. Two possibilities:

1. Lewis had become crazed enough to try to lure him with the text so they could shoot him down. That way he could prove his loyalty to the PUMAs. Perhaps he had been the one

who'd fired the RPG, or he'd been shooting one of the automatic rifles. But this was a ludicrous scenario. Why would they waste their time on such a stunt and force themselves to abandon their hideout? And Lewis wouldn't do that to his father…would he? They were a violent group. If they'd managed to brainwash Lewis, who knew what he was capable of?

2. Most likely, they discovered Lewis tried to contact him. That would mean his life was in danger before Ed ever showed up.

But if they didn't know whose helicopter they'd brought down, Ed hoped to hell they didn't watch or read the news. Because if they found out, they'd be asking Lewis some harsh questions—or worse.

Still staring at the murky water beneath the deck, Ed pictured himself fully healed, addressing the PUMAs, each of them roped onto an individual chair.

You parasitical cowardly slime. Hell-dogs who eat their own shit. You virus, you cancer, you flag-waving scum.

Lewis stood next to him under his protection. A jar of sulfuric acid appeared in Ed's left hand, a medicine dropper in his right. It was a simple matter to insert a few milliliters into a helpless vomit-bag's ear, a great pleasure to watch him scream. Afterward, pairs of nostrils presented another pathway and after that, eye sockets.

You killed, now you die. Ed, the chauffeur of death, transformed to the emissary of vengeance.

But he was not a hero. He was a fuck-up standing at a railing overlooking a harbor, losing sight of the harbor to indulge in a stupid fantasy.

Maybe that oil tanker or another one like it could use an extra crewman.

But he knew he would stay. On his third or fourth circuit

along the harbor almost an hour ago, he'd decided that, although he could never bring back his helicopter passengers, he could at least attend their memorial services. It was time to find out when and where those events would occur.

He moved away from the harbor back toward the town center where he'd paid for a cheap hotel room. Next to an army surplus store, coyotes serenaded the moon—yip yip baw-oooh—he needed to get rid of that crazy damn ringtone. He took the phone from his pocket, stared at Nancy's number, felt the panic growing more familiar, and let the call go by.

Maybe tomorrow. If she called. If she didn't conclude he was an asshole.

In another minute, as he stepped into the hotel lobby, the voicemail ringtone sounded. All the way down the dim and musty-smelling hallway he held the phone in his good hand, and although he kept it silent he felt her voice seep up his arm into his heart. In his room he played the message.

"Where are you, Ed? I'm parked across from your house right now and I don't care if you're inside and don't want to see me, I just want to know you're okay. I'm going to keep calling until I know you're okay. I'm going to make myself a bitch to the FBI and the Forest Circus and the CIA and the fuckin' president until somebody tells me for real you're okay, but I won't believe a word they say until I hear it from you. If you want to spare them the blithering rants of a crazy woman, call me back just so I know you have a voice and you're breathing. I don't care what you're doing, but I do care about you. Call me, and that's an order. Call me. Call. Me."

While the mailbox management options droned, Ed stared out the window at the passing traffic. If he didn't call right away, she'd survive. He had a right to some time, didn't he?

No.

It was loony, he knew it. but he took a few steps back from

the window to the narrow space between the bed and the television, cradled an imaginary football he named fear, and drop-kicked it out the window across three blocks and into the bay. Boom. It was a helluva kick, the best one he'd ever made.

He left his room, walked the dingy hallway with its faded red carpet out into the dampness and down to the ferry terminal as dusk veiled its entry into the gray-dimmed day. He let his body find another rectangle to lap, this one a little park pathway 100 yards past the ferry terminal, and allowed the momentum of footsteps to draw out his phone.

Nancy put him on speaker, told him to wait while she took the next exit off I-90.

"Where are you?" she asked after a minute had passed.

"Port Angeles. Fifty-three degrees, wet but not raining."

"I'm going to keep with what I said I wanted to know. Are you okay?"

"I don't know. You said I wouldn't be okay and you were right. I'm sorry I…I couldn't answer your call."

"You can't shake me. If you don't want me, that's one thing. Just tell me. But if it's something else, all this shit, this mess—"

"Have you heard? Do you know what this is about?"

"Just what's on the news."

He hesitated.

"Something to do with your son," she said.

"Did you know when you spent the night with me you were sleeping with someone who'd fuck up this badly?"

"Ed. What do you...no, that's not true."

"It is true. And they fired my ass this very morning and I deserved it, too, but that's not why I'm over here. I'm over here because the fucking reporters know where I live and they want me to puke out all my regret in front of cameras for all America to see. But I can't stay here because I need to go to the memorial services of the people they shot up on my helo. I don't know why but I just have to. I was on my way back to the hotel when you called and I...I'm a fuckup, that's all."

"Ed, no. You're not."

"They're dead because of me. I know I didn't shoot them but they wouldn't have been there if it hadn't been for me. It was my idea. It was a stupid dumb fucking thing to do. I'll never get over it for the rest of my life, and I shouldn't get over it because it's just not the kind of thing to get over. Everyone wants me to feel all right and stop blaming myself, and I understand why but there it is staring me in the face every moment. Take me out of the picture and Detective Rosario bakes cupcakes for her daughter's birthday instead of being dead in the back of my helo. So, no, I'm not okay. I'm a fucking mess."

"Why don't you hide out at my place? Three reporters showed up while I was hanging around by your house, but I never told them who I was or anything at all except I was a friend and didn't know where you were, either. They'd never know to look for you at my place."

"I'm a mess and a fuckup, and I can't even talk to you. That's how much a mess I am."

"Ed, did you hear the message I left for you a couple days ago?"

There was the one with the word *love*.

"Yes."

"What did I say?"

"You didn't know everything then. You don't even know now. Remember that text message the morning after? It was...no. . .It was..."

"Ed. Ed. I said I loved you."

He paused in his walking again at the edge of the harbor. Lights pinpointed misty gleams across the dark waters from a spit of land separating Port Angeles from the strait. He leaned onto the damp wooden rail.

"I don't know how you feel about me," she continued, "and you don't owe me a damn thing just because I said that, but they almost got you, too, and when I realized that, I just about keeled over. I think I know something about you after all these years, at least I hope the hell I do, and that something's called loyalty. I'm the same way. I'm not going to go running off on you."

He pictured her hazel eyes obscured in her dark pickup parked on a mountain road off the freeway, and a kind of yearning bubbled up like a hot spring from the earth. He almost sobbed from its overflow.

"I don't know how to interpret silence, Ed."

"You're more than I deserve."

"I don't know about *deserve.* I don't know if that's part of the calculation."

She was amazing, a saint full of forgiveness.

"When are you coming home? To me? You know how it is. I could get called to a fire any minute. What the hell you doing in Port Angeles?"

The next morning, with an arm and hand pulsing shots of pain, Ed drove without medication around the southern reaches of the Puget Sound then north through heavy traffic until he arrived at Seattle Pacific University for Detective Rosario's memorial service. He wore sunglasses, and, when it ended, he hurried away unrecognized, found the freeway, took it across the mountains, paused shy of Easton to take an Oxycontin, and finished the trip to Nancy's house.

CHAPTER TWENTY-SIX

She was home, five hours before the end of her workday. When she greeted him at the door in a forest green shirt and mid-thigh yellow shorts, he recalled what he'd read about opioids impacting sexual functions. He wondered what she might expect in that department. She wrapped her arms tightly around him, leaned her head against his shoulder, and held him a long time. Her hair was soft and smelled like coconut.

It made no sense to him how a woman so lovely and so strong could leave work early to greet a man who'd fucked up the lives of so many people.

She released her hold, stepped back, smiled.

"It's good to see you," she said.

"You're beautiful."

"I've had time to get rid of the fire boogers."

"Is something baking?"

"Biscuits. Welcome to my refuge. I've cast a spell, made it invisible to all members of the media. As long as you are here, they shall not find you."

Half an hour later, spooned against her naked body, he kissed the skin between her shoulder and neck. On this afternoon, at least, he enjoyed immunity from the pain medication's bedroom side effects. And even though bullet wounds relegated him to lying either on his back or his left side, Nancy had guided them into delightful accommodations.

"Biscuits smell good," he said.

"Shit!" She bounded out of bed, treating him to the sight of her tight buttocks scurrying out of the bedroom. A moment later he heard the clatter of a baking sheet, silverware, the tear of paper towels. She returned, her furry triangle fetching his focus though she carried two biscuits in each hand.

"For a minute I thought I'd forgotten to turn off the oven," she said.

Careful to keep weight off his right arm, he sat upright on the side of the bed. He took a bite—melted butter, warm sour dough, soft inside, a slight crunch on the outside. "These are good."

"I put something else in the oven."

Ed set his paper towel and the biscuits on the nightstand. He leaned forward, flicked his tongue, elicited a squeal.

"Something in the oven?" he repeated.

"Not that one. The one out in the kitchen."

"I like what I'm eating in here."

"You glutton! I've got second helpings, though, and thirds. But out there I've got chicken enchiladas."

"That sounds great. But you're the best treat." He leaned forward again.

She pushed against him, grasped the back of his head. "Ooo. Ooo. Oh my. Have your fill, hungry boy."

When he moved to the living room while she returned to the kitchen, he kept the television off, even though the Mariners were in Boston playing the Red Sox. Instead, he sat in a rocking chair made of a dark varnished wood with a white seating pad, and he surveyed his refuge.

Her furniture didn't come from Ikea. Everything appeared to be at least seventy years old, items that transported him back to his grandparents' home when he was a little kid: a head-high bookcase of cherrywood, a couch with off-white cotton upholstery embedded in a curving wood backrest, an open roll-top desk on which she kept a laptop computer and printer, a wooden swivel chair with padding light blue like a robin's egg, a cedar hope chest atop which stood a DVD player and a small flat-screen television. Several multi-colored oval throw-rugs covered sections of wooden flooring. A big ceiling fan with walnut-colored blades spun medium speed. What he liked best about the living room was a giant 1960s poster of Smokey Bear, wearing blue jeans and a ranger hat, pointing at him and admonishing, "Only YOU can prevent forest fires."

He stepped outside, stood beneath the covered porch. It was a modest home with a 1930's exterior, faux shutters, wood siding lime green, and trim the color of basil. A weeping willow thirty feet high dominated a small front lawn. Beyond the homes across the street, the sound of semi-trucks revealed her proximity to the freeway.

At the fire base Nancy exhibited a hard exterior, left no doubt who was in charge. He felt privileged to look through to the interior, comfortable like the living room, surprising with a woman's touch. Spicy tomato aromas drifted from the kitchen. After today, he'd do the cooking. She'd be working, and he wouldn't. Any minute the phone could ring and send her anywhere in the Western U.S. But his phone would no longer summon him to such dispatches. And when the reporters surrendered and withdrew from the quiet isolated contrast of his house, what would he do then?

Chapter Twenty-seven

Dry wind pushed against his truck while he sat in the driver's seat, watching the Ellensburg High School gymnasium parking lot fill with vehicles. Holding hats down on their heads, mourners in formal attire trudged toward the glass double-doors. Two days ago, no one among the thousands at Seattle Pacific University noticed him. Yesterday at the large church in Issaquah, his gray stubble beard and sunglasses provided a thin mask as he stood with a group in the back corner of a church for Agent Bishop's funeral. Wary, he watched the cameras more than the speakers. Whenever anyone in the crammed press section panned a camcorder, Ed lowered his head to study the service program. He only half-heard what the FBI executive director, who'd flown from Washington, D.C., had to say. Lots of talk about capturing the PUMAs. How Bishop and the others had at least disrupted their cowardly brand of terror.

Here at Sheriff Stewart's ceremony, he doubted he'd escape notice, not among his rural neighbors, friends, and perhaps work colleagues. He'd be obliged to say something and *I'm fine* would not suffice, would sound cold, indifferent to the victim he had delivered to death. *Not so good,* he'd have to say, and he practiced those three words and knew them to be the truth.

To the media he'd say the same thing he would have said at the other services if one of them detected him. He'd say *this is the sheriff's service. I'm not talking.* He'd rehearsed those words, too.

News flash. The Firehawk pilot who could not evade militia killers could not elude the media, either. Watch closely as we fire barbed questions in faux-sympathetic tones to break him so that our audience can see a real person suffer a live meltdown. We leave it to our viewers to decide if that same shaky demeanor contributed to the disastrous decision leading to the deaths of three brave law enforcement figures.

But he wouldn't play his part, not today.

Three minutes before the ceremony, with the parking lot full of cars, Ed donned the sunglasses, stepped onto the baking asphalt, and strode toward the gym. Outside the doors two men watched him. One moved toward him just as he stepped on the sidewalk.

"You're Edward Kline, aren't you?"

Ed kept moving. The man walked with him.

"I'm Joseph Williams from *Time* magazine. Can I buy you a cup of coffee after the service?"

Ed stopped at the door.

"No."

"I saw you at the other services. I left you alone out of respect."

"Thank you."

He opened the door and entered the foyer. Adhered to a large trophy case, oversized photographs of Stewart in all stages of his life greeted the visitors. Above the photos, a giant hand-painted sign on white butcher paper proclaimed, *We miss you, Sheriff Darrin!* In the wide, narrow room, a half dozen individuals clustered on both ends where signs invited them to write messages. From the gym a choir sang "Precious Memories." With the *Time* reporter quietly dogging him on his right, the other man entered a different door, a young guy wearing dark blue slacks and a black shirt. He cut off Ed's pathway.

"Edward Kline. Stephen Moore from *The Sun.* United Kingdom, right? We'll pay you for your story. Substantial."

Before Kline could react, Moore grasped Ed's sports jacket and deposited a business card into a side pocket. Ed whirled at the invasion of his person.

Moore took a step back, simultaneously holding both arms from his sides. "No harm," he said. "Quite the opposite. Five G's."

Ed passed through the open doorway to the side of the bleachers where a crowd, cramming the floor, ignored an usher's plea to move to the seats.

After squeezing through the crowd and around the corner to the front of the bleachers, Ed stopped. Across the floor on the opposite side, hundreds of uniformed law enforcement officers sat solemnly. Next to him on the first row a young woman shifted her tear-lined face to look around him toward the choir. Ed spun a half-turn, hissed at the *Time* reporter behind him.

"Go away. Sit somewhere else."

He darted to a small spot only three rows up. The choir finished, left a soft buzz of whispers and clearing throats to take its place. On the floor beneath a basketball hoop a photographer pointed a telephoto lens directly at Ed, who hadn't had time or peace to obtain a program and no subtle means to hide his face.

Somehow between yesterday and today they'd figured out who he was. Another camera copied the first one while, from farther down the bleachers, a portly man in his forties emerged from a roped-off section for family members. Behind the lectern, he attached a lapel microphone to his suit and announced the ceremony would begin, requesting news media to vacate the gymnasium floor out of respect for the sheriff's family and friends. Ed refrained from blowing him a kiss.

He learned that the Foothill Baptist Church choir singing at the service counted as one of its members every Sunday the roguish Sheriff Darrin Stewart. The director told how Stewart sometimes tried to veil his chronically late arrivals to rehearsal—on all fours he'd crawl up the floor on a side aisle, or he'd enter from the back, scurry behind a little bookcase, tiptoe in until close behind the director, and scamper to the group when she turned to get another hymnal from the front pew. One time he sauntered to the group wearing an oversized trench coat and an old Richard Nixon mask.

"I expect him to come dashing out one of these locker rooms, wearing a skirt and a mop-head, but he's with Jesus now, pranking the angels." She laughed and then she cried. "It won't be the same down here on earth."

More tributes followed. Stewart's wit and hijinks eased the pressure-cooker work of protecting a large rural county with an undersized staff, but out in public he insisted on professional conduct. Speaking on behalf of his widow, Stewart's sister-in-law explained that Mrs. Stewart could not talk about her husband without weeping, but as soon as she finished relaying her sister's sentiments, a trim blonde in a black dress strode to the lectern, grasped the microphone from its stand, swept reddened eyes left and right to both bleachers.

"Not everyone loved Darrin," she said. "There are bad people in this world. But to me he was the dearest man on this entire planet."

As she returned to her seat, the only sounds were the tread of her shoes and sniffles among the audience. Across the gym, numerous law enforcement officers brushed hands across their cheeks.

Afterward, Moore stepped toward him as soon as he exited the outside doors.

"If it's the money, my regrets. Less or more, none if it suits your principles."

"This is the sheriff's funeral. I'm not talking."

"Respect, yes, I see. Good. Who do you want to tell your story, Mr. Kline? The FBI? Your boss? Your ex-wife? Or you?"

"Christ, man!" A voice behind interrupted the exchange. "He said no. Leave him be, for God's sake!"

"Ah! My regrets then. Mr. Kline, it's your story. A chance to tell your side. You have my card." Moore nodded once, looked past Ed, advanced toward the murmurs inside the foyer.

Only then, at the edge of the parking lot, did Ed stop moving.

He turned to the voice behind him and saw it was Dale Everett, the helitack captain who'd sat across from him in the now-crashed Firehawk dozens of times this season and harnessed with the rest of the crew in the seats behind him hundreds of times before that. He'd never seen him in formal duds, a charcoal gray dress shirt and an emerald-green tie, his rusty hair ruffling in the late morning wind.

"You're in our thoughts all the time, Ed."

"Thanks."

"Miss you, man. Miss how you challenge me. What you know about fire. I can bank on you to take care of us."

"You back on board? They told me they'd bring up another bird."

"Yeah, we're good. It's not you, but we're good. When you coming back?"

"I don't know....Well, that's not true. Not this season, I do know that."

"That's rough."

"Listen, I'd talk more, but these reporters. I'm trying to keep a low profile."

Everett nodded and looked back toward the gym. There was no one near them. "Yeah, I get it. You need to drop by the base. Throw some darts, have a beer, play some poker. We'll take your money."

"You bet."

"I mean it. We miss you."

"Just need a little time."

"Don't be scarce."

"You bet."

"Stewart, man, he was a character. When I was in high school, he busted me for underage drinking. Of course, he wasn't sheriff then. Scared the hell out of me, but I didn't touch a beer for another nine months before I got the nerve back up. Sure as hell was a lot more careful. He'd hang out, shoot hoops with us after school."

Ed knew the words he should say. Sorrow. Regret. The wind pressed into his chest, tumbled everything inside.

"What the hell," said Everett. "Saving democracy, are they? Bastards."

An awkward look took hold of Everett's face, and he glanced away, a sure signal that like millions of other Americans, he'd heard about the helitack pilot with three law enforcement specialists trying to find his son.

"It's okay, Dale. It's the truth."

"I'm sorry, man."

"So am I."

"You take care of yourself, Ed."

"You bet."

His legs steered him to the truck and he drove out of town in a kind of autopilot; he parked and sat almost catatonic near the freeway at the far corner of a vast truck stop. He unzipped the small pocket of the daypack in the passenger seat, swallowed an Oxycontin pill with a swig from his water bottle, turned on the ignition, covered the thirty-five miles to Nancy's house. When he arrived, his legs would not let him out of the pickup and so he restarted the engine and drove away.

Chapter Twenty-eight

In the Maruf District of Kandahar, his last year flying Black Hawks for the Rangers, Ed learned first-hand the meaning of helplessness. It was bad enough that the endless folds of dry and mostly barren mountains sequestered passage for the Taliban back and forth from refuge in Pakistan, bad enough that he and the coalition soldiers could not trust the Afghani villagers or the Pakistani military on the other side. But the most helpless feeling arose in regard to a man named Juma Tareen, a military overlord who took an eleven-year-old boy as a sex slave. *Bacha bazi,* they called it—boy play. The Ranger platoon had to collaborate with Juma Tareen but could not interfere with Afghani cultural norms in the process. War permitted them to oppose evils perpetrated by their enemy but not by their ally. When they saw the warlord bring the boy into his quarters at their Forward Operating Base, they could do nothing.

Among the platoon, words grew harsh about Juma Tareen, but more bitter toward the unseen and unknown leaders somewhere up their own chain of command who had decreed their impotence to quash the rape of a child. That was one pissed-off platoon, and he recalled his own resolve that in the future he would not stand idle if evil sprouted in his own neighborhood.

Well, here it was. Evil.

He stood beneath a swaying cottonwood next to the Yakima River outside Cle Elum. With a muffled roar, the Yakima rushed in a wide path, the land on both sides flush with cottonwoods, pines, and willows. He threw a stone and the river swallowed it, and he felt the same damn way he did in Kandahar.

Powerless.

When the PUMAs fled north the night they shot him down, only two access points offered them a way out, and just up the road was one of them. If he drove that road south across Cle Elum Ridge into the Lt. Murray Wildlife Area, he would eventually reach the abandoned PUMA compound. No doubt the FBI had already combed the canyons and creeks, analyzed tire tracks, photographed every square inch with its fleet of drones.

It was ludicrous to think he could find something the FBI overlooked, but he remembered the sheriff's widow, Delgado's little girl, and Lewis. He walked to his pickup and started the motor. It was time to honor the resolution he'd vowed in Kandahar.

Away from the river, the road turned to gravel to become Forest Road 3350. For a few miles, occasional gravel driveways cut among the trees toward unseen houses and cabins until the powerline reached its last pole. Paralleling the road, barbed wire drooped from tree trunks and rotting posts until a deeply rutted logging path splotched with wheatgrass and blue chicory flowers invited him to probe west. Less than a mile away, flanked by half-grown firs twenty feet high, he stopped in front of a ditch that a backhoe had dug across the path, probably by a logging company to keep people like him off their land. He left the truck, hopped the ditch, wandered up the road, found nothing.

Farther south another logging road twisted down to a dry

creek, followed it upstream, then switch-backed up the same mountain until it faded to an overgrown track and soon afterward ended among the trees. He turned around and pointed his rig back toward the main forest road.

Ed knew that dozens of these turns webbed the mountains. The few that didn't dead-end would circle back to the same road, tiny unmarked pink squiggles on the oversized road atlas he still kept from his hunting days. If he didn't count the involuntary grounding the PUMAs forced upon him a week ago, the last time he'd wandered through this territory was with his old army buddy, Hank Baker, when they each bagged a buck. Shortly afterward, Hank had joined Gibraltar Defense Services and disappeared. He could be anywhere in the world. Probably coordinating security for some despot dictator in Africa or Southeast Asia or maybe a sheik in Saudi Arabia.

He missed Hank. Those were good times.

The third road he chose ascended a rise through a section of knee-high pine saplings. Half a mile up where it swung left against an embankment, he stopped at a landing, treaded among shards of shot-up beer bottles, examined a naked mannequin strapped atop an orange mildewed hide-a-bed sofa. Within a black permanent marker circle where the heart would be, gunshots had created a jagged hole eight inches across.

"Got places where the bullet casings outnumber the rocks," Stewart had said on Bessie's last flight, with no thought that within that same hour he'd be strapped in the bird like the mannequin offering itself for target practice.

Well, sheriff, where to now?

Ed returned to the forest road, climbed four miles, bypassed logging avenues left and right. He paused at a summit bearing more rocks than trees, peered southeast at ridges half-bare and otherwise scrubby receding toward the dry Columbia basin. Down the other side, he kept south through timber and hardwoods to the bottom, bypassed a junction of dirt roads, crossed a trickle of stream on a single-lane board-planked bridge. Now cratered with chuckholes, the route became Forest Road 3330, ascended a north-facing slope until at the top it split, each branch following a fork of the same creek.

Two wood barricades and a sign forbade choosing the eastern option.

Crime Scene—Road Closed

Trespassers will be prosecuted

Halfway out his truck, he snapped a hand to his head too late to prevent the wind from pilfering his fedora. He hurried around the other side, ensnared it from a bramble of vine maple, and plucked out cheat-grass stickers. He pushed the sweat-damp brim farther down his brow, walked in his dust-covered dress shoes to the barrier, noted the tracks of multiple big rigs circumventing the roadblock. He wondered if Suzuki would be among the G-men down the road cataloguing every item in the compound, including leftover trousers.

A shadow circled the big three-way intersection. Above him a red-tail hawk patrolled for unwary rodents. How's the view, he said aloud. Someday he'd reclaim that view.

He'd come back tomorrow. Maybe they'd be done looking and he could have a turn.

By the time he returned to Nancy's, she'd already arrived from work. He apologized for not having dinner ready, said he needed to hike around and clear his head after the funeral. Said he'd done his hiking around the Yakima River outside Cle Elum, didn't mention the other part of his day.

"What's that on your forehead?" she asked.

"I don't know. Maybe a little sunburn."

"You ought to check it in a mirror."

Clustered in the size and shape of a sweatband, a pink stripe of bumps crossed his forehead.

Poison oak. The wind had flung his hat into more than vine maple. No wonder it felt like ants with needle-tipped legs were crawling across his forehead.

"You still keeping your radio off?" she asked when he returned to the living room.

"Yeah."

"Heard something about the PUMAs on the way home."

"Yeah."

"Another threat."

They opened Nancy's laptop and found the latest in the *Seattle Times.*

PUMAs threaten government buildings

The Patriots United Militia of America (PUMA), already responsible for seven killings in three separate incidents this month, left new threats today at both the state capital building in Olympia and the Henry M. Jackson Federal Building in Seattle. Mail clerks at each location opened small lightweight boxes that held inside bubble-wrap packaging a single business-sized envelope bearing a single word: BOOM. The envelopes enclosed identical letters authorities believe to have been composed on the same typewriter used for other PUMA communiques.

"We're still here," began the letter. "We assume you'll try to increase security measures now. We assume you'll try to reassure people. But will it be enough? Citizens, please avoid all government buildings for the next two weeks. Your friends, the PUMAs."

FBI task force spokeswoman Karen Harrison declined to detail all the security precautions being implemented, but she did reveal that additional concrete barriers would be installed around numerous unspecified government buildings. More law enforcement personnel will be stationed within and around these buildings, and the governor's office has requested the federal government make available specially trained units from Joint Base Lewis McChord.

State lawmakers asserted they would not be intimidated from continuing their third special session to complete the state biennial budget, already two months overdue. Budget negotiations resumed two days ago after Democratic and Republican caucuses chose new leaders to replace the ones the PUMAs assassinated.

Ed turned away while Nancy kept reading.

Lewis could have written the PUMA communique. Or arranged the delivery. He could be preparing a bomb. Or he might be dead, like the passengers in his helo, a casualty of Ed's stupidity.

The next morning after Nancy left, he went to his house to pick up his orange hunting vest. He found eight business cards lodged between the door and door frame.

Seattle Times...The Issaquah Press...CNN...KING 5 TV Seattle...KUOW National Public Radio...Wall Street Journal...New York Times...The Sun—another card from Stephen Moore, this one with a number written on it: $5,000.

Ed tore the card into eighths, threw it like confetti off his porch.

Inside he found five business envelopes shoved from beneath the door:

The San Francisco Chronicle...ABC News...Benton and

Thomas, Attorneys at Law...Samuel Tucker, Media Relations Specialist...Office of the King County Sheriff. . .

He gave thanks again for Nancy and for her house, wondered when he'd be free enough to spend a day in his own home, walk the trail to the creek and the cool shaded grass.

Almost two hours later with his forehead itching like hell, he stood at the barriers partially blocking the road that led to the old PUMA compound. He raised his eyes up the reddish-brown bark of pines, the gray scaly bark of black cottonwoods, up into the canopies of needles and leaves. He detected no cameras or signs of disturbance, but in case he overlooked something, he offered a "Hi, mom" wave before returning to his pickup and creeping past the barrier. About a mile away from the PUMA compound, he left the road and drove through an opening in the trees across a mat of dried needles and leaves. He parked, hoping the shadows of the woods would obscure the pickup's gray metal exterior.

If he heard voices or engines or rhythmic bangs or anything else human, he planned to turn back and resume exploring the web of logging roads outside the barriers. He began his approach like a deer, a few steps at a time, pausing and chewing on the situation and perking his ears for predator sounds, except that deer did not wear bright orange vests. If they did, perhaps more of them would survive hunting season.

At the edge of the road he heard nothing, but he was still at least a mile away. Keeping inside the woods, he froze at the end of a curve.

The noise of an engine—did it come from where he had begun? He pointed an ear north. No, not from there.

It was above him, like a small plane. He stepped onto the road, squinted at the midday sky. Nothing.

Dread and adrenalin mixed in his body. He knew that sound from Afghanistan. A drone. To the Taliban it was the angel of death.

Law folks didn't need tree canopies to hide their cameras. They used the sky.

The sound grew neither louder or softer, neither approached or receded. It stayed in one spot. His spot.

A rock on the road offered itself for a hard kick, but he left it there and took a long breath instead. He'd accomplished only one thing. Some FBI grunt staring at a monitor on which nothing happened day after day finally had something to do. Glad to enliven your day, he thought before pivoting back toward his truck. He managed to get his rig out of the woods, but a minute afterward, two black SUV's appeared over a small rise. The first one stopped at an angle lest the idiot in the gray pickup think he might just drive on like a distracted birdwatcher. For a moment he and they waited and watched each other until Ed decided he'd better get out—slowly, with his hands as visible as he could make them. As soon as he opened his door, two men exited the SUV, one on each side, using the front doors with their FBI insignia as shields. One had a mike and his words ricocheted among the trees and up the road and off Ed's chest.

"Keep your arms away from your sides and move slowly to the front of your truck. Stand on the driver's side."

He complied, and then everyone remained in place for a while, long enough, he figured, for them to run a check on his license plate and conclude the owner was a certain stupid-ass Edward Kline who thought maybe No Trespassing didn't apply to him. That he had certain rights denied to everyone else because the PUMAs shot him down and killed his passengers. Two men from the second SUV joined the ones in front of him.

"Edward Kline," called the driver.

"Yeah."

"Stay where you are and do not move. We are going to approach you. If you make a sudden move you will be shot."

"Roger that."

Holding pistols, all four spread apart and advanced until the lead man handed his weapon to the man next to him so that he could pat down Ed top to bottom. Satisfied, he took a step back. He looked about twenty years younger than Ed, had a shaven head, sunglasses, an army green Kevlar vest with gold FBI letters printed on the front.

"What are you doing here, Mr. Kline?"

"Guess I'm being a damn fool."

"Explain."

He took a breath, shook his head side to side. "Only a damn fool would think he could find something you guys overlooked."

"You're the same Edward Kline the PUMAs shot down?"

"I don't know. I don't feel the same."

"You're not exactly in a good position here. Cut the bullshit."

"Same guy. Haven't learned a damn thing."

"Sit down."

The man walked back to the SUV, talked to someone on his radio while the other agents remained, still wielding pistols.

The shiny-headed agent returned. "I've got every reason to cram you in the back of our rig and haul you off to federal detention in Seattle so we can interrogate you." He placed his pistol in a holster beneath a suit jacket.

"Wouldn't blame you if you did."

"We're sorry about what happened. Getting shot down, wondering about your kid. But now we've got to start wondering."

Ed nodded his head.

"Maybe we don't know everything there is to know about your connection to the PUMAs."

"What?" Ed felt his eyes widen, his pulse quicken.

"Suppose you're here for some other reason? Do you mind if we search your vehicle?"

"No, I don't mind. If I were you, that's what I'd do."

The lead agent nodded at one of the men, and while everyone waited Ed heard behind him the glove compartment open, papers rustling, the seat pushed forward, the metal clatter of his tire jack and tow chain. The pickup door shut and the man returned to his place among the others, all of whom by then had holstered their pistols.

"You claim you're here to find something we didn't find," the lead man resumed.

"I don't know what there is to find. I'm not saying I know something's there."

"You were there before."

"Not willingly."

"You had a chance to look around."

"I did. I already shared that information with Agent Suzuki."

"We know. Anything you didn't tell him?"

"No."

"Then why are you here?"

"I told you. I'm an idiot."

"That's not working for me."

"Not working for me, either."

"Let's try again. Why are you here?"

"I understand why you're doing this. I—"

"Good for you. Why are you here?"

"To look around. If you guys were done."

"What do you mean if we were done? You saw the road

sign, I assume. No trespassing. Crime scene."

"I admit I did."

"You parked your truck in the trees."

"Yes."

"Why?"

"If I found out you guys were still here I was going to go back to the truck and leave."

"Why?"

"Didn't think you'd exactly welcome an amateur."

"But if we were gone you were going to poke around."

"Yes."

"Why the vest?"

"If you *were* still here, you might have a taste for venison."

"Put yourself in my spot, Mr. Kline. You seem like a smart man. They say you served in Afghanistan. A man breaches the security perimeter. Hides his truck. Sneaks in the woods toward your position. What do you do with him?"

"He's damn lucky he doesn't get shot."

"Damn lucky. What do you do?"

"Assume the guy's going to clack off a suicide vest. Maybe shoot him just in case. Take him in. Check him out every which way. If he's not there to test our defenses then what the fuck for? Let his beard grow longer in lockup."

"So you get the idea."

"Yeah."

"Wait here some more. I'm thinking my supervisor might want to talk to you in our office."

The lead agent returned to his SUV, spoke again with someone. Ed contemplated the headlines. *Helitack pilot shot near PUMA compound. Helitack pilot detained by FBI.* He imagined himself calling Nancy from lockup.

No, he couldn't imagine that. Bessie was gone. At this point in his life, Nancy was all he had.

"Why should we let you go?" the lead agent asked when he returned again.

"I don't know. I don't mean any harm."

"What if we did let you go?"

"I suppose you need some kind of promise."

"That would be a start."

"And an apology."

"Wouldn't hurt."

"Damn, I'm sorry. And not just for me. Especially not for me. I'm sorry I put you through this. You could have killed me and you'd have been justified and you'd have felt shitty afterward. And I promise I won't cross any police lines or any other law enforcement lines, but I don't know about any other kinds of lines. But I won't cross your lines, that's a promise."

"I can't guess what you're going through, sir. But you can't do this kind of stuff."

"I know."

He returned to Nancy's in time to prepare tacos for dinner. While they were eating, someone knocked on the front door.

"Ed," called Nancy. "It's Agent Suzuki from the FBI."

He gave thanks again for Nancy, this time for having the discretion to withdraw to the dining room. He stepped onto the porch, closed the door behind him.

"Mr. Kline," said Agent Suzuki, his arms folded across his chest, head tilted left and eyes regarding him with disapproval.

"I know, I know. I'm sorry."

"Why?"

"A long time ago I made a promise. I can't let it go. I need to do something. I thought maybe if you guys had cleared out, I'd poke around, maybe find something. Wasn't trying to be super sneaky. Did they tell you I was wearing a hunter's orange vest?"

"Yes."

Suzuki adopted an appraising look, the same one he and Dr. Cisneros gave him at the hospital in Ellensburg. Hell, he ought to give himself the same scrutiny.

"How many years' experience do you have analyzing crime scenes, Mr. Kline?"

"I know, I know. God, I'm sorry."

More appraisal.

"Do you know where you'd be right now if my colleagues had not contacted me?"

"I can guess. Not good."

"I told them to make you a little uncomfortable before they let you go. What's going to happen after this? Do we need to place you under surveillance?"

"No. I told your men—no crossing law enforcement lines forever and ever."

"You can go wherever any other citizen can go."

"I took up your time and I took up your resources. I'm taking up your time even now."

"This is true."

"This isn't me. I'm not myself. Do you have children?"

"Yes."

"I pray to God you never find yourself in my situation."

When they finished, Ed returned to Nancy and his uneaten taco.

"What was that about?" she asked.

"Just giving me an update. They haven't found anything yet."

"I've got some Calamine in the medicine cabinet for that rash. What did you do with the hat?"

"Heard if you pissed on it, it'd neutralize the oils."

"Did you try it?"

"After I finish this taco."

"You just set it out in the yard brim up and tonight when it gets dark I'll take care of it."

"Appreciate that."

"I'll hose it out when I'm finished."

The next morning, he started where he left off the first day, quite a few miles from the forbidden boundary. He set his odometer at zero and logged forty-five miles of dead ends, little dumps where creeps had piled garbage bags, an old fire pit with scorched beer bottles, a spring gurgling out the ground and forming a mini-marsh ten feet wide, a bloated deer corpse beset by yellow jackets and vermin, a twisted smashed 1940s green pickup cab rolled off an embankment and buried in a tangle of shrubs. Lots of items tattered with bullets—a watermelon on a stump, a white double-door refrigerator-freezer, a faded life-size cardboard Yoda, an old RCA console television set, an oversized poster of three tabby kittens. Bottles and jugs.

The next day near noon in the quiet dry heat, a mile down a weedy graveled path, a stenciled sign warned "Trespassers may be shot," a not unusual welcome in the rural sticks. For another mile he guided his truck around big rocks before resorting to his feet where the single-lane track ended at a waist-high pile of branches. Past the branches, deeply shadowed beneath the trees, an eight-foot chain-link fence topped by three strands of barbed wire surrounded a brown metal building with no windows and three garage doors, brown like the rest of the building. Years of needle-fall cushioned the grounds both inside and outside the enclosure.

He walked a circuit, scanned the woods, heard only jays and crows, found nothing. He retrieved work gloves from his truck, unpiled the branches, brought his rig parallel to the gate, climbed onto the cab. With his eyes, he measured the drop and the probable impact on his body were he to jump over. How long would it take for anyone to find him on the other side of the fence with a broken femur or fibula?

He grasped the top wire with his good hand, barbs between his fingers, lifted one leg over, probed with a toe for a gap in the links. If he slipped, he'd shred his arms, maybe slide crotch-first onto the barbs. He took a breath, concentrated his weight and balance onto the little toe-hold, swung his other leg off the cab and over the wires and there he hung, five feet from the ground holding himself up mostly by the one good hand. With the bad hand, he stabilized himself, gasped through a shot of pain as he released the top wire and quickly snatched the top rail. One more repetition put him on the ground.

Near the building where the needles thinned, boot prints showed in the dirt. All the doors were locked. Between the fence and building, pines crammed the enclosure, and at the base of one of those big trees, obscured by grass, a black pistol lay like a discarded beer can.

A person would miss a firearm if he had only one or two. But what if he had bushel? Ed stilled his movements, listened half a minute, used his handkerchief to pick up the pistol. It was a Beretta M9, armed with a fifteen-round clip, the very kind he carried holstered everywhere he flew, walked, or drove in Kandahar. Making sure the safety was on, he tucked it in his back pocket, studied the ground, used his boots to brush aside decomposing branches.

Thank you, sheriff, for leading me here.

It was easier to climb up over the fence onto his truck than it was to get inside the area. He opened the passenger door, set the pistol on the seat, picked it back up and pocketed it again. What if he ran into somebody? Someone dangerous? What if there were a surveillance system he hadn't detected?

But the gun could be evidence, more than a pair of pants.

Could be a careless gun nut who owned the place, totally unconnected. Maybe a small-time logging contractor. But what if it were the PUMAs? What if Lewis's prints were on that gun?

He left the gun in his pocket, decided he could figure out what to do with it later. He repeated his inspection around the outside perimeter, farther from the fence where the trees and the ground duff beneath them thinned. On a patch of dirt, he found a tire track, looked forward and back, saw a gap in the trees wide enough for a vehicle. He followed the gap as it turned south through an understory of half-grown elderberries and brush until the path widened and stopped at the edge of a ravine. Luggage-sized stones and brush cluttered the downslope left and right but not below where he stood. Here the path plunged unobstructed a hundred feet to an algae-pasted pond, like a boat ramp steep as a ski run into a brew of watery slime.

In the murk, something pale and white angled flat beneath the surface. To get a closer look Ed hunched down then lay flat on his stomach but couldn't quite discern its identity. He rose and probed the stability of a desk-sized rock to the right of the plunge-line, leaned against the hill, lowered himself off the edge. Grasping scrawny branches, he controlled his slide down between rocks, paused halfway to the pond, looked again.

A vehicle. The back end of a van maybe with a window. He slid down another twenty feet.

It looked like a passenger van—and next to it, dark green like the water, another van.

Well, sheriff, another spot.

Chapter Twenty-nine

The next morning, Ed was waiting where the pathway began off Forest Road 3330 when Suzuki and the bald-headed man, who gave his name as Agent Alexander, showed up. After they stopped at the shade-darkened fence, Ed walked them to the path through the trees, showed them patches of tire tracks, stopped at the slime pond surrounded almost completely by steep drop-offs. He loaned them the binoculars he brought this time.

"That's some kind of vehicle, all right," said Suzuki before handing the binoculars to Alexander.

"See the other one?" asked Ed.

"Barely," said Alexander.

"It's there. Two vans. And the wind hasn't already blown dust across the tracks we saw behind us. Those vans couldn't have been there very long. Want to climb down and look closer? I managed it most of the way with one arm."

"Not yet," said Suzuki. "We'll bring a team. First we need to talk with the property owner. We have zero authority to do any searching here."

"If I blew an engine on an old rig, I could get at least a few hundred dollars for it at the junkyard. Two rigs—that'd be more than five hundred."

"What would it cost to have it towed?"

"Negotiate that with the junkman."

"People trash their cars in the woods."

"That night they shot me down and abandoned their compound? Remember I told you earlier I saw them go by. Didn't have headlights on, had a couple of guys jogging ahead to show the road. Two rigs were vans with all seats occupied. Couldn't see much but I did see silhouettes. There was a cargo van and a pickup."

They returned to the fenced storage.

"You said you found something interesting here, Mr. Kline?" asked Suzuki.

"See those three pines up there with all the grass around them?"

"Okay."

"I'll show you what I found."

Ed walked to his truck, retrieved the Beretta in a freezer bag from beneath the passenger seat.

"Interesting," said Suzuki. "What did I tell you about removing evidence? You could have left it there. How'd you get in there?"

"Climbed it. As for the evidence, think about it this way. You guys don't have authority to go get a gun lying in the grass inside a fence on someone's private property. But suppose some idiot goes and gets it and hands it over to you. What are you going to do then?"

"Find who it belongs to."

"Serial number's still there, right below the slide. I kept my prints off it, used a handkerchief to pick it up."

"So here's the scenario. You think those vehicles may be the ones you saw go by you when they abandoned their compound. Maybe they were spooked about the vehicles, ditched them in the pond. You're thinking this gun might be theirs. Maybe they had other assets here, other vehicles, possibly weapons."

"Add to that people moving in a hurry, moving in the dark. Easier to drop something and not notice. That's the exact same kind of gun they issued me back in the day. You've heard about all the weapons that disappear in the military. Could be one of those PUMAs had access to them, ex-military or knows someone who is."

"You're aware it could be none of these things?"

"Only one way to find out."

"Tell you what, Mr. Kline."

"You can call me Ed."

"I need to keep saying Mr. Kline. This is business. I've also got something interesting to share with you."

Suzuki fetched a thick binder from the now-dusty SUV, stood next to Ed, turned through pages of aerial photographs.

"Ah. Here we are. See anything?"

"Nothing but trees."

"That's right. How about this one?"

"Is that the pond?"

"See anything in it?"

"No."

"There you go," said Suzuki. "If I wanted to hide stuff, I'd pick these places."

"Probably won't find fingerprints with the rigs in the water like that."

"Chances are near zero. We'll have better luck on that storage building, maybe on the Beretta, too. I wouldn't be a bit surprised if it turns out an ordinary yahoo wondering what happened to his gun owns this place. But we'll check it out. If we can't get the owner's permission, we might be able to get a search warrant. A big maybe. The bit about the two vans will help. So you have my thanks. Let me ask you a question, however. Suppose they were here. I don't mean a week ago. Yesterday. Say they still had assets here and posted a guard or two with those M16s."

"Guess you'd have to find out some other way because I wouldn't be here to tell you."

"Exactly."

"That's not going to stop me," said Ed. "I made you a promise and I'll stay out of your zones. No one else is with me so no one else is going to get shot. And I said I'd share anything I find and here's proof."

"If this does turn out to be significant, it's fortuitous you found it."

"I feel like I didn't find it myself."

"What do you mean?"

"The sheriff. Stewart. I know it can't be real, but… Ever since his funeral it's like he's been helping me, like I'm still here so he's using me to look around."

"And what's the sheriff telling you now?"

"I don't know. But what I'm telling him is thanks. If this turns out significant. Even if it doesn't."

Suzuki switched on the emergency room appraisal look then smiled—the first time Ed had seen him smile.

"Tell your sheriff I say thanks, too. And that he needs to steer your butt away from danger."

The next day, a westerly breeze broke the monotony of what had been a long stretch of stale heat. Although the poison oak on his head was drying up, Ed didn't wear a hat, and so now through the thinning hair atop his head, he added sunburn to his other wounds and ailments. On his way to the warehouse, Ed counted eight different rigs going by the opposite direction: a sheriff department's white SUV and light green sedan, three black unmarked SUV's with tinted windows, a Jasper's Road Services flat-bed tow truck, two civilian pickups. No news media vehicles, however. Where the pathway met Road 3330, four men stood near two parked rigs, one a sheriff's patrol car and the other a dark blue sedan. Two wore blue FBI polo shirts and two wore deputy uniforms. Ed stopped and left his truck on the opposite side of the road.

"Can we help you, sir?" asked one of the deputies.

"You guys bust a kegger?"

"Might be."

"Dope grow?"

"Sir, this isn't Twenty Questions."

"I know! Some passenger vans went for a swim. Is that it?"

"Okay, show us your ID. What agency you from?"

Ed opened his wallet to reveal his driver's license.

"Any other ID?"

"Wait a second," said one of the agents, who looked up from the wallet at Ed. "You're the helicopter pilot. I heard you tried to break our perimeter at the PUMA compound. What are you here for now?"

"I found those rigs in the pond. Met with Agents Suzuki and Alexander yesterday, showed them around."

"So we heard."

"I saw the tow truck."

"Okay."

"Is Agent Suzuki here? He's the one I'm working with."

"He might be."

"Can you radio them to find out?"

"Why?"

"Look, I know I'm nobody or worse than that, a pain in the ass. But I helped you guys, too."

"Possibly. We don't know anything yet."

"He gave me his cell number. Why don't I give him a call right from here?"

"Cell phone? Out here? Good luck with that. We'll call him. You wait here."

The two agents walked down the pathway out of earshot, strolled back a minute later, and handed him their radio.

"Mr. Kline," Suzuki said.

"Yes."

"What can I do for you?"

"Last night I got on the county auditor's website and it showed how this piece belongs to a man named William Sweeney."

"So it does."

Suzuki did not fill the pause that followed.

"I was hoping maybe you could tell me, but… I know that's kind of stupid."

"If we have information we'll share it in a statement. If anything involves you, we'll try to contact you first."

"Yeah."

"I'm sorry, Mr. Kline. It's an active investigation. I'm sure you've seen the news. They're threatening government buildings now."

"Yeah."

"The one thing I can say is thank you again for tipping us off to this place. And if you find anything else, please tell us."

"Yeah. I will. Thanks for talking to me."

In the afternoon, wind blew from different directions and a single big cloud billowed into a thunderhead north back toward Cle Elem. Ed logged 30 miles on his odometer. More dead-end logging roads beyond which walking revealed nothing but forest in various stages of growth. On a hillside, a bear foraging on serviceberries. An old brick-red railroad caboose marred by graffiti on a ten-yard section of track with nothing else around it except beer cans. A stripped-out primer gray Chevy Nova with the windows shot out and bullet marks pocking the doors and side panels. Squirrels in trees chastising his invasion of their territory. Lots of does and fawns.

That evening Nancy said she had to be back at base by 11 p.m.

"They're predicting lots of lightning, beginning about midnight. We're bringing in additional crews from the west side."

Her work boots were dusty and there were salt lines on her tee-shirt.

"Had us up Davis Peak doing trail maintenance. Steep and hot, more than enough to maintain my popularity with the crew. How about you?"

"Still hiking around Cle Elum, south. Thinking I ought to get a fishing license."

"First thing on my agenda's a shower."

He had just set the pot on the stove to heat water for the fettuccini when she appeared at the entry wrapped in a maroon towel, her black hair still wet and her thighs and calves firm and damp.

"I never show it to the crew but I feel it a little bit more every year," she said. "Today it's my lower back. Can I prevail upon you for a little massage?"

He'd come to like her room: the bed with its hand-carved scallop atop the apex of its curved wooden headboard and the wide wooden ceiling fan overhead and the faint aroma of smoke from her boots. She sighed while he rubbed her back and didn't object to explorations higher and lower and on the flip side, too. He used his good hand on her feet and her toes, squeezed and kneaded calves, quadriceps, hamstrings, slid the base of his wounded hand up and down her legs.

"Come up here," she said, and as they kissed, she pulled the back of his shirt up over his head. They broke for a moment while he completed its removal.

"I never know when I'll be back," she said.

"Whenever it is, I'll be here as long as you'll have me."

In the afterglow while the wind played patty-cake with the curtains, they lay atop the sheets. She rolled her head to look at the clock.

"Three hours," she said. "I can handle the hoofing, the smoke. Don't cut line like I used to, but that's not my job so much these days. Harder to stay awake. That last fire in the Gifford-Pinchot, counting seven hours transportation, we put in 28 hours on the first shift 'til they had enough crews to send us to fire camp."

"I never had to deal with that. No flying at night. That's with fires. Not with war."

"Add an hour for briefings after I put the crew to bed and before I wake them up. Then when I'm out there scouting and looking out for the crew, if I let myself sit five seconds I'd be out like a drunk."

"You've still got fire in your blood, though."

"I'd miss it if I moved behind a desk. Still a fire junkie."

"I'll get the pasta going."

"Let's wait a minute." She propped herself on an elbow. "How are you doing?"

"I'm okay."

"You can talk to me, you know. Tell me what's on your mind. What you see on your hikes. I understand why you don't talk much right now. But if you ever feel like it, you can say anything at all and it won't faze me. Just get it all out."

"Saw a bear today."

"Oh?"

"Far from me, though. Up a hillside."

"What else?"

"Lots of deer."

She lay quietly, ready if he had more to share.

What would she think if he told her he spent hours every day on a fool's errand looking for his son?

"He's...Lewis...he's on my mind a lot," he said.

After a night of thunder mumbling from far away, Ed explored the last of the logging roads and pathways he had not yet covered. Down dry creek bottoms and up to broken concrete where lookouts once stood. Six-site campgrounds with outhouses and century-old hitching posts. Dried-up deep ruts where months ago high-clearance trucks had churned up mud. Extended families of turkeys and quail. Spooked range cattle trotting among stands of oak. Remnants of cabins weathering among pines. Another junk heap shooting gallery, this one featuring Marilyn Monroe and Chewbacca and a china cabinet. He spotted a lone coyote with mottled fur in a yellow-grassed field, and an odd sense of kinship bubbled up in his chest.

Billowing islands of cumulus materialized from nothingness, puffed themselves high and wide, joined forces, growled menace. In early afternoon beneath the gray he sat on his tailgate eating dried pears while a sliver of sun spotlighted amber ridgelines. A breeze brushed his finally itchless forehead, although the sunburn atop his head preached the gospel of hats. Road dust carried whiffs of precipitation but no moisture fell. Tomorrow he was due in Ellensburg for an appointment with Dr. Cisneros. He hoped he had not been too rough on his arm and his hand.

He looked again at the road atlas, flipped from page to page, traced dotted lines north of Interstate 90, skipped to another page back south beyond the Lt. Murray Wildlife Area down into the Yakima Indian Reservation and the area below that around the Columbia River Gorge. Hundreds and hundreds of miles of unpaved roads. He could use up years and still not cover it all.

At the pathway to the warehouse or garage or whatever it was, the same two vehicles and the same four men stood in the shade of the clouds. He waved and they nodded their heads and farther down the road he turned a U and headed for Nancy's place.

She had left a message on the answering machine indicating she'd be home at the usual time but that the next day she and the crew were leaving for Lake Chelan where three lightning fires burned out of control. He'd been there with Bessie in years past, once on a blaze that took out 200,000 acres.

"Might be gone a while," she said at dinner. "One of them's grown to five thousand acres already."

Like the night before, nothing resembling rain had come from the now-broken clouds over their own heads. The breeze had stiffened enough to lob fir cones against the dining room window.

"Maybe I'll sleep a couple of nights at my own place," he said. "See if the reporters are gone."

"We've got two places now," she said.

"If you had to pick one, which one would it be?"

"This place is bigger but your place has a better location. Only I wouldn't want to live there if I lived by myself."

"I like where I live, too. But you've got nice things here."

"What are we talking about?"

"I know."

Someone knocked on the door. Nancy answered it, called from the living room that it was Agent Suzuki again. Apparently, Suzuki had asked her about the fires up north because when Ed reached the living room, she was telling him her crew was heading that way tomorrow morning.

"I respect the work you do," he said. "I just want to update Ed. He's helped us out the last few days."

Her eyes met Ed's and she looked a little miffed as he stepped out onto the porch. The sun had dropped behind western mountains but plenty of daylight remained. Weeping willow limbs tussled with the wind, muffling freeway sounds.

"You're actually going to update me?" he asked.

"You're on my way home. The media started making phone calls to us about it. They've heard something. We'll feed them what we can at a conference in Ellensburg tomorrow morning."

"What did you find out about William Sweeney?"

"He's one of those Patriot Party guys. Says he's never set foot on the property all his life. Says a man named White met him at a party meeting in Spokane and asked him how'd he like to own some land. This White guy gave Sweeney the money to buy it and set White up with a post office box. The only stipulation was that he handed over the keys to the PO box and never set foot on the land and in five years he could have it free and clear just for letting them use it. This White guy said if Sweeney ever did show up, he'd never make it back home. Sweeney said he didn't have a problem with it at all, said there was no law against it that he knew of and if there were such a law, he didn't submit to that kind of authority. Didn't remember much about White's physical features even after we reminded him about obstructing justice."

"I'll be damned."

"Same thing with the vehicles. There were three vans and a pickup in that pond, just like you saw going by the night they shot you down. Bought with cash in Renton, registered to another Patriot sympathizer named Anthony Bates, a whole PO Box setup for keeping the registrations up to date. The only catch with Bates is that he's dead. Shot execution-style two years ago and left lying on his front yard for the neighbors to see. Whatever they're driving now has to be registered to someone else because Bates never bought another vehicle again. These guys cover their tracks."

"Do you think it's them?"

"That's what we're going to tell the media tomorrow. From tire tread analysis, we know the vehicles in the pond had been at the compound."

"What about the gun?"

"Belongs to Uncle Sam. U.S. Army."

"Figures. Wasn't mine, I can tell you that. What about fingerprints?"

"We've got prints from the warehouse, not from the vehicles. They've all been altered. They put Z-cuts on their fingertips, and it totally fouls up the computer identification process."

"I didn't think you could do that."

"It's not something we publicize. Bottom line, Mr. Kline—

we're not any closer to identifying or finding the PUMAs. They could be anywhere. We're assuming they're still in Washington, but we don't even know that for sure."

A ring tone sounded. Suzuki took a phone from his pocket, noted the number, asked Ed's pardon, and stepped away toward the street. In a moment, he called to Ed, asking if Nancy had television.

She was sitting in the old rocking chair when Ed stepped inside with Suzuki. She picked up the remote and found CNN.

"Just a moment, just a moment," an unseen reporter urged with sirens in the background while the camera zoomed across a brick plaza to a large building with a blown-out glass façade expelling smoke. A half dozen SWAT officers ran from the plaza into the building. On the plaza behind cement planters with little trees, more SWAT officers stood holding automatic weapons.

"We've got a man here..."

Something jostled the camera and the angle yanked up and they could see it was a tall building stacked with windows recessed behind thick concrete. The camera moved back down to the entry.

"...a man who says he was inside..."

The view zoomed back and they could see the camera had to be across the street because now it showed firefighters standing around two fire trucks, Seattle PD squad cars, four ambulances parked on the brick plaza, lights flashing on all the vehicles. Off to the right a group of civilians with their hands behind their heads submitted to searches by more SWAT officers.

"...before the explosion..."

Abruptly the camera zoomed back to the entry where a SWAT officer waved an arm just as teams of firefighters began running hose toward the building past the officers holding weapons.

"...bring it...bring it...bring the camera back to me..."

The building scene blurred, and there was a man in a television studio who said they had iphone footage from a survivor and then on the television screen a blonde woman reporter in a crowd of people appeared with the sound of excited chatter and sirens. She wore a cream-colored suit jacket over a blue blouse and stood next to a twenty-something man with a green button-down shirt and tousled hair.

"I have with me Kyung-sook Lee. He fled the building after the first drone smashed through the glass above the doors. The business day having been finished, few people were in the lobby, and the doors were locked. Mr. Lee, tell us what happened."

"A big thing like a little plane. I saw it coming from outside. I dove for the wall. It crashed through above the doors. I looked up and it was against a big desk."

"A drone."

"Yes, a drone. Big as a cookstove. It had some kind of audio player inside it. It said 'live free or die' three times. Then it kept saying 'evacuate evacuate evacuate.' The people, they were bleeding from the glass but the guards, they unlocked the doors and told us to get outside so we did."

"But you took some video."

"With my phone."

"And you've let us download it so that we can show our viewers?"

"Yes."

"Back to you, Brent."

The man in the studio said, "Here's that dramatic footage."

A grainy video panned an office building lobby. A few people lay on the floor, while others in hunched positions scrambled different directions. Low-grade audio captured the sounds of shouting. The panning stopped at a white blunt-nosed drone with horizontal wings in front and angled wings in back. It lay among chunks of glass on the floor in front of a big lobby desk, but then it receded quickly from view as Lee backed out of the building.

The news camera switched back to the reporter and Mr. Lee.

"What happened next?"

"One of the guards, he kept saying get back, get back all the way to the street and so we did. And then another drone, it zoomed down through the first hole and there was a big explosion and the guards, they were still there."

"And you have that on your phone also?"

"No, no…"

"Can we turn it off?" asked Ed.

"I've seen enough," said Suzuki.

After Suzuki left, Nancy returned to the rocking chair while Ed remained standing looking out the front window.

"I'm sorry," she said.

"He's either with them or he's not, and if he's not, where is he?"

They listened to the wind and then she asked the question he dreaded.

"What did Agent Suzuki mean about you helping them these past few days?"

"I didn't want you to worry."

"Well, I'm worried, so let's hear it."

"I *have* been hiking," he said, directing his explanation at the window. "And driving logging roads and looking. It sounds crazy, but I can't just sit around. And I wouldn't believe it if I didn't see it myself, but I actually found something they didn't. A brown metal building with big garage doors in the middle of nowhere beneath some trees, and then past there, down a ravine, some vehicles dumped in a pond. And there was a gun on the ground outside the building. It was a Beretta, just like the one I had in Afghanistan."

"Can you come over here? I want to see you when we talk about these kinds of things."

Ed walked to the couch and sat.

"Suzuki says it's the PUMAs. He told me the FBI figured out they'd bought it through a front man. But he said they weren't any closer to finding them."

She hesitated, as though formulating a response.

"Whatever roof we share," she said, "your place or mine or a fucking Motel 6 in Timbuktu, truth has to reside there, too. Do you understand what I'm saying?"

"Yeah."

"All the years we've known each other and all the shit you're going through gives you a little bit of wriggle room. If you don't want to tell me something you don't have to. You get to decide. Just say you don't want to say it. But you misled me, Ed."

"Yeah."

"I don't expect you to be your normal self. Hell, I wouldn't be my normal self."

"No."

She rose from the rocking chair, sat beside him, leaned her head carefully on his bandaged arm.

"I love you, Ed."

"And that puzzles the hell out of me. I love you, too. I'm sorry."

Chapter Thirty

In the middle of the night Nancy stood at the bedroom doorway, called for Ed to look out the front window. They donned flannel shirts and sat on the porch.

Past the waving willow limbs, out on the street, an empty paper cup tumbled across the asphalt. In the black tunnel of the northern sky, beyond the interstate's glow of moving headlights, distant lightning strobed.

"Tomorrow's destination," observed Ed.

"Like we didn't have enough to do already."

"I'd fly if they let me. Seems like I ought to be there."

Solitary clouds drew dark curtains across the stars. Thunder rumbled, and the lightning crept closer. Barbed and white-hot, it harpooned the eastern sky.

But the air smelled dry.

In the morning, on the way to Ellensburg, past Cle Elum where the timber thinned and the hills turned dry, Ed swiveled his gaze between the freeway and the northern horizon out the driver's window, and he watched a smoke column grow 30,000 feet high. Blood surged in his veins. For years, such a sight meant he'd reverse course, head to the fire base. He'd take the pilot's seat, rise from the ground, face the dragon.

But now…

He pulled away his gaze, concentrated on the road. His

heart hurt.

"Cleaning twice a day like I showed you?" Dr. Cisneros asked in the examination room an hour later.

"Yes, doctor."

A rough thin sheath, red like a dark cherry, formed a crater where the bullet had pierced his palm. He winced when she pressed against the skin outside the circumference.

"Has it been giving you much pain?"

"Not until just now."

"Sorry about that. Pain medication help?"

"Stopped taking it. Sold it to a pill-popper for 10 cents a tablet."

"Shall I call the police?"

"No, he'd be long gone. He was hitchhiking to Spokane."

"But you're still here."

"I'm still here."

"How about your arm?"

"It's good."

While the nurse cleaned and rebandaged his arm, Dr. Cisneros typed notes on her laptop then stepped outside. The nurse finished and left, and the doctor returned with a different question.

"How's the other wound?"

"What other wound?"

"That's what I want to hear."

"Oh. That one. Still there. How long does it take to heal from the knowledge you led three people to their deaths?"

Dr. Cisneros closed her laptop and turned her chair away from the desk to face Ed. She brushed a strand of her dark brown hair away from her eyes and rubbed her chin briefly.

"You should look me up on Yelp," she said. "My failure is there for all the world to see. Google me. It shows up within the first two pages. Doesn't matter how many lives I've saved. One time three years ago the wrong tests confirmed the wrong diagnosis and led to the wrong outcome, not so bad as malpractice but enough to put a tally on the ugly side of the ledger. Was it my fault, was it fate, or was it God? I've got the same malady you do. Disease can perpetrate an ambush the same way people can."

"Let's start a club. There's got to be a cop or a climbing guide or some teenage driver eligible to join."

"If you consider how blind luck or fate or God or whatever you believe separates out all the near misses, you'd have a harder time finding someone who's not eligible."

"I'd feel better if I could take those PUMAs and drive them face-first into the ground with a post-hole pounder."

"You'd have to wait in line for that privilege."

Ed took a look at the thick layer of gauze wrapped and bound around his palm. "I don't know if I want that other wound to heal. Absolution may not be a healthy outcome."

"All right. Tell me then: how debilitating should we allow it to be?"

"Let me know when you find out."

As Ed was leaving the parking lot, coyotes raised hell in the cab of his pickup—baw-ooo yippety-yip-yip. He found another parking space and stopped.

"Agent Suzuki. Didn't know if I'd hear from you again."

"I'm on my way your direction. Are you at Nancy's house or yours?"

"I'm in Ellensburg after a doctor appointment."

"Where can I meet you?"

"Have you got some news?"

"Yes."

"Good or bad?"

"Let's just meet and I'll share it then."

"Not good."

Suzuki did not respond.

Not good.

Agents Suzuki and Alexander were waiting in their black SUV when Ed arrived at his house.

"Let's hear it," Ed said after they settled into the living room.

Suzuki did the talking. "Last night while everyone was dealing with the drone attack, somebody managed to work around computer restrictions in a Bellevue library. This individual uploaded a PUMAs recruitment video and sent it to 14 anti-government websites that we're aware of. There may have been more. These sites posted the video, adding their own disclaimers against violence. They've gotten wise that way, careful to reject violence but at the same time advocating it through innuendo. This video is filled with propaganda. It has training footage. It includes advice about forming small militia cells. In that part of the video, the PUMAs include footage of two so-called *trial* scenes of your son. We've confirmed that the individual is indeed your son, and then...."

For a moment Suzuki averted his eyes, and then he faced Ed.

"The video shows your son being executed by pistol shot."

Ed couldn't move. He was empty and he was full. The room was still and the room was racing.

"I detest those bastards," said Suzuki. "We're going to catch them."

He was buried, smothering.

"Thank you for telling me," he said.

"It looks as though your son never did participate in any of their actions."

Ed nodded.

"They're going to fuck up," said Suzuki. "When they do we'll pounce."

"What about his mother?" asked Ed.

"Someone is with her right now. This video, it's going to come out. We can't stop it."

"His sister?"

"I'm sorry. We thought you might want to…"

"Of course. That's our job."

He closed his eyes, then opened them. How could he protect Sarah from this? She would be devistated.

"Does it say...does the video say why they killed him?"

"It does in the trial scenes. They caught him trying to get away."

"Before or after I showed up?"

"The first one before, the second one after you showed up."

"So it's me. Again."

"Before you go blaming yourself," said Alexander, "they'd have had to get rid of Lewis sooner or later. It's clear that Lewis was an insufficient believer if not of their cause, then certainly of their methods."

"What about...what about the body?"

"Unknown," said Suzuki. "We have no idea. Mr. Kline, if you want to talk to someone. Ms. Avila, she's probably still on that fire?"

"She is."

"We've brought a business card. It's a...kind of counselor, someone who helps people get through this kind of thing."

"I'll be fine, thank you."

Suzuki took the card from his shirt pocket, scrutinizing Ed at the same time. "This video," he said. "There isn't really anything to see. They're brutal and they're full of their own glory."

"And?"

"It's already out but so far the media doesn't know about it."

"You're worried I might see it."

"There's nothing to be gained by watching it."

"Okay."

"So do you think you will or won't?"

"Watch it?"

"Yes."

"I don't know."

"If you do, we have a version that does not include the...the execution. Just ask us for it and we'll give it to you. If you don't...it's probably better if you don't."

"I'll watch it."

"The whole thing?"

"I don't know. Yeah. Probably."

Suzuki nodded at Alexander, who opened a small briefcase. He held up two DVD's in clear plastic cases.

"Disk A—cut. Disk B—all of it," said Alexander. "We'd rather you get it from us than go searching the net or seeing it on social media."

"You can always take a hammer to it," said Suzuki.

"That's a tempting idea."

Ed found his legs, stood up, held out a hand to Suzuki.

"Good of you both. Gotta be hard to do. I need to talk to my ex. We have work to do."

"Let me give you this card, Mr. Kline."

"I'm good. If you're worried I'm going to knock myself off, don't worry. One death in the family is bad enough."

"I'm going to leave it right here on the table just in case. And you know you can call me anytime."

"Yeah, I do. Thank you."

They shook his hand and moved toward the door.

"Hey, my kid," said Ed, prompting them to pause. "He's innocent. He's got guts."

He picked up the photo with the salmon.

"That's him. That's the real Lewis."

"He looks happy," said Alexander.

"They're here. The PUMAs are around here somewhere. I want to kill them."

"Mr. Kline," said Suzuki. "We want those bastards as much as you do. That's our job."

"I know, I know. What the hell can I do anyway? Thanks a lot, gentlemen."

Chapter Thirty-one

What could he say to Sharon when it was his action that finalized their son's death sentence?

But he picked up the phone and called her.

They agreed he would be in Redding the next day. They'd hold the memorial service there. He'd stay in a motel.

They cried.

Afterward he staggered out behind his house, started the trail to the creek, stopped halfway there, sat on an old stump. In the grass on both sides of the foot tread, bumblebees nuzzled on purple clover and a dust-brown rabbit bounded for the trees. Jays squabbled over perches and higher still, a solitary crow circled. All moved through life as though nothing had changed, today the same as yesterday as tomorrow. But it wasn't true. The planet had spun off its axis.

He'd been home full-time when Lewis was three and four-years old. The kid was a climbing machine—he frightened the bejesus out of Ed one day when he climbed a bench and then the barbeque and stood on it looking across the space between him and the kitchen window, nothing but patio cement below him, grinning with a toddler's I-gotchya peek-a-boo. Curly brown hair like his momma's. Give him a football and he'd run from one side of the yard to the next, giggling at the improbability of outracing his daddy for a touchdown. He was good with the kid two houses down, handing his neighbor one

Matchbox car after another until the other boy had a big pile on the carpet.

Same way all growing up. At age six he wrapped his favorite book, full of pictures from Disney movies, wrote "Daddy" on a card, put it under the Christmas tree. The look on his face when Ed opened it and held it to his heart—that captured the joy of giving. Widest damn smile—it'd stretch his eyes flat, and if it didn't make you smile back, you had no soul. Had the same curly hair, browner. When Lewis was nine he was heartbroken the day of Ed's departure for another deployment, yet he said only, "Don't feel bad, Dad. We'll be okay." Brown hair sticking out like flaps above his ears and above his forehead. Learning at an early age how to force a smile.

Eighth grade Lewis fought two boys between classes at school because they were taunting a girl for having a flat chest. One of them split Lewis's lip so badly he needed stitches. Fighting's not the way, the vice principal said at the time. He could have informed an adult. Like hell, Ed remembered saying, and he took Lewis fishing during the period of suspension. Brown hair cut short. Smile not so wide against the pull of four stitches angled on the center of his lower lip.

In tenth grade, Lewis camped once a month rain, snow, or shine with Troop 217, delighted when his Assistant Scoutmaster dad was home to join the adventure. What was that lake? McKenzie. Rain enough to sink Noah's ark when they did that hike around the lake, and what did Lewis do? Gave his rain poncho to that scrawny kid who'd forgotten his. If they had a merit badge for heart… What did he get for merit badges that year? Geocaching. Signs, Signals, and Codes. Kayaking. Some others Ed couldn't remember.

One time in Kandahar, he'd looked back from his pilot's seat just as the medic switched cloths on the head of a wounded man blithering syllables. Behind an ear—a chunk of bony skull, a coil of bloody pink brain. The man died.

Lewis.

Wherever he was, Ed prayed it would be a place of smiles, a place without wounds.

He prayed—not certain to whom—for his own spirit, for his own inner wound, that he might have strength for Sharon and their daughter Sarah and his old in-laws, both of them still kicking in their eighties. That at least for the service, he might push aside the guilt weighing on him like a backpack stuffed with rocks. That he might drive his truck without the image of the man in his helicopter popping into his mind and blocking his view of the road. Because now that man looked like Lewis.

South on Highway 97 across the Columbia River and into yellow hills of winter wheat, 500 miles before Redding, Ed turned on the satellite radio. What would everyone be hearing on the news? Knowing would help him prepare for all the people in Redding. And the media, if they were there. If he heard something about the PUMA video, he could turn the radio off. Or not.

On CNN: "Homeland Security officials have determined that the drones used to attack the Henry M. Jackson Federal Building were launched and directed from the rooftop of a nearby building. From the building, the flight path was a diagonal line down through the glass above the entry. The drones themselves were a simple model, purchasable for less than $1,000 each. They'd been modified, one with a voice recording and the other with a bomb."

On FOX: "Americans would not feel so much anger if the government would simply get out of their lives..."

On MSNBC: "Certain politicians preach a brand of hatred toward the very same government that employs them. They inspire these fringe wackos. . ."

Back to CNN: "The Patriots United Militia of America, perpetrators of numerous deadly attacks, released a communique this afternoon. 'We told you,' said the communique. 'Avoid federal buildings for two weeks. Two weeks have not yet passed.' The communique goes on to offer a ceasefire if the President publicly states his willingness to negotiate with the PUMAs in order to convene a new constitutional convention."

On NPR: "Terry from Scranton, Ohio, you're on the line."

Terry: "I'm not a bit surprised so many people in that Pew Research survey say they support the PUMAs. Remember that cattle rancher in Nevada with all those militia people aiming their rifles at the BLM? How about the ones who took over the Malheur Wildlife Refuge? Pretty popular with a certain crowd, weren't they? They'd have been even more popular if they'd started shooting."

Moderator: "Terry, let me remind you, the survey indicated the majority of self-described Conservatives opposed the PUMAs. Twenty-six percent expressed support."

Terry: "That's a hell of a lot of people. Extrapolate it and you've got millions of Americans cheering on terrorism, as long as it comes in the form of White guys and the government's the target."

Moderator: "Let me ask our guest, Ms. Taylor from Pew Research. What do you make of those numbers?"

Taylor: "They're distressing, certainly. But the United States has seen this type of sentiment throughout its history from both the left and the right. In the 1960s and 1970s we had groups like the Symbionese Liberation Army and the Weather Underground who enjoyed support from many individuals on the far left. We had magazines like *Ramparts* argue against the government's legitimacy and imply support if not outright advocate for armed resistance. It's not just a right wing or a left wing phenomenon. It's something about America. Early after the turn of the 20th century…"

Back to CNN: "According to Reuters International, at least two U.S. militia websites have posted a video produced by the Patriots United Militia of America, in an attempt to recruit other like-minded individuals to join their campaign of terror…"

On his desk at home the video sat unopened and unwatched. Ed put his hand to the radio knob but stopped short of turning it off.

"CNN has learned a third group, calling itself the Freedom Militia Shasta Squad, has also posted the video. In addition to its recruitment pitch, or perhaps even as part of that pitch, the video shows the trial and execution of one of its members, Lewis Kline, for what the PUMAs call treason. As our viewers may recall, on July 31st the PUMAs shot down a firefighting helicopter piloted by Lewis Kline's father, Edward Kline, as he flew over the PUMA compound to search for his son. Although Edward Kline managed to escape, the PUMAs murdered three law enforcement officials who were also on the helicopter. Lewis Kline becomes the 11th known individual killed by the PUMAs in four separate incidents in a span of two weeks. We'll bring you more right here on CNN as more information becomes available."

When CNN switched to a commercial about IRS tax relief, he turned off the radio.

He hated hearing his name and his son's name and worse,

his son's name linked to those bastard killers. He was a great kid and he didn't kill and he wouldn't kill and that's why they had to get rid of him. Alexander said so. It wasn't only because Ed had found them.

But the reporters would be in Redding. Sirens would go off at the offices of the *Redding Record-Searchlight* and KRCR television news, and then the whole national media would park outside Sharon's house.

Twenty minutes north of Bend, a dozen coyotes blared an oratorio inside his shirt pocket. He parked off the highway atop a high prairie occupied by dried grass and scrub brush.

Nancy. Wherever she was.

"All I've got is a few moments," she greeted him. "You know how it is. Even though fire camp has reception there's no way to charge the phones."

"You don't know, do you?"

"What?"

And he told her. From several hundred miles away, Nancy said what she could, did what she could. Just as many years ago he had done with Sharon when she needed him, except the mileage separating them numbered far into the thousands. Half the globe.

Fifteen minutes later Nancy called again. He parked off the highway where a half-dozen Herefords stared at him from the other side of a barbed wire fence.

"It's all arranged," she said. "They'll give me leave, and Bill can run the crew. He's next in line whenever I retire anyway."

"Wait a minute. What for? Your crew needs you. I'll manage."

"Ed, this is not a normal thing. People take leaves for bereavement."

"I don't...I'm going to be fine."

"Sure you'll be fine. You're always fine. Couples do this, you know. Support each other when someone special dies."

"How will you get out of fire camp?"

"I'll get a ride. Kitchen crew going to town for supplies. Local paramedic when his shift's over. I can fly out of Wenatchee. Rent a car. I'll figure it out."

"You don't need to do this."

"What are you trying to tell me, Ed? You don't want me there?"

"No, I...that would be great."

"Then I'm coming."

"Well, thanks."

"And I've been thinking. You can't escape the press this time. At least your ex-wife can't. Unless she's got a hideout. They'll be there before you are. You have a plan for that?"

One of the steers, mostly brown with a white face, turned away from the fence.

"I've been trying to think about it," he said.

"I'm no expert about it, but they've given us supervisor-types some training. I don't run the show on the biggest ones, but I'm the one who does the talking on the littler ones. Reporters don't go away. They require feeding. But there are ways to manage them and reduce the hassle. We can talk about it when I get there."

After checking in at the hotel, he sat at the edge of the bed, the television off and the curtains closed. He called Sharon's cell, but it was her husband Tom who answered it.

"She can't take all the calling," Tom said. "The media somehow got hold of her number. I'll go get her."

"They're all up and down the street," said Sharon after Tom gave her the phone. "Sarah's arriving tomorrow. I don't want her to see this. It's bad enough."

"Is there someplace you and Tom could go?"

"I don't want to subject our friends to this."

"Maybe you could stop by the mall for an hour. What are they going to do? Follow you in the stores? Then, I don't know, maybe have someone pick you two up?"

"I don't even want to step outside. I don't want them taking my picture. Tom went out and tried to get them to leave and they left the sidewalk, but I can still see them in their vehicles across the street and Tom says they're down at the end of the block, too."

"I have a friend who knows something about this. Says we've got to feed them. Can you have Tom tell them we'll have a statement and we'll answer questions at noon tomorrow? And then tomorrow I'll do it. You don't have to come out. Maybe if they know they'll get to talk to one of us they'll leave if Tom asks them to and then they'll come back when it's time."

"You sure you want to do that?"

"No, I don't want to do that. Do you?"

"No."

"I'll do it. I'll ask my friend for some advice."

"So you're accepting advice, are you?"

He let the question go. She was stressed, and who wouldn't be?

Later that night Nancy called from her home. She was going to get some sleep and leave early the next morning, but she would not arrive before noon. She gave him some strategies for the press. Give them facts. Write out a statement. Express confidence that law enforcement would bring the PUMAs to justice. Most of the reporters would be respectful, would understand Ed and Sharon were not seasoned politicians and they were grieving. If anyone was rude just answer blandly and ignore the individual after that. Had they gone away after Tom told them they'd talk tomorrow?

Yes, Ed said, as far as Sharon could determine.

"That was a good idea, Ed."

"It was your idea, not mine. I'd have probably started cussing them out. Still might."

"The more emotion you show..."

"I know, the more they'll play it up. You told me. I'm glad you're coming."

He walked three blocks to a grocery store, bought a spiral-bound notebook, savored the temporary anonymity. At the hotel, he used up fifteen pages to write three. He wanted to think about Lewis, not the media, and so that was the focus. He'd told Suzuki and Alexander that Lewis had guts. He'd say the same thing to the reporters. Then he'd tell them to get the fuck out of his life. Or he wished he could.

By one o'clock the next day he'd survived the ordeal. The last of the microphone- and camera-wielding horde had abandoned the front lawn of Sharon's ranch-style home, the media vans had left, and the neighbors gawking from across the street and various other doorways had retreated to their air-conditioning. He sat on the cement steps in front of the house, retrieved from his shirt pocket the dozen business cards they'd given him. One by one he tore them up.

His heart still pounded. His jaw felt tight.

But they had treated him kindly. Listened quietly without interrupting when he droned through his statement. Raised hands and waited their turns. Departed when he said they were finished. He visualized what the photographs and the video would show: a middle-aged man missing half his hair, what remained mostly gray, tired eyes, a tight, halting voice. No excitement here. Just grief.

Among the questioners, one asked if he regretted flying his helicopter to look for his son. Ed was ready. Yes, he regretted flying over the PUMA compound. At the time no one knew that's what it was. He would do anything to avoid the loss of life. But like any ordinary father, he had been working with law enforcement representatives to look for his son, using every means available, including the helicopter.

"Do any of you ladies and gentlemen have sons and daughters?" he turned the tables and queried them. "Then surely you understand."

At the very end he shocked himself. Words and emotion he never planned spilled from his mouth.

"As for the PUMAs, I have something to say to you. How dare you equate yourselves with our founding fathers and slaughter innocent people at the same time? You cannot use liberty as an excuse for murder. You shall come to justice, and if I could stick the needle in your arm to end your existence I would do it. You do not stand for America. You stand for evil."

It was that upswelling from a deep place inside him that set his heart beating even faster, that kept it pounding as he sat alone on the hot steps. Yes, the media were gone, but the PUMAs, the men who'd murdered his son—they remained. He'd kill them if he could.

They held the ceremony two days later, a private one, although that did not prevent the media from establishing a parking lot enclave. To deliver real-time grief across the nation, the video-pointing crowd pressed against the roped walkway established for guests to arrive and leave the small nondenominational church isolated among oaks and yellow-grassed hills east of Redding. And although Nancy's presence at his side did not bring his emotions to the level of comfort, her closeness and her hand in his helped soothe the pain.

Chapter Thirty-two

Back home the next day, with Nancy continuing north to rejoin her crew, Ed eyed the PUMA videos on the end table next to his padded rocking chair. Though they made no noise, their presence chirped like a smoke detector with drained batteries. They would not permit rest or a cup of coffee or watching the Mariners with a chance to climb back to .500 if they beat the Astros.

Maybe Suzuki was right—there was nothing to be gained by watching them. He grabbed both DVDs, stepped out to the garage, picked up a sledgehammer.

At the edge of the woods behind his house he set DVD A, the one without Lewis's execution, on a mostly flat rock. Smoke from all the fires on the eastern slopes had thickened, a fog in the middle of summer, gray tufts a hand-grab away, an inversion saturated not with dew but with soot and grit, remnants of incinerated grass and brush and trees. Flakes of ash drifted like snow. The air smelled like burned cheddar cheese in a toaster oven.

He hunched low, swung with his good arm. In the smash of plastic, a shard popped off the stone, zipped toward his face. He yanked back his head, too late to avoid a poke in his left eye. He swung his bandaged hand up to cover the eye, moaned, stood and staggered. After a moment he lowered his hand, found he could still see the rock and plastic chunks at his feet blurry through a watery eye.

What the hell was that? Some kind of fucking metaphor? They'd already pierced his heart—why not his eye, too?

He placed the second DVD on the stone, squatted on bent knees, raised the hammer. A jab in the eye would not stop him from spitting on the fucking PUMAs, stop him from obliterating their…

He reconsidered. Maybe that first shot truly was a message.

He stood up and blew out a breath.

Up north the fires scorched even more land, would likely keep Nancy away for quite some time. If ever he could bring himself to view the video, shouldn't it be now? Whatever he had to feel, he could feel it alone. If he wanted to, he could break a window.

He returned the sledgehammer to the garage.

Inside his house, he made a pastrami sandwich, brought it, a pickle, and a beer to the front room where the Mariners did what the Mariners did, bases loaded with nobody out and left them that way. A strikeout and a double-play and a big fat zero on the scoreboard. Game over.

The remaining DVD yammered at him like an idiot pressing a finger to the doorbell and not letting go even if you set his pants on fire and he burned until only a blackened skeleton remained, a little bony digit stuck on the damn bell. Open me up. Open me up.

He opened it, grasped it as though a frisbee between his thumb and forefinger, the rest of his fingers curled, and it would have been easy to open the front door and fling it out across the road and into the woods on the other side. At least the damn thing wouldn't poke him in the eye that way. Probably come back like a boomerang and whack him in the head.

Instead, his hand obeyed the chirps and the buzzing, placed the DVD into the player, turned on the television again.

"The duty of a true patriot is to protect his country from its government," began a deep-toned digitally altered voice reciting words from Thomas Paine. The screen switched to black-shirted men in black balaclavas scrambling in a clearing among mixed pines and firs. Ed immediately recognized the background song, Sammy Hagar's "Remember the Heroes."

Ed had heard the song plenty. He paused the video, fighting an impulse to fly out his chair and kick the hell out of his television. Hagar meant it for real veterans returning from real wars—for example, Ed himself—not a bunch of murdering thugs playing soldier. An old TV show scene surfaced in his brain, a black-and-white episode where a guy heaved a bowling ball through his television set. He was glad he didn't have a bowling ball, glad he'd left the sledgehammer out of reach in the garage.

He looked at the frozen image—Lewis could be behind one of those masks, perhaps the one dashing to the right of a parked pickup, wielding a pistol just like the one he'd found on the ground at that storage site. But Lewis had resisted and now he was dead. Maybe it was another PUMA with a similar build.

He tapped play, pressed fast-forward, stopped it, reminded himself to watch and listen. They might have fucked up somehow with this video, might have slipped a detail that pointed like a neon arrow to where they were or who they were. He assumed the FBI already had studied every image beginning to end, re-digitalized it, run it through computers for geographical matches. The same FBI whose satellites and agents couldn't find rigs in a pond.

Back close to the beginning, the video resumed with a 15-minute pseudo-analysis of ratifying conventions, definitions of patriotism, the rights of communities, the conspiracy between large banks and governments around the world. While the altered voice rambled as though narrating a Ken Burns documentary, still images provided the only visuals—John Locke, Thomas Jefferson, Mel Gibson, Frederick Douglass, idle lumber mills, Asian factory workers, a kid eyeing a pair of running shoes on sale for $80.

Not a single clue.

A dozen men returned in balaclavas and camouflage uniforms and caps, stood in a line across the top of a hillside, backed by a mountain behind them, a rising sun off camera casting upon them an angled glow. A man in the middle with an American flag. Three of them with Lewis's physique.

"We do not enjoy our work," the voice intoned. "We wish dearly that our mission would be unnecessary, that the unholy cabal of politics and payola had not conspired to usurp the rights guaranteed to us in the Declaration of Independence. We wish an international conspiracy under the guise of the United Nations had not stolen from us decent wages and honorable work.

"We did not ask for these injustices, but we will not yield to them. We shall not stand idle before tyranny. Those among you who've been studying already know about the unconstitutional powers arrogated by federal and state governments, the illegal taxations and financial treaties, unauthorized overreach, a standing military numbering far more than lawfully permitted. You know that the people are entirely within their rights to form local militias by a factor of 25 to 1 over the U.S. Military, and you know the measures politicians have taken to prevent the people from accomplishing this bulwark against government tyranny. You know the urgency of the moment. How sad it is that we've reached the state described by Thomas Jefferson when he said,

'The tree of liberty must be refreshed from time to time by the blood of patriots and tyrants.'"

Murky footage of a helicopter cut onto the screen, an explosive bam, smoke-tailed mini-rocket, a burst above the tail rotor, autorotation, a hard landing far across a field.

"Go go go!" someone shouts, and three figures burst from behind the camera onto the field, sprinting with weapons toward the downed bird.

Bastards. They'd filmed that, too.

The video blinked to the opening clip of black-shirted men scrambling with pistols around a parked pickup truck.

"Keep your groups small. Do not recruit or accept any recruits you have not personally known at least two years. Far too many patriots who naively admitted undercover government agents now lie in prison cells or graveyards. Plan to *win*. Practice your plan again and again and again, anticipate every contingency, then separate yourselves from the pretenders: carry out the plan."

Back to the line of twelve with the American flag.

"You may think the odds are too overwhelming, that it's insane to strike a government backed by the most powerful military in the world. But if George Washington had allowed defeatism to dominate his spirit, he would never have trudged through snow and across the icy Dover River overnight on Christmas Day with his ragtag patriots, and we would never have gained the freedom that since then has been stolen from us one illegal law at a time. Beware traitors in your midst and be prepared to administer cold justice, as Washington himself did when he ordered his men to immediately execute Benedict Arnold should they ever capture him. Though it may rip at your hearts you must make a clear example of anyone who betrays you."

When the footage switched to Lewis, Ed sucked back a

breath and his thumb darted to the pause button.

Lewis sat by himself on a metal chair against a plywood wall. Behind a shaggy brown beard, he poked his tongue at a gap where a tooth had been. His bottom lip looked double the size of his upper one. His right hand and fingers fidgeted against the side of the chair. Ed recognized the classroom he'd seen by cell-phone penlight the night they shot him down. He'd seen the same single chair positioned in the same spot.

He resumed "play."

"I saw a Burger King and I wanted to go there," said Lewis—the first words Ed had heard spoken by his son in almost a year. Except it wasn't Lewis's voice. Lewis never spoke through fear, not the Lewis Ed knew.

"I wanted to get away. My whole goal was to disappear."

"Mister Kline..." an off-screen voice began. The same voice as the rest of the video, digitally altered. "If I were to attempt to do the same—to leave—what would happen to me?"

"I guess..." Lewis looked down at his feet.

"No guess. Certainty."

"You'd be...killed."

"We are called to meet a very high standard. Each one of us: an information device, a danger to our brothers. As much as we might fantasize silence, we would be found. The enforcers for the corporate-financial syndicate have effective methods. In the end, we would talk."

"Mister Kline, look at me."

Lewis looked up.

"We are all equal, none of us more privileged than another. Therefore, Mister Kline, what is the penalty for your action yesterday?"

"Die."

"Louder, so all may hear."

"Die. I fuckin' die."

Ed pressed "pause" again. He noticed his own hand, the bandaged one, tapping the wooden frame of his rocking chair. He felt as though he were shivering.

So that was it. And it happened before he showed up with Bessie. Lewis had tried to escape.

Did he need to see any more? Wasn't this enough?

He took a breath and resumed the video.

In a new scene, Lewis sat on a wooden chair. The walls were metal, perhaps a steel pole-building with florescent lights. Again, he sat alone.

A big chunk of Lewis's beard below the chin was missing, but across both cheeks hair frizzed outward. His lips didn't fit together right. The symmetry of his face had been bent askew. As before, he fidgeted, flapped one hand against his thigh, held his other arm outstretched, twisted it behind his neck. A single gray blanket sagged around his figure, leaving his bare upper chest and lower legs exposed. He wore black boots. Although the footage revealed nothing about who stood or sat in front of him, his eyes stared as though striving to remember a song, striving for another time and place.

What had they done to him?

Again, an altered off-camera voice addressed him.

"Traitor Kline, you are accused of surreptitiously betraying the physical location of your comrades' headquarters, exposing them to potential military ambush, capture, and death. How do you plead to these charges?"

"All I wanted to do was leave." His words emerged distorted, as though he suffered from a handicap or speech impediment.

"Your motivation is irrelevant. Answer the charges."

"I partially communicated my location." He rubbed his fingers together, scratched his nose, twisted in his seat, but his eyes stared motionless as though occupying a different body.

"Eyes up here, soldier. The location matches that of your colleagues, correct?"

"Yes."

"Then you plead guilty or innocent?"

He clutched the top of his head, twisted the other way, blinked. He returned a hand to his thigh, tapped nervously.

"I plead stupid."

"Let the court take note that the accused is refusing to plead and thereby avoiding the answering of charges. On behalf of the accused…"

"Stupid. Stupid for getting sucked in. Stupid for…"

"Soldier!"

"...sending codes!"

"Ah, sending codes. Was that how you betrayed us?"

"At the store. Remember? The rolling grapefruit?"

"Quit wasting our time."

The image blinked, and Lewis reappeared with a rag stuffed in his mouth and his hands tied behind the chair. The eye-stare had not changed, but the fidgeting shifted to his foot, tapping the concrete floor.

"You betrayed the location of your brothers in arms. We had no way to determine whether or not the modified Blackhawk helicopter contained an armed contingent such as an Army Special Forces unit of the type Traitor Kline's father routinely transported in overseas war zones. Such a unit would represent an immediate threat to the lives of the entire militia. Therefore, we shot down the helicopter and killed all but one of its occupants, including, perhaps, your own father. Do you see what your perfidy has cost? Nod your head for *yes* or shake it for *no*."

Lewis began humming through the cloth.

"This militia was forced to implement Tactical Retreat Scenario Number Three and abandon its compound. This militia's capacity to train and carry out actions is temporarily constrained, but we shall resume operations sooner than the enemy expects."

Again the video blinked and the next image portrayed Lewis outside, a breeze blowing his tangled hair, his hands apparently tied behind his back. Behind him a hillside in shadow rose steeply, bearing only sagebrush and yellow grass.

"By the time the Patriots United Militia of America releases this video, the news media will have trumpeted how the federalistas found our headquarters. Learn from this. At some point they will find you. When they do, you must already know how to escape and how to reassemble. Not one of our soldiers has been captured or killed.

"The price for restoring freedom from tyranny is high. The soldier before you was not always a traitor, but he turned out to be weak. No single individual is more important than the welfare of the militia. Without the militia, there exists no pathway to freedom. Freedom will not be given to you. The acquisition of it will hurt. Steel your hearts to do what you must do."

There was a pause and then a hand holding a pistol pushed into view inches away from Lewis's right temple. A shot fired.

So much blood. Such a quick fall.

"We remain strong, and we will strike again," said the voice.

Chapter Thirty-three

Outside the bedroom window a metallic bang varied its rhythm depending upon the ferocity of gusts, awakening Ed at 3:06 a.m.

Bam. Bang. Bang-bang-bam-bang-bang.

Calm during daylight, wind-charged at night—weird weather for this time of year, the kind that snatched the lives of firefighters. If Nancy were out with her crew, he hoped the forecasters had inoculated them against the ambush of wind. Were he out there with them and the hour be daylight, they'd ground him for a different reason this time—winds too strong.

He recalled how last month he aligned himself with fire officials in their obsession for caution. Rules saved lives. Now he didn't care, not for himself. Smoke-fog or winds on the verge of gale—it was only life.

He shook his head. Weird weather birthing weird thoughts.

Bam. Bang. Bang-bang-bam-bang-bang. Something had lodged itself in the damn rain gutter.

He donned a pair of jeans and sneakers, strapped a headlamp around his forehead, walked out bare-chested to peer at the noisemaker. A pine cone hung off a limb the wind had crammed into the rain gutter and now it played like a clapper against a steel drum. With the aid of a ladder, he pulled loose the unwanted instrument, tossed it into the woods. Still on the ladder while the wind blew warm against his shoulders, he gazed at stars no longer clogged by soot, their gleam brilliant far from any town or freeway.

Where did the spirit go? Where was Lewis?

Back inside he lay awake, agitation knocking not in the form of a pine cone but instead like Lewis's hand against his thigh, like his booted foot against the floor.

Guilty of sending codes...

Guilty of sending codes...

As though the mattress bore an electric prod, he jolted out of bed, turned on lights, pushed the DVD into the player, searched for the second kangaroo court. With the volume turned up so loud the digitized voice offscreen boomed, Lewis's hand taps pattered like droplets dripping unevenly.

Tap. Tap tap.

That would be "B."

Tap. Tap.

That would be "A."

Tap. Tap tap tap.

That would be "C" or "K."

One tap, then five. An "E."

Five taps, then two. An "R."

"Answer the charges!" thundered the electronic voice.

Lewis wore a faraway look.

Except maybe it was a look of concentration.

"Stupid! I plead stupid!"

Unlike the first "trial," Lewis, anticipating his fate, refused to play the game, the only hint of fear in the form of ceaseless tapping.

Except maybe it wasn't fear.

Another B. An A. C or K. E. R.

BAKER. Lewis had repeated the exact same letters.

The video blinked and Lewis reappeared, this time gagged.

But not gagged. His feet spoke. While his body fidgeted as though beset by ants, there was a pattern to his feet.

B-A-K-E-R.

"Not answering the question?" snarled the full-volume voice.

But Lewis was answering a different question, one the accuser had not asked.

BAKER.

What was the question?

Ed had been delighted when Lewis chose Signs, Signals, and Codes for one of his tenth-grade merit badges, because he could help his son work through the requirements. By the time he retired from the army, the military had replaced Morse Code with satellite-based communications, but he had learned some basic signals and location codes early in his service. As it related to take-offs, landings, and taxiing, he understood semaphore signals. Although the merit badge required specific competencies and demonstrations, it did allow scouts to explore other kinds of codes.

And so it was around a family campfire in April that Ed used his marshmallow-roasting stick to teach tap code to Lewis, Sarah, and Sharon. By combining the C and the K into one box, the remaining twenty-four letters fit the rest of a five-by-five grid: A through E on the top row, F through J on the second row, L through P on the third, and so on. The first set of taps referred to the row, the second one to the column. Military pilots especially knew about tap code and hoped the enemy did not. Ed told them how Senator John McCain and other captured pilots used the simple five-by-five grid to communicate even while isolated in separate cells in North Vietnamese prison camps. Tapping disclosures of what their interrogators had asked, they managed to keep their stories consistent.

It was so simple they could do it in their heads, without a paper key. Ed still remembered something of what everyone tapped that night with marshmallow sticks against the rocks around the firepit.

"Love U," tapped Sarah.

"Big fish," tapped Lewis.

"Stay home," tapped Sharon.

He had thought Sharon was teasing—but it was the last camping trip they ever took as a family.

Seven years later Lewis remembered. Wearing only a blanket and boots, his front tooth missing, lip swollen, jaw perhaps broken, he adopted the code used by other beaten and abused prisoners. Unlike McCain, Lewis didn't tap the code from an isolated cell. He did it directly in the face of his captors.

BAKER. Like the man or woman who bakes bread? Bread or money or… Why would he tap that?

What about a place? Could Lewis have signaled their location that way? Mt. Baker. A snow-blanketed peak in northwest Washington, it was a long way from there to the kind of dry land where Lewis took his last breath. Why would they go so far out of their way when if they were holed up around Baker, they could find a million isolated places to kill a man? The same with Baker Lake, just off the east side of the mountain.

What about Seattle? Wasn't there a Mt. Baker district?

Ed went to his bedroom, turned on his computer, found the Mt. Baker district against the west side of Lake Washington east of downtown. From there, another two-plus hour drive to cross the mountains into sage country. He did another search for Baker in eastern Washington. No such place existed.

A place or a thing or a profession or maybe a name.

What if it meant nothing at all? Lewis could have tuned out his ordeal by zeroing in on a song, could have been tapping to its beats. But five different times exactly? Even after they stuffed his mouth and bound his hands?

Baker. Mixing, kneading, rising. Pastries. Rolling, shaping. Joe and Jane Baker, up long before the sun, baking chocolate muffins for the morning coffee crowd.

Or Hank Baker.

Hank.

That didn't make sense, either. His old buddy in war and for a while in peace, now part of some terror group that shot him down and murdered his son?

Ed had known Hank for more than a decade, operated in the same unit out of Joint Base Lewis-McChord, saw combat together that first year in Afghanistan. By then a platoon leader, Hank stayed a year with special forces after Ed retired. Demanding of himself and others, professional, dedicated to his men, Hank never talked about hating the government. He worked his first civilian year for the Postal Service in Moses Lake before hiring on with an international security firm and taking short-term assignments around the world. He said he missed the Rangers, felt like he should still be "in country" with his men. A lot of soldiers were like that—hated their time in combat zones but missed it when they were home.

The last time he'd seen Hank was more than three years ago. They'd gone spring turkey hunting around Hank's old cabin up some canyon west of Wenatchee. After Hank took his discharge from the Rangers it had become a tradition, turkeys in April and deer in October. Three years ago when he didn't hear from Hank, he assumed security work must have prevented him from being home. The next year he figured the same thing and when this spring arrived without a phone call, Ed figured maybe Hank had moved on. But all of this took place after Ed's marriage collapsed. Lewis had never met Hank or heard about him.

Ed's computer screen provided the only light in his room, though light from the living room where he'd watched the DVD spilled in. He rubbed his chin and sighed. He couldn't picture Hank mouthing wacko notions like 25-to-one Armed Power Ratios or following anyone who did.

Maybe it was a different Baker. There had to be hundreds of them in Washington state alone. But if Lewis was actually using tap code, he wouldn't spell Baker for nothing, would he?

What if he meant it specifically for Ed? Maybe he knew or hoped the video footage would find its way into the world for his father to see, which would mean somehow he learned his father knew this man Baker.

Where was Hank? He googled the name Henry Baker, found a list that included a computer scientist, a botanist, financial manager, college football placekicker, restaurant owner, and a 1970's hippy comic book character. On the third search page, a link to a small announcement from the JBLM newspaper summarized his honorary discharge and his tours of duty. "Henry Baker Moses Lake" yielded a White Pages phone number, but Ed already had that on his cellphone. No searchable records existed to connect Hank to a security contractor, but that's the way international security companies liked it.

Hank.

He could wait a couple of hours so that it was actually morning by most people's definition and then call that Moses Lake number. But what if Hank was the message that Lewis tapped?

Hank. Standing nearby or actually pulling the trigger on his son? Unthinkable.

Baker. What else could it be?

What if the *k* were a *c*?

Bacer. What the hell was that?

An online urban dictionary defined the word as *baby talk for a cute face.* That didn't work. Googling Bacer as a surname led to a pediatrician, a Louisiana legislative representative, and a circus trapeze artist.

He ought to call Suzuki, but what good would that do at 4:15 a.m.? He'd call him later. A few hours wouldn't matter.

Think like Lewis, he thought.

Baker.

Fuckin' Hank Baker. What else could it be?

Lewis knew his father knew tap code, and somehow he knew his father knew Hank Baker. And he revealed Hank's identity on camera while facing death in a small room of tormentors.

Hank, you bastard. I'll kill you myself.

But if Baker were a PUMA, he'd have more firepower and more allies. All Ed had was a Marlin 336 hunting rifle and a Remington shotgun for turkeys. If he couldn't kill Baker, maybe the FBI would.

As he expected, at 4:30 a.m. when he called Suzuki, all he reached was voicemail.

"Don't want to prejudice you to find something when

maybe there's nothing to find," he said. "But I suggest you look up Tap Code if you don't already know what it is and then reexamine the PUMA video and see what Lewis is trying to communicate in the second so-called trial. I won't tell you the word but it looks to me like he repeats it five different times. If you conclude I'm not hallucinating, give me a call. I might know something more than what Lewis is telling us."

Something like the cabin Hank owned out of Wenatchee where they headquartered for the turkey hunts. Couldn't exactly cram a militia in that one-room log structure with a little toilet and shower room off to the side. But it sat off the road on a twenty-acre piece, forested with pines and oaks, affording plenty of space for expansion. Anyone living within two miles constituted a neighbor. People out there would not think it odd or threatening to hear automatic weapons fire, although they might wonder how much cash the shooters were blowing on ammo.

No more Lewis existed to justify poking his head in the woods where the PUMAs might be. He needed to keep his ass out of the way this time. But suppose Suzuki was on vacation? Or when he saw the voicemail was from Ed, he decided he had other priorities?

He got dressed, gathered what he needed, and headed for the truck.

He'd be more careful this time.

Ten miles south of Wenatchee: Yip yip yip-yip baw-ooo! Baw-ooo! Baw-ooo!"

Fuckin' ringtone.

He glanced at the passenger seat where he'd put the phone,

saw the number belonged to Suzuki, pulled off the highway.

"Baker," said Suzuki. "Either that or Bacer. Is that what you meant?"

"You learn quick."

"You mentioned you might know something more."

"Maybe. Henry Thomas Baker. An old special forces buddy of mine. Haven't heard from him in three years."

"I didn't catch a first name, only Baker. What makes you think it could be this particular Baker?"

Ed told Suzuki about teaching Lewis tap code and about his hunch that Lewis was communicating that name to him in case he ever saw the video.

"You might want to get your people together, check Chelan County auditor records if you haven't already done that, look for some Baker property west of Wenatchee."

"We'll do that. Are you saying Henry Baker owns it?"

"Yeah. Been there with him."

"If you don't mind my asking, what are you doing now?"

"Thought I might go to church later this morning. Why you asking?"

"Church sounds like a safe option, Mr. Kline."

"You never know anymore. Could've said that about government buildings a week ago."

A few miles closer to Wenatchee, where pines and brush ceded ground to apple orchards, smoke daubed the rising sun red, cast the scent of incinerated conifers. An easterly breeze pushed ash and soot across the road, cluttered with the tree limbs and unripe fruit dismembered by last night's blow.

On the other side of town, closer to his destination, filtered sunlight tinged smoke primrose as it boiled 10,000 feet above the hills and bent west with the wind. At the beginning of the gravel road, a sign warned away motorists.

Extreme fire danger. Local residents only.

He sat in his cab a moment, then picked up his phone.

"You're better than I deserve," he replied to Nancy's voicemail greeting. "You're the only way life's any good for me right now. So be safe, my love."

He ended the call, looked through the smoke screen to the unpaved road, took a deep breath, and drove past the warning sign.

Chapter Thirty-four

Ed wondered how quickly Suzuki reacted to this Baker possibility, if even now the FBI had a drone overhead, if somewhere a surveillance specialist peering at a screen was shaking his head at the appearance of the same damn gray pickup. Maybe around the next bend he'd see the same two black SUV's that cut short his retreat the last time he'd ignored a road barrier. As he proceeded slowly along the gravel, fire-cloud swallowed more and more sky while ash flakes spilling through the air grew larger, some half a finger long.

If there were PUMAs out here, the fire threatened them more than an ex-helitack pilot wielding only binoculars.

Half a mile from where he remembered the cabin to be, a path embedded with large stones climbed off the road to his right. He parked his rig fifty yards up, silenced his out-of-range phone, donned his backpack, camouflaged in a green pattern like the attire he wore. After pressing the pickup door one soft click partway shut, he studied the hillside, ducked beneath some branches, and began the climb, avoiding twigs and oak leaves, moving silently across rock, bare dirt, compact needles.

A hundred yards up he turned left, paralleled the out-of-sight road, squeezed through skinny passages and waist-high chutes among the thicker stands. Wind arm-wrestled limbs and boughs, lifted and scattered loose soil and stray leaves, smothered the sound of his bootsteps. Unseen beyond the woodland tangle, an air tanker rumbled low. Its presence meant more than the pink ammonia-smelling storm it would drop in the fire's pathway. With air operations this close, drones would be prohibited. Both Ed and the PUMAs, if there were any, could move without detection from the sky.

He picked his way up a small knob less dense with growth, high enough to see a monstrous billowing cloud lift beyond the nearest ridge, lofting a mushroom top bright gray in the early sun, larger by far than an hour ago. It was only mid-morning. The day would grow hotter, the winds stronger. A small spotter plane swept parallel to the crest and behind it a DC-10 crawled into view, dumped its curtain of pink rain, the two aircraft no larger than a gnat and a June bug against the smoke. It seemed fire officials aimed to stop the flames from breaching the crest, but Ed foresaw trouble holding back the burning beast.

No heroics, he reminded himself. Find out if Hank was in the cabin, if something like the PUMAs were there, then get the fuck out before flames overran the place or, worse, the militia spotted him.

Squinting his eyes against the siege of wind-blown grit, he backed away from his fire show perch, turned downslope, ducked and twisted around brush until he detected a gap in the treetops where the road would be. He hunched low, moved in ten-foot increments, reached the top of a fifteen-foot embankment above the road. Just as he'd hoped, he'd overshot Hank's driveway, but he could see it angle off the road and out of sight, no mailbox, nothing so stupidly obvious as a gate and a guardhouse. If they had sentries they'd be hidden.

He glanced at his watch. Forty-five minutes had passed since he left his pickup. He eased off his daypack, unzipped a pocket, removed his field binoculars. For the next twenty minutes the only movements he detected included two rabbits sprinting into the open and then back into the shadows and a family of eleven turkeys parading across the road. No human voices or activity. Silenced by the wind and smoke, smaller birds hunkered out of sight. Ed crawled back from the edge into the cloak of woods and contoured the road farther away from Hank's driveway so that he could maintain stealth when he crossed to the other side.

He returned to the edge of the road, ten feet above the surface this time, broke out of the trees, took a side-step down the embankment. A vehicle engine hummed as though navigating a far-off highway, but Ed knew the deceptions of wind, hurried back up, squatted on a knee behind a pair of half-grown pines. A green Forest Service fire engine emerged around the corner heading toward the fire. Below him at the passenger window, a woman wore a dirt-covered yellow Nomex fire shirt, a bandanna over her hair, soot on her face. Wherever they'd been toiling, they were being diverted to the blaze gobbling grass and trees his direction.

He waited another minute, dropped to the road, and crossed it. In the woods on the lower side where down the road Hank had his cabin, Ed peered with and without binoculars into the brigade of trees. At his back now, the same wind that blew grit past his eyes would also hurl away from his hearing any human sounds arising from the cabin area. He moved twenty yards, watched and waited, moved another twenty yards, repeated the process three more times until ahead of him the trees opened to a clearing and fifty feet into it the cabin stood, calf-high yellowed grass on the side and behind it, a large area of packed dirt in front. The logs composing the side wall were smooth and weathered the color of cardboard. There was nothing around the cabin, no new buildings, no vehicles, no voices. Nothing but ash and cinders flowing across the grassy flat.

This was no compound.

Still, someone could be in the cabin and Ed wouldn't know it. No window looked out from the fifteen-foot side wall, but Ed remembered a small one in the back above a sink and bigger one in the front on the left side of the door. After waiting five minutes, he moved to the last tree at the edge of the clearing, waited some more, then strode to the back corner on the side of the cabin. He pressed his ear to the wood, felt his heart beating, felt his lungs constricting in the smoke and stress.

From the front of the cabin a sudden flapping coincided with a wind gust, a tarp most likely, but what if someone had quietly opened the front door, someone with a gun waiting for Ed to round the corner? He hunched low, traversed the back side of the cabin beneath the small kitchen window, crept up the opposite side to the front corner, took a breath, risked a peek.

Nobody. A plastic blue tarp wrapped over firewood and weighted with rocks rustled beneath the long overhanging eave.

He crouched low, snuck to the bottom corner edge of the window. A green curtain covered the dusty glass, offered no clue about occupancy except that it appeared dark inside. He could knock on the door but if for some freaky reason Hank was in there and Hank was a PUMA, he'd know why Ed had shown up and that would be the end of this expedition. But it was clear no one was there and only paranoia suggested otherwise.

He rose full-height, walked by the window onto the wooden step in front of the door, his legs coiled, ready to flee. It was locked. If he had his truck he could get a crowbar to pry open the door, but his truck was half a mile away, farther than he could run if suddenly flames shot through the trees and onto the grass.

He turned, looked across the front of the clearing to the edge where the gravel driveway rose and disappeared around the

Ponderosas on its way to the road. The picture he'd imagined had not materialized, and his purpose for this exploration crumbled. Maybe he ought to return to his truck and get the hell out.

BAKER. Five times. That was no mirage—even Suzuki saw it.

He'd come all this way, snuck through the woods like he hadn't learned a damn thing the last time he tried it, and for what?

Unless...

Maybe he hadn't found Baker or anyone else stirring, but that didn't mean he would not find a *thing* or an artifact to remove all doubt, to implicate Baker the way Lewis had tried to tell him. Lewis meant his message for Ed, and he would not fail his son, would see his mission through to the end, whatever that would be.

He stepped away from the door, drew back a leg, shot it karate-like into the wood below the knob like they did in cop shows and it felt like someone had smacked his heel with a two-by-four and it wrenched his knee at the same time. He hopped on the leg he hadn't used, brought his karate-not leg to the ground to keep from falling, found he could support his weight.

Well. Time to try the window. He took one of the rocks holding down the tarp, cocked his good arm, paused. He stepped back again, hunched down, lifted the wooden step.

Bingo. A single brass-colored house key, spotted with dirt, in the pathway of a troop of black ants. He bent down to pick it up, heard a footstep, whirled around, ready to dive for the ground.

Nothing. The clatter of a windy forest. He shifted his eyes tree to tree, concentrated for another set of eyes or a leg or a foot. Paranoid again. He could taste adrenalin like a coin on his tongue. He'd never been jumpy in war, not even when they shot at his helo.

He let himself inside, closed the door, flipped the light switch. Electricity still worked. Reconsidering, he turned off the light, just like the night they shot him down, when he entered their barracks building.

The stench was terrible, like a septic tank. Muted daylight seeped through the curtain, revealed shadows without detail—the ghost of a table and two wooden chairs, a pot-belly stove, a row of cupboards against the back wall, a kitchen sink, a little two-burner stove on the counter, against both side walls a single metal cot, each with a nightstand and reading lamp. He retrieved his phone, turned on its flashlight. Rodent droppings spread among thick dust on every surface and explained the scratching sounds from across the room, faintly audible above the wind. Except for the profusion of turds and dust, nothing, no papers or books, lay on any of the surfaces. He opened the nightstands. Nothing.

He walked past the table to the back of the room, provoked squeaks and tiny foot scrambles, opened a cupboard beneath one of the counters, recoiled from a more concentrated odor of excrement. The penlight revealed nest snarls of shredded paper and foam along with more turds. He held his breath, kneeled, slowly waved his light the length of both shelves. Nothing. The cupboard below the other counter held a kettle, a large covered pot, a cast iron frying pan containing a sauté mix of turds. He opened the single cupboard above the left-hand counter, and a fat gray rat shrieked with pointy teeth and terrified eyes, leaped past his head onto the floor, sprinted away. He felt his legs buckle. By instinct with his good hand, he grabbed the counter at the edge of the sink, felt turd pellets crushed against his palm, let go again, held his balance.

The plague—sure, why not? It would fit well into his current life sequence. Except for the Nancy part. What would she say if she knew he were sneaking around like this?

He twisted his backpack off one shoulder to reach the front pocket, wiped his palm with a tissue then squeezed onto it a long shot of hand cleanser. On the shelf that doubled as the rat's launching pad, a plain office file, its bottom portion shredded to supply rodent nesting, held the ubiquitous layer of dust and turds. With tissue paper, he wiped clear a spot on the counter to set the folder, fidgeted with his phone, selected the camera option. Something knocked against the outside wall, but this time Ed didn't jump, recognizing the sound of a pine cone or twig the wind had tossed. Smoke found passage into the room, mixed with the aroma of rodents and dust.

The first document was a multi-page xeroxed copy with the heading *Dissolution of Marriage.* His wife had dumped him, the divorce final less than a year after the last time he'd seen the bastard.

That proved nothing. Once the loss of his wife removed the necessity of dwelling in or near a town, it would have been just like the Hank he knew to hole up in this cabin. Hank and he were alike that way.

Beneath the court document, there was a copy of a contract with Gibraltar Defence Services, an underlined space for a re-signing bonus filled with the number $131,000. For a moment sorrow surfaced—Ed recalled his own contract with Pacific Aviation Services predating the signature he later scrawled onto his own dissolution papers. But Pacific Aviation didn't pay like Gibraltar.

Adrenalin. He and Hank took different highways to attain the need for speed, the rush creating its own moral code. Six weeks ago he channeled his particular version into the Firehawk, one of the good guys doing good deeds. It was all changed now.

Why am I here? he wondered. Why did he feel compelled

to get there before the cops?

There was nothing else in the folder. Ed peered back into the upper cupboard, found a few plates and bowls and mugs, reexamined the lower cupboards, contemplated and rejected a notion to remove the shredded paper snarls to look for words or pieces of words to reveal truth, to vindicate Lewis's last communication. He opened both drawers, found silverware, extension cords, a sewing kit, a deck of half-chewed playing cards. He stepped back to the front area, wiped the floor clear near both side walls, lay near face-down to peer beneath the cots.

Nothing.

With his penlight he followed the cracks between the floorboards for some sign of a secret opening. He lifted the dining chairs in case a document had been adhered to the underside.

Nothing, nothing, nothing. Nothing in the whole damn cabin.

BAKER.

Lewis sent him here. It wasn't just the video. It felt right, like he was supposed to be here. Like Sheriff Stewart helping steer him around the old PUMA country.

The sound of an engine rose above the flailing trees and the whoosh of wind. The engine stopped and a vehicle door opened.

Ed darted beneath the window, lifted a curtain corner for a peak.

Sitting in the driver's seat of a white king cab pickup, wearing a form-fitting gray tee-shirt, was Henry Thomas Baker, looking just as powerful as he had during his Ranger days. A little mountain of topsoil capped with a long length of garden hose filled the pickup bed. Hank had arrived to save his cabin from fire.

Chapter Thirty-five

Ed figured he had about ten seconds maximum. PUMA Hank would know why Ed was there. Probably he'd have a gun, and he'd kill Ed.

Still hunched in the gloom, he dashed for the kitchen, grabbed the frying pan, shed his daypack, hurried back behind where the door would open.

A not-PUMA Hank meant serious shit. By the time he finished with not-PUMA Hank, he'd be facing either a felony assault or a murder charge. If he hesitated, if he didn't flatten Hank's skull, he'd risk Hank killing him. But if he did—as he must do—he risked prison for the rest of his life.

He couldn't glance out the window, couldn't risk alerting Hank that someone was inside the cabin. He could only listen.

Truck door shutting. Footsteps barely audible in the wind. Key in door knob, the start of its turning. A pause and the key withdrawn.

"Shit," Hank muttered from outside. He must have noticed the knob was unlocked. A scrape of wood—a lifting of the step.

"Sonuvabitch," said Hank.

Sonuvabitch echoed in Ed's mind. Now Hank would be alert. Might have his gun drawn.

Footsteps sideways along the front past the window.

No sound. Where was he? Did Ed leave bootprints behind for Hank to see?

Yes.

Sonuvabitch.

No sound. But a slow turning of the knob.

The door shot open, slammed into Ed against the wall, ricocheted back, stopped.

Hank burst in. A gun in his right hand, he pivoted toward Ed, just as Ed rushed around the door and swung the frying pan like a hammer down on Hank's skull. The force of it shot pain like an awl into his wounded palm, like a branding iron on his arm. His legs buckled and Hank staggered while still whirling the gun at Ed. A deafening bang pounded the rat-shit air.

Ed swung the pan like a baseball bat across the hand with the gun. Hank grunted but held the pistol. Before he could point it, Ed thrust the pan upward, and clipping Hank's jaw, and then he threw his whole weight into a tackle. They crashed onto the turd-covered floor. Hank twisted beneath him, pointed the pistol up. Another gunshot flashed, the sound of it pounding Ed's ears. Beyond all feeling, lit only by the smoky light from the partially open door, he smashed the frying pan side-first like a piston onto Hank's mouth, his nose, his jaw, each blow eliciting a grunt or a shout like he'd turned Hank into a macabre squeeze doll, and then when he sensed a diminishment in the struggle, he changed the angle of the pan and whacked the flat end of it against the side of Hank's head.

No more groans, the body beneath him limp, the arm flat on the floor, the hand open, the gun unattached a foot away. Heavy breathing, his own breathing, his chest heaving and lungs gasping.

He sprang up, dropped the skillet, snatched the gun, backed two steps, peered down.

He'd rearranged Hank's face. Nose crushed and twisted. Teeth missing from the open mouth. Lots of blood, enough to mix its smell with the rodents and tinges of smoke. But Hank was breathing and his body quivered and his eyes were open.

Another step back and he flipped on the light and his eyes strained against the brightness and he was panting and the anger sloshed inside him. Adrenalin buried the pain from his bad hand and arm.

"How 'bout we finish it right now?"

He pointed the pistol at Hank, whose eyes showed no awareness.

But instead he stepped into the kitchen area, retrieved the extension cord, rolled Hank's heavy body to the side, bound the wrists together harshly behind his back, dragged him two feet and tied the female end of the cord to the leg of the pot-belly stove. He examined Hank's wallet—no credit or discount or insurance cards, no coffee drink tally cards, no family photos. Certainly no PUMA membership card. A driver's license and cash—nine twenties, two one-hundreds, a five and two ones. In the other pocket a Gerber folding knife, coins, keys on a chain.

He lifted Hank into a sitting position with his back against the stove. Hank's chest still quivered, his breaths were short and rapid, his eyes glazed. Blood dribbled from his nose and mouth. He choked a moment, then coughed out a splatter of blood.

Ed hoped to God Lewis hadn't been referring to a different Baker.

"Wait here," he said, a little dig at the big man who wouldn't be going anywhere for a while.

When he exited the cabin, the wind shoved against him and ash flooded across the culvert of sky. He squinted into the blowing smoke across the clearing toward the trees, could see no red or orange flames through the gray screen, could hear no fire pops or snaps. But the beast was close. How long did they have?

At the truck he noticed in addition to the topsoil and hose, Hank brought a shovel and a mattock, and inside on the passenger seat he'd brought two fire extinguishers.

"Looks like your cabin might burn after all," he said aloud. He opened the truck, pulled everything out of the glove compartment—napkins, maps, registration and insurance cards, vehicle manual. In the inside door slots more maps, a box of bullets. Beneath the front seat a first aid kit, a paper coffee cup, an energy bar wrapper. Behind the back seat a tire jack, jumper cables, road hazard reflectors, fire extinguisher, tow rope, loading straps, twine rope, an old towel, a mini-donut package wrapper.

Nothing nothing nothing. Nothing in the cabin. Nothing in the truck.

Only Hank.

His arm and his hand resurrected pathways to the part of his brain that registered pain. It felt like someone with a baseball bat swinging for the bleachers had struck his arm, like a chainsaw had spun its steel teeth into his palm. He was sweating and shaky and he had to piss. He walked back to the front door. Showing no more strength than a Raggedy Ann doll and no more awareness than a junkie leaning on a park bench, Hank struggled impotently to pull away from the stove.

Good.

He returned to the truck and took Hank's thin rope. After urinating on the front grill, he withdrew his iPhone, found the Voice Memo icon. Back inside the cabin, he closed the door, set the phone and the gun on the counter separating the front section from the kitchen area, retrieved his daypack, applied more hand cleanser. When he began wrapping rope around

Hank's forearms, Hank yanked backward, rolled down, swung a leg short of contacting Ed. But the movements were weak, a pro forma resistance that gained nothing for Hank except Ed's backhanded punch to his fractured jaw, inducing a loud yelp.

"Hold still," said Ed. He resumed the winding of rope, tied the end around the stove, then removed the extension cord. Hank's lower arms, including the palms of his hands, looked more like a tight roll of rope.

He picked the pistol up off the counter, placed a chair in front of Hank, and sat down.

"Thanks for the rope," he said. "How's it going?"

Beaten and bloodied with a concussed head, Hank allowed no moans from mouth or fear from eyes. Beneath the bare-bulb overhead light, his face wore red gashes and the yellows and purples of swelling skin.

"You the one who killed my kid?"

No reaction.

Ed exaggerated a deep breath.

"Mmm. Smell that smoke. Like the barbeque pit at our old FBO. I kind of like this scenario. Here you are, not going anywhere. How long do you think it'll take the flames to reach the cabin once they hit all the dried grass out there? I'd say less than a minute, wouldn't you? All the dried needles underneath, old leaves. I'm thinking I'll water your cabin with some of that gasoline you got in the back of your truck and leave the rest of the can sitting against the wall and then I'll stroll on out of here. Won't be any bullet holes in whatever's left of your skeleton, the rope will burn up, it'll be a big damn mystery when they find this cabin torched and the remains of a human lying inside the foundation."

He stood, stepped past Hank to the counter, pressed the Memo icon on his phone.

"The hell you doin?" Hank gurgled and slurred his words. His chin and jaw were split open, bleeding, crooked. He was missing several teeth and those that remained were either hanging or jagged remains.

Ed sat back in front of Hank. "Justice, Hank. Justice for my son."

"Whatayou...whatayou...the hell."

"Don't pretend, Hank. I already know."

"What."

"I found you, didn't I? Twice. At your old compound and now here. How'd I do that?"

Hank waited.

"I had help. Lewis. A traitor to you but a hero to me. That's how I already know you're one of them. Lewis. And he did it right in front of your face. You ground-pounders don't know about tap code. Lewis used it to communicate your name in that second kangaroo court scene you released on your PUMA video. Henry Baker."

Ed leaned forward. "Tap. Tap-tap-tap-tap." He poked Hank's forehead with the rhythm. "That's a *D*, Hank. Tap. Tap. *A* Tap. Tap-tap-tap-tap. *D*. Dad. Then he tapped your full name. I'll bet you thought he was just nervous, but he wasn't. FBI already knows, too, and if they haven't already figured out this place they will soon, and when they get here they'll see a burned-down cabin and they'll see a blackened bone fragment and maybe a hunk of charred skin and if you've ever had dental work they might figure out it's you.

"So let me ask you again. What's it matter? You're going to die. Did you kill my kid?"

"You're jus' like ee." Hank couldn't bring his lips together.

"What?"

"We're the say."

"No, we're not the same. I don't murder people."

"Not yet."

"Touché. Score one for Hank. Let me amend that statement. I don't kill *innocent* people."

"You sure?"

Was he? A mixture of horror and dread threatened to paralyze him—he had nothing to prove anything. And he'd destroyed this man's face.

But there was a way to find out—something Suzuki had told him.

Ed rose, picked up his phone, and turned on the flashlight again. He knelt behind Hank and pointed the beam down at the fingertips poking out the constriction of rope.

The fingertips were marred. He felt relief and dread—relief that he hadn't committed felony assault on an innocent man and dread for what he would have to do to this guilty one.

"You must have well-rested fingers, because they've sure been catching a lot of zz's. Etched and scarred enough to obscure your prints. Just like the ones at the compound where you fuckers shot me down and killed my passengers."

He stood and looked down at Hank.

"Don't give me your innocent shit. You're a PUMA. But there's one thing I don't know. Are you the one who killed my son? Or did you watch?"

"No."

"No what?"

"Didn't watch."

"Did you pull the trigger? Is that your hand in the video?"

"I liked your kid. Soldier Kline. Good kid."

"You killed Lewis."

"Sorry."

He wanted to cry. He wanted to scream.

"You did it."

"Yes."

Ed pressed the pistol against Hank's temple.

"Like this? You fucking bastard." Hank showed no reaction, no fear. One finger squeeze and what a fucking mess he'd make out of Hank's brains. It would be a lovely sight.

Then he backed away, looked at his phone. The memo recorder was still operating. He sat in the chair again and waved the phone in front of Hank's face.

"Pardon me. I forgot to mention—these proceedings are being recorded. You know something about that, don't you? Except you used video and my kid nailed your ass and you didn't even know it."

Ed stopped the recording.

"Let's have a little chat off the record. How do you want to die, Hank? One way or another, I'll make sure this cabin burns. Would you rather be dead before then? Let's say you got loose and we struggled and the gun went off and it killed you. If the fire's hot enough, all they'll find is ash."

"You're just like ee."

"No, I'm not just like you. Choose your justice. Die now or burn later."

"Now."

Ed raised his arm, sighted the pistol at the forehead between the eyes, moved his finger to the trigger. Hank stared without emotion. Boom—it would be so easy. It would feel so right.

But he lowered the pistol.

"Wait a minute. You missed some funerals. You should have been there. My kid's funeral. The people on my helo. Guards. Senators. Moms. Dads. Sons. Daughters. Sisters. Brothers. Cousins. Husbands and wives.

"Do you believe in the constitution, Hank? No answer? Ambivalent, perhaps? Let's ask another question."

"Shut uh."

"Shut up? How's your nose feeling?" He rose from the chair, leaned forward, squeezed the blood-caked contortion of cartilage. Hank sucked in a breath. His back tightened. A whimper escaped.

"Not so good, huh? How about your head?" He touched the spot where the last frying pan blow had struck, then slapped it. Hank cried out, and his eyes showed fear.

Ed sat again. His bullet wounds throbbed. When could he ever give them time to heal?

"The voice, Hank. That voice in the video. It's you, isn't it?"

Hank didn't reply.

"Your jaw hurting you? Would you like me to check it? Remember, you're in the last stages of life. This is your death bed. It won't matter if I or the whole fucking world knows it's your voice on the PUMA video. Is that voice—"

"Yes."

Hiding the phone from Hank's view, Ed tapped the memo icon to record.

"You, Henry Baker, you're the voice on the PUMA video. Yes or no."

"Yes."

"You killed my son and you're the voice of the PUMAs."

"Lih hree or die."

"What?"

"Lih hree or die."

"Lih hree. Live free? Live free or die."

"Lih hree or die."

"You speak for the PUMAs and you kill for the PUMAs

and so let's consider those funerals you missed. You never met the family and friends of the people you killed, but you can meet them in a court of law. While the government you hate houses you and feeds you and dresses you up."

"Kill ee."

"I should kill you, but I won't. Let's let the government..."

Hank raised his eyelids. Another vehicle engine contested the wind's monopoly of sound. Ed pocketed the phone and hurried to the window.

To his left across the clearing dark smoke almost black boiled above the pines, slanted with the wind across the sky directly overhead. In front, from behind the trees that climbed along the driveway toward the road, two Forest Service green vehicles emerged, both of them crew transport trucks. As they turned at the bottom of the driveway the words above the top of the passenger windows nearly stopped Ed's heart:

Snoqualmie Hotshots.

Nancy's crew.

Chapter Thirty-six

They were supposed to be outside Lake Chelan, sixty miles away. They must have been diverted to protect structures—like the cabin.

What was Nancy going to think when she saw the scene inside? Because she was going to look—Hank's pickup assured that she'd investigate.

Ed turned out the lights, locked the door, squatted low beneath the window, ignored the chuckle that Hank squeezed through his mangled mouth.

The two crew buggies parked one behind the other and the figures in the windows stirred as they gathered gear. Nancy and Bill, her assistant supervisor, strode toward the cabin. Ed ducked his head close to the rat feces on the floor. A rapid knock pounded the door.

"I saw a light in there," Bill said.

More pounding rattled the door.

"Ugghhh!" Hank called.

Sonuvabitch.

Ed bolted up, unlocked the knob, jerked open the door, stepped outside.

Nancy stepped back, seemed about to lose her blance.

"Ed! What the fuck!" Her eyes zeroed in below his face, to his side…

Because he was holding Hank's gun. He'd forgotten it was in his left hand.

"It's okay," he tried to reassure them.

"Ugghhh!" Hank bellowed loud as a moose, advertised pain and fear. Beyond Nancy and Bill, other crew members in dirt and soot-crusted yellow Nomex shirts paused from their preparations, stared toward Ed.

"What the hell's going on here?" demanded Nancy.

"He's a PUMA. This is a PUMA cabin." Ed engaged the pistol's safety, stuffed it behind him inside the waistband of his pants.

"Who's in there?" She would leave their relationship in the bud. He could see it in her eyes. They didn't look at him like he was Ed, like a man she loved, like anyone she recognized at all.

"His name is Henry Baker. I just found out today and I came here and I know I shouldn't have. He showed up, and he'd have shot me if I didn't stop him."

"Are you fucking crazy?"

Before he could answer she whirled toward the crew. "Hold up!" she called, then turned with furious eyes back at Ed.

"There was no one here," he said. "No one had been here in years. And all of a sudden, he drove right up."

"What did I tell you about poking your fucking head where it's not supposed to be?"

"I know, I know."

"Ugghhh!"

"Is that your gun?"

"It's his."

She gestured toward the door. "I want to see him."

Ed didn't move. "It's—"

"Now."

"You wouldn't—"

"Damnit, Ed, open the fucking door before we throw you out of the way and do it ourselves."

Ed turned, opened the door, stepped back into the dark and rancid interior, moved to the side so Nancy could see what she demanded to see. The cabin was so small that she could have reached Hank in two steps if she wanted.

Nancy gaped at Hank's mangled face. Revulsion…rage…what was in her face? It didn't matter. Their relationship was finished.

"All I had was a frying pan. He had a gun."

"He's crazy," slurred Hank through his open mouth.

"No. I've got it all on my phone. He confessed. You bastard. You killed my son."

"Crazy."

"Fuck you, you lying sonuva—"

"Enough." said Nancy. "Back outside." At the foot of the steps, she took the radio from its holster. "Strike Team, this is Avila with the Snoqualmie Hotshots. We need law enforcement ASAP. Two males on the premises, one tied to a woodstove with his face beat all to hell, the other claiming the one tied up is part of that PUMA militia gang."

"Avila, this is Watkins," someone from the other end replied. "Are you safe?"

"Ugghhh!"

Hank's yell was primal. A warrior's yell.

"What the hell was that?" asked Watkins.

"We're safe," said Nancy.

"We'll get people there as quick as we can."

"Copy. Paramedics, too. We've got fire coming at us. It's defensible but we could use an engine."

"Copy that. An engine you shall have. Probably faster than law enforcement."

Nancy turned to Bill. "No saws. Hand tools. Cut the grass twenty feet wide at the edge of the forest, then burn out. Safety zone's this parking area. Have someone move the trucks over to the far side away from where the fire will hit and point them toward the road."

"Got it," he said. He hesitated.

"What do you need?" she asked.

"What are you going to do?" He gestured toward Ed. His eyes, too, regarded Ed as a stranger, a criminal, someone to avoid. And yet, he'd known Ed almost as long as Nancy had.

"I'll handle Kline."

Kline. No longer Ed. Even while adrenalin continued racing through his veins, his heart sank.

"There's a bunch of garden hose in that pickup," he said, "and a faucet's out back."

Bill looked toward Nancy.

"Yeah, go ahead," she said.

Bill walked back to the waiting crew, their postures wary at the sight of Ed, the helitack pilot who'd been kicked off their shared base at Snoqualmie Pass.

"Ugghhh." The noise from inside the cabin could not have been reassuring.

Staccato pops snapped across the sky. Ed half-ducked, jumped back a step. But Hank didn't have the gun. Ed did. They looked southwest to the woods, the true source of the shots, the sound of pine pitch exploding in flames approaching 2,000 degrees Fahrenheit. Through the turbulent smoke rising above the trees, they felt the fire's thrust. A vanguard of glowing cinders among flakes of ash blew at them.

She turned her eyes back at Ed.

"Did he hurt you?"

"I got him before he got me. He fired off a couple of shots, but I was on him and he couldn't really aim. My arm hurts like hell and so does my hand."

"I can't deal with this. It's too much."

"I could have killed him. He admitted killing Lewis. I had his gun and I put it right against his head, but I didn't shoot."

"I don't even know you. Why didn't you call the police?"

"I did. But I got here before them. And I didn't know he'd show up. But I'm the same. I went by the book. I didn't shoot him."

Already, hotshot crewmen had advanced to the edge of the forest. In a single line, they cut divots of grass, tossed them with shovels and McLeods into the green, away from the trees and the fire within. Bill walked past them, dragging a hundred feet of garden hose.

"I've got a crew to run. You stay here and—"

Tires skidding on dirt and gravel pulled their attention toward the driveway. A moss green Voyager van slid to a stop on the downward slant, its front end off the driveway, a foot short of smashing into a tree. The driver reversed onto the path, gunned it to the flat.

"Get the fuck away from here," Ed muttered. "Get your crew out of the way but don't make it obvious. That van's got PUMAs in it."

"How do you—"

"Get away. Contact fire camp."

"You, too, Ed," she whispered. "Go with me." Whatever she'd been feeling up to that point, now her eyes showed fear.

"No. I'll take them. Get your people out of here."

Keeping her eyes on him as though to fix him in her memory, she stepped back before turning and marching through the smoke toward her crew, just as the van slammed to stop next to Hank's pickup, five feet directly in front of Ed.

Chapter Thirty-seven

The driver turned off the engine and for a moment he and his passenger and Ed eyed each other. They both looked young, the driver low in his seat with crew-cut ink-black hair and Latino features and the other with a buzz cut and narrow face with a tapered chin.

"Ugghhh!"

The good thing about smoke was that the men in the van had their windows rolled up. Maybe they hadn't heard Hank, but that wouldn't last long. Perhaps, thought Ed, he should have shot Hank through the vocal cords. He put on a smile, stepped to the driver's side.

"Howdy, guys," he said as the driver lowered the window. Both occupants declined to return the greeting, opting instead to harden their stares. They sat in bucket seats, the driver's hands both on the steering wheel, the passenger with his left hand on the arm rest but his right one concealed near his door.

"How'd you manage to get through?" Ed asked.

"Logging road."

"You must be here to help Mr. Baker."

Puzzlement flitted and disappeared from the driver's eyes. Ed moved his good arm—not the one he'd normally use for the purpose he anticipated—to the pistol handle tucked behind his pants.

"The one that owns the cabin," Ed offered.

"Yeah, that's right," said the passenger.

"Ugghhh!"

"What's that?"

Ed whirled the pistol at the men while moving back one step.

"Freeze!" he commanded. But the passenger twisted rapidly toward him.

Ed fired and missed, spider-webbed the side window as the passenger spun toward him with a gun in his hand and the driver thrust his head back against his seat. Ed aimed again just as the other gun barrel's horizontal arc neared his chest. He fired, winced in anticipation of the other man's shot, but it never came. The man's head slammed against the window and a dark fluid splatted onto the cracked glass.

Ed blunted the split-second horror, pointed the pistol at the driver's head.

"Don't move."

The driver kept his head back against the seat, his eyes wide in terror. Beyond the van across the clearing, the hotshot crew had fled, leaving behind a line of sod.

With Hank's gun pointed at the driver, Ed used his other hand to open the driver's door, then stepped back.

"Show me your hands."

The man complied.

"Get out."

The man complied.

"Hands in the air and turn away from me."

Ed jammed the barrel between the man's shoulder blades, patted his body for a weapon. Baker had stopped making noises. Perhaps he recognized Ed as the voice that prevailed.

"Where's your gun?"

"Don't have one."

"If I look in your truck and find out you're lying, I promise you I'll kill you."

"Under the seat."

"Good boy. We'll leave it there for now. We're going to walk very slowly toward the woods on the fire side of the clearing and if you keep being good boy I won't kill you."

Smoke-choked wind clogged Ed's lungs. His eyes stung. Tears formed. It was hard to breathe.

"What the fuck is this?" said the man after a half dozen steps.

"Shut up, PUMA boy. Walk."

The man coughed a smoker's cough, but he kept walking.

When they neared the edge of the grass next to the bare dirt the hotshots had exposed, Ed told the man to stop. A roar like a train and spattering snaps reverberated somewhere behind the smoke.

"Fuckin' hot!" cried the man.

"Your left hamstring or your right one." Ed had to shout just to hear his own voice. "The next word you say, you get a bullet. Two words and you'll get two bullets."

He yelled into the woods.

"Nancy! Bill! It's safe now!"

No one answered. No one emerged.

"Nancy! Bill!"

Nothing. Where had she taken them? Were they in the woods, closer to the flames—too close?

"Turn around," he told the man. "We're going to walk back toward the fire crew buses. No talking."

He wondered how long he had until the flames hit.

They reached the dirt parking area. "Sit your ass down and put your hands behind your head," he said. As a safety zone, the parking area was small, less than half a football field in size.

Even though dirt would never burn, the flames surrounding it could get hot enough to fry their lungs.

"You can talk to answer my questions. Understand?"

"Yeh."

"That fire's going to hit any minute. When it does, it'll slam right across all that dried grass and eat that cabin for lunch with your buddy inside. Would you like to save him from burning?"

"Yeh."

"He's tied to a wood stove. I fucked up his face with a frying pan so he's not looking real good. I can lead you there and have you untie him and if either you or Baker makes any sudden moves, I'll kill you both. Are you willing to untie him?"

"Yeh."

"I don't know why I should save him. He killed my son. I'm the helitack pilot."

"What are you talking about?"

"Playing stupid, huh? Maybe we can wait here and let Baker fry."

They waited a moment. The man coughed again.

"It's difficult to breathe, isn't it?" said Ed.

"Yeh."

"We can hear the fire before we see it. Can you hear it?"

"Yeh."

"Do you think Baker hears it?"

"Why do you keep calling him Baker? He's not Baker."

"He's not?"

"He's Cap…" The man stopped himself.

"Go on."

The man was silent.

"Whatever his name is, if you want to save the murderer in that cabin, first I need you to tell me the truth. I don't think we have much time. You're a PUMA, aren't you?"

The man was silent.

"Don't be shy. The man in the cabin already told me. Not that he needed to. I already knew, just like I already know about you. We can wait here and watch the flames burn the cabin or we can save him and then watch it burn. I'm Lewis's father. Do you understand why I would feel no remorse in watching the man in the cabin die? That's a question, PUMA boy. Answer it."

"Yeh."

"That's better. Let's get this on the record, shall we?"

He took out the iPhone, pressed the Memo icon.

"Your name please."

"Diego Marquez."

"And you're a PUMA."

Silence.

"Are you a PUMA?"

"Yeh."

"What's PUMA mean?"

"Patriots United Militia of America."

"I think it means murder."

"Means freedom."

"How free is my son? How free are all the people you've killed?"

"We warned them."

"The man inside the cabin. What did you say his name is?"

No answer.

"We can wait."

"Captain White."

"Captain White."

"Yeh."

"Is he a leader?"

No answer.

"That's a helluva a roar coming from those trees."

"Yeh."

"He's a leader?"

"Yeh. Can we go now?"

"Get up."

On the road, multiple engines sounded and a set of brakes squeaked. Still out of sight, they turned onto the driveway. A fucking damn parade, Ed thought. Who's next? If it's more PUMAs he'd get his ass out of there quick, up through the trees toward the road. Maybe that was where, from a less direct route, Nancy took the crew.

A Chelan County sheriff's SUV sped into view, followed by a Wenatchee Police patrol car. Both stopped fifty feet away. Doors opened and officers popped out pointing guns.

"Drop the gun!" one of them shouted.

Ed spread his fingers off the grip for the officers to see, tossed the gun away from the PUMA, raised both arms high.

"On to the ground! On your stomachs."

On the ground Ed kept his head tilted up at the deputies. Two dashed at him, two at the other man, and a knee thrust onto his back. Before anyone could yank his bullet-wounded arm and hand, Ed placed his arms behind his back. Metal gripped his wrists, and the handcuffs clicked tight. The second officer frisked his body for weapons, pulled out pants pockets, emptied the contents.

"The phone's on voice recorder," one of them said.

"Turn it off," said the other.

"There's a man in the cabin," said Ed. "He's dangerous."

"Is he armed?"

"No. That gun I threw down—it's his. He's tied to the

wood stove. He's a PUMA—you know who they are?"

"Sergeant Rawlins, you need to see this." Ed turned his head toward that voice, saw one of the Wenatchee police officers peering into the van.

The man standing next to Ed walked to the Voyager, looked in, then looked back toward Ed.

"I did it," said Ed. "You'll find he had a gun. He pulled it on me so I had to do it."

"Crazy motherfucker," said the man who called himself Marquez.

"He's a PUMA, too," said Ed.

"Bullshit."

"He's recorded on my phone admitting it."

"You had a gun pointed at me. What was I supposed to say?"

"Shut up, both of you," said Rawlins.

Another deputy, still behind the open door of the sheriff's SUV, called toward them. "Sergeant Rawlins."

"Yeah."

"Fire people say the road's cut off. Fire's on both sides of the road both directions. Torched somebody's pickup. We're going to get hit any minute."

"Send the hotshot crew back down here and the engine crew, too. Get the aid car in here."

His face sideways in the dirt, Ed suppressed a sob. Nancy was safe.

Two officers went into the cabin. The deputy watching Ed stepped into his line of vision, opened Ed's wallet.

"Edward Kline?"

"Yeah."

"The helitack pilot."

"Yeah."

In a couple of minutes the officers exited the cabin, Baker handcuffed in front of them, his mouth contorted open, coagulated blood pasted across the lower part of his face and forming a dark dripping pattern on his shirt. As he neared them, Marquez lifted his head.

"PUMAs!" Marquez called the name like it was a football team, but rather than passion, Ed detected fear in the young man's eyes, fixed and following Baker's enfeebled steps. Baker gazed forward. Maimed and bloody, he bore himself as a soldier.

"PUMAs!"

This second call demanded Baker's attention. While the policemen prodded him forward he turned and looked down at Marquez.

"Ee quieuh," he said.

Marquez looked puzzled as Baker marched past.

"Shuh uh."

"Shut up," said one of the policemen.

Hank Baker wouldn't be narrating any videos for a while. That, at least, gave Ed a small satisfaction.

An old red fire engine groaned down the driveway, across the dirt clearing to the grass at the edge of the woods where smoke continued billowing at a slant with the wind. Pops behind the smoke announced imminent flames. The sound of boots prompted Ed to turn his head toward the driveway.

With Nancy in the lead holding a shovel, a line of hotshots hustled past them toward the line they'd begun cutting before a peril different than the burning kind pushed them into retreat. A paramedic van came down the driveway and parked near the police cruiser. Ed realized all these forces had been waiting on the road above them while fire had cut their exits both directions. Now they were all gathered on Hank's property.

Law enforcement and paramedics joined the prisoners as spectators trapped in a small arena while the firefighters labored against a racing horde of flame. The hotshots made quick work turning up dirt the full length of the woods at the same time the engine crew laid out hose and started their pump. He could see Nancy say something to Bill, and then the hotshots split into two groups, one remaining next to the woods and the other against the hillside below the road.

In both groups, crew members removed fusees from their firepacks, struck the flare-like sticks, lit the grasses at the edge of the woods. Flames jumped off the ground, gobbled scraggly willows and vine maple, leaped to the pines, ziplined straight up the bark as though pulled by a magnet. Crowns burst into fiery balls, spinning and roiling, blowing out chunks of wood against the backdrop of black smoke.

Flames launched fifty feet above the trees, bent improbably against the wind. Somewhere back in the forest, the main fire sucked at the one lit by humans, pulled the flaming gyroscope of hell into the wind back at itself. When the two fires met, a fireball loud as a rocket exploded above the trees, heated the underside of heaven itself.

Nancy gave a nod to someone at the fire engine, and its crew opened up the water, dousing the main edge of fire with one length of hose and doing the same at the far east end behind the house where a finger of fire raced on ahead toward Wenatchee fifteen miles away. More fire swept close and raced through the woods above them between their position and the road, and the heat of it drew a new batch of sweat from Ed's inner reserves.

For a long time they waited, a half hour, an hour, Ed was not sure how much time had passed, ninety minutes and more. They let him pee when he asked and sometime during the interval they allowed him and the other two off their bellies to sit on the dirt. No one asked questions. The firefighters busied themselves mopping up flames at the edge of the clearing. The paramedics did what they could with Baker's head and face. Black smoke thinned, revealing a charred forest full of smaller blazes with tendrils of slate-colored smoke and a sky bleached white.

Finally, someone must have given the all-clear, because they put Baker with two deputies in the aid car, Marquez in the back of the police car, and Ed into the back seat of the SUV. They drove slowly down the road several miles blackened on both sides with occasional engine crews hosing flames until they reached untouched vegetation where the fire turned west.

Chapter Thirty-eight

Knees bent, Ed lay on his back on a concrete bench, stared at the pastel green concrete block wall, away from the caged lightbulb glaring in the middle of the holding cell. An overabundance of bleach and chemically scrubbed surfaces failed to mask the odor of sweat and the rodent excrement wafting from him in the broiling cell.

He turned his head, looked through the bars across the small booking room. On the other side of a Plexiglas barrier, a disinterested middle-aged woman peered at a computer screen or security monitor or whatever it was. Probably playing solitaire. Probably had air conditioning, too. Past his feet on the other side of a three-foot high concrete partition, a stainless steel toilet-sink unit sat center-stage, a monument to his confinement. Over the course of a week, he wondered, how many men had that lady seen from the waist up while they urinated?

With no cell phone, no watch, nothing in his pockets, he had no way to determine how long he'd been in the holding cell, but it seemed nobody worried about time or when they'd get around to telling him what came next. He made himself rise, trudged to the toilet-sink unit, pressed dribbles of water from the faucet, smeared it on his face and beneath his shirt at the armpits, but all he accomplished was a temporary liquid essence to the rank smell. His body forced him to account for the abuse of its capacity—his arm and his hand in a full rebellion of pain, his lower back throbbing as though hammered with a wedge, his empty stomach burbling up bile.

But Hank was suffering even more, and that gave Ed a little satisfaction.

He sat and waited. He'd stay confined until he died if he could have Lewis back, if he could know that outside this imprisonment, his son lived and grew and learned and flourished. If the others could have their lives back, especially Rosario so she could bake cupcakes for her children's birthdays into perpetuity, he'd confess to murder and take the blame for all of it. He'd had a good life. Let the young people have theirs.

But the image of Lewis's last moment assaulted his mind, emphasized a gruesome finality. Where was Lewis now? Ed rarely considered existence beyond his last breath, but now that his son was gone he began to hope that Lewis was not completely obliterated. From whatever dimension he occupied, could Lewis perceive his father had bested his killer?

Do you know, Lewis? I've avenged you.

Would Lewis forgive him, if he knew what Ed had done on his behalf? Or had he forgiven Ed the whole time?

And Ed wondered: when would he forgive himself? Should he?

Others still lived. Nancy and Sarah. What would Sarah think when she learned her father had killed a man and disfigured another, even if both were scum? Hank—scum. One of the few good friends he'd ever had. If Hank evolved to feel regret, he'd live locked up to brood upon his sins, and every shackled breath would punish him more than death. Never in his craziest dreams did Ed envision that the next time Sarah looked at him she'd be looking at a father who had killed. She might approve of the reason why, but something would change between them.

He'd forever altered the bond he had with the living, hadn't he?

And that same bond, tied so intimately with Nancy—had it unraveled? Her knowledge of his capacity for violence surpassed theoretical. She'd seen his handiwork sculpted on Hank's face, saw him wielding a gun, probably heard the gunshots. She showed him no recognition as she marched by him on the way to the flames after the deputies retrieved her crew. He had as much of a chance of keeping her as the Mariners did of winning the World Series.

At last a pair of deputies entered, one holding on outstretched arms bright yellow clothing with a small travel-sized bar of soap and a rag. They waited outside the bars while he cleaned himself and changed into his Chelan County Inmate uniform. They used rubber gloves to remove his old clothes. After handcuffing him again, they brought him out to the small room beyond his cell, where they took his mug shot, obtained fingerprints, asked him basic questions such as address, date of birth, and so forth, even though they already had his wallet and identification. He used his one phone call to leave a message with Suzuki, whom he assumed already knew where he had landed. No doubt the man had other priorities at the moment.

"What are the charges against me?" he asked.

"That will be the prosecutor's call," answered the oldest deputy, gray-haired with small eyes recessed behind thick brows.

"When will I know?"

"Within seventy-two hours of your arrest."

They escorted him to an elevator and brought him to the real jail, a skinny corridor of cells sealed from the world by an iron door with a Plexiglas window.

His cell featured two plastic slabs, each topped by a thin

mattress, embedded like bunk beds into a concrete wall. Only two steps away on the other side of the cell was a steel toilet-sink unit.

Seated on the top plank with his feet draped over the side, his roomie was young enough to be his son. He was medium-sized with butch-cut brown hair and a fleshy nose that looked as though it may have encountered a concrete wall at full speed. One forearm graced a Virgin of Guadalupe tattoo while the other one featured a human skull smoking a doobie.

"Hey, gramps," his roomie said. "You bring some drugs?"

"Two packets working through my small intestine. Next time I shit, we'll have a party."

"No shit?"

"Yes, shit. *No shit* means no party."

"Ha ha!"

Ed sat on the floor, leaned against a wall. Even with the pain, he felt as though he could fall asleep if not for the haunting footage of the day that kept looping through his mind.

"What you here for?" asked his roomie.

"They haven't told me yet."

"What you do?"

Ed recalled news accounts of prisoners ratting on other prisoners, not that he had anything to hide.

"Took care of some business," he said.

"Yeah riiiight. So you in manufacturing or selling?"

"Neither."

"So what's your gig, gramps? You here for something."

"You really want to know?"

"Nobody got any secrets here."

"All right. I'll tell you what they'll probably *say* I did. I'm not saying I did any of it. Breaking and entering. Then the stupid owner showed up, so there's felony assault and battery and then false imprisonment after that. Then a couple of his friends showed up, so now you've got murder and another false imprisonment. Brandishing a firearm."

"Hooo-weee, you a badass gramps."

"Just answering your question. What about you?"

"Meth."

"Better quit that stuff."

"I prob'ly should. Fucked me up pretty good. They haven't decided what to do with me yet. They gonna send you to the big house, you know that?"

"No, they'll let me go."

"Bullshit. They gonna strap you down and shoot you up with strychnine. Sweet dreams and no bedtime story."

"You wait and see."

"You fuckin' crazy."

"That's right."

"They ain't gonna let you go."

"Haven't you heard? It's not what you know. It's who you know."

"Bullshit."

"Have a little faith."

"You the crown prince of Wenatchee? You diddling the mayor's missus? Or more like his grandma?"

"Connections. That's all I'm saying."

The man shook his head, then lay on his back.

"They give me a champion bull-shitter," he said to the ceiling.

Up and down both sides of the corridor of cells, voices chattered, punctuated by guffaws and amplified by concrete acoustics. Ed recalled reading about cases like his. Individuals who'd killed some despicable character, someone who'd raped a daughter or sodomized a kid. They ended up in prison despite the favor they'd done society.

Vigilantes.

He wasn't a vigilante, was he? He just happened to be in the wrong place at the wrong time. Kill or be killed. They were PUMAs.

Maybe they'd put Hank and him in the same prison. They'd decide they needed to make an example of him. Don't try this at home, kids. Maybe his roomie was right. Bull-shitter.

After what seemed like a couple of hours, the guards let them out two cells at a time, walked them to a dining room, its decor consistent with the rest of the facility—steel round tables with three steel seats, each unit bolted into the cement floor. Dinner consisted of a peanut butter and grape jelly sandwich, a small bag of tortilla chips, three lemon-sugar cookies, and individual juice punches, overseen by armed stewards who did not ask how they liked their meal.

"They give us dinner at lunch," said his roomie. "Today was chicken chunks puked in gravy."

"You should join the army if they let you," said Ed. "You heard of MREs?"

"Naw."

"Meals Ready to Excrete. Wild turkey surprise. Hockey pucks."

"Fuck, I'd take that. I'd eat a football. It would have more meat than what they give us here."

Two hours later a guard appeared outside Ed's cell.

"You've got a visitor," he said.

The guard brought him to one of those rooms with a table, the kind that on television always had a two-way mirror and a couple of detectives listening from outside. Suzuki was there with half-closed eyes, wearing a tie and rumpled blue shirt, and a deputy stood by the door.

"I can't get you out of here," Suzuki said after they sat down.

"Okay."

"The county has your case. The initial charge includes murder but that doesn't mean they're going to arraign you for that or for anything. They have seventy-two hours to make up their minds. It's up to the prosecutor to decide."

"What have you found out? Did you hear about my iPhone recordings?"

"Yes. And we've listened to it. And one of them's talking. Admits he's PUMA, happy to brag about attacks they've already made, says nothing about what's ahead. Says wherever they were, they'd be gone by now. Says they've got properties but he doesn't know where they are except the one where we...I should say *you*...captured him. We wouldn't have been able to investigate that property, not with a wildfire burning around it and restrictions in place. But we did obtain a search warrant. We were going to go in as soon as the situation allowed it. But they'd have been gone by then."

"Okay."

"Their presence would have been a danger to the fire crews, but they'd have probably kept their mouths shut and no one would have known who they were. You're the reason we have them in custody, Mr. Kline. I know this has been a terrible time for you, but at least you have that."

"You catch the part where Marquez says Baker is a leader?"

"Yes. Would you like a lawyer, Mr. Kline? Because I'm about to ask you to tell me what happened. I can come back tomorrow if you want a lawyer present. I'm told you've been read your rights—do you recall the individual elements of it?"

"Yeah. And no, I don't need a lawyer. I'll tell you the whole thing."

"Including the part about how anything you say can be used against you in a court of law?"

"Like to see the prosecutor who'd bring charges. Like to see the jury that'd convict me."

"I happen to agree with you, Mr. Kline, but remember, I'm not in control of those decisions."

"I could have blown him away. Had him tied up. Had his gun right in my hand. Boom! There goes the fucker who killed my son. Thought about doing it. But I didn't. Let him face his victims. Turn his ass over to the government he hates."

Suzuki took a voice recorder from his briefcase and set it on the table. "Let's start from the beginning. This morning when I called you—it appears you were not on your way to church."

"Hey, Kline."

Was it daylight? Where was he?

Oh. Jail. Lights on all night. He remembered thinking he'd never get any sleep.

"Yeah."

"You're out of here."

"No fuckin' way!" called the man on the top bunk.

"What'd I tell you?" said Ed.

He rolled out the bottom bunk. His back felt as though clamped in a vise, and his hand and arm felt like it did the day after they shot him. Dr. Cisneros was not going to be pleased.

"Get outa here, gramps. Kill a dude and they let you out. Do meth—they throw away the key."

"Remember to quit that shit."

"Speakin' of shit—you leave me anything?"

"Aw hell, I flushed it."

The deputy held the jail door open.

"What time is it, sir?" he asked.

"One a.m."

In the booking room they told him they were releasing him on his own recognizance. He had to sign a paper promising to remain in the county of his residence, maintain contact with the court, and to comply with a handwritten statement that he would "Cease all activity to locate and apprehend members of the Patriots United Militia of America." They gave him Levis too small so that he couldn't snap the top snap and a white shirt so big it might as well have been a muumuu.

"Can't keep a hero locked up," said the deputy processing him out. "Sheriff says to let you go, judge says no bail. You're all over the news. Helitack pilot captures militia leader."

"They killed my son. Fuck all that other shit. I want my son back."

"I'm with you, Kline. You'd better get ready. We cleared the media out of the lobby, but they're waiting outside. They know we're letting you out. Your daughter's Sarah?"

"Yeah."

"She's waiting for you. Says she'll take you home. I'll go out with you, help you get to her vehicle."

"Do I have to say anything?"

"What do you mean?"

"To those jackals out there."

"Lot of people fantasize about doing what you did. All the families of all the victims. Now think about all the additional victims those three PUMAs won't be able to create because they're in custody or dead. I know you'd trade it all for your kid. I know it's not a happy day for you. But it is for a lot of other people."

"Do you happen to know about a pickup that burned up on that fire?" he asked the deputy. "I had a pickup parked about a half mile from the Baker cabin off the main road on the other side. I'd like to know if the one that burned was mine."

The deputy said he'd check, wrote his work cell phone on a business card and gave it to Ed.

Sarah, wearing a plain lime green blouse and blue jeans, popped up from a chair as soon as he entered the lobby. Her tight hug launched a shot of pain up his arm and around his neck, and when he gasped, she let go. Camera flashes from outside the windows prickled his eyes. High powered flood lights lit the heads and shoulders of a human herd as well as the backs of two deputies with trooper hats standing in front of the doors. But they were quiet.

"How'd you get in here?" he asked.

"When I heard the news, I tried to call and the line was always busy. Finally I left and on the way, an Agent Suzuki who said he was from the FBI called and told me he'd meet me and help us."

"He's a good man."

He looked at the booking deputy. Flashes continued peppering his eyes.

"Officer, could you please go ahead of us and tell them I won't have anything to say? Tell them I need some rest, and I'll make a statement later."

They waited a minute after the deputy left, then braced themselves as they stepped out into the crowd. But it was quiet. Flashes blinked and camcorders panned, but nobody barked questions or called his name. Whatever the deputy had said, it subdued the entire group into something that felt like respect. No one trailed them as they cleared the group, and they left on the silent nighttime streets.

"They know where I live," he said. "There was a place I was staying, but I don't know if I can stay there anymore."

"My place, then," she said. At the next traffic light half glowing through the fog of smoke, she did a U-turn, pointed them west.

Out of town, smoke mist hovered among spectral orchards. Sarah slowed and turned into the vacant parking lot of a farm machinery business.

"Everything okay?" he asked.

"Just need some air," she said.

They stepped into the warm night, the stillness of it eerie after a wind tunnel day. Across the road hovering over the silhouette of a long mountain ridge, a pale red dome of fire curved beneath the stars. He walked to the front of the car where she stood, saw her tears glisten in the parking lot lights.

"Honey." He hugged her and she pressed her face to his shoulder. He had created this, too, the tears of the living, the tears of his daughter.

"I'm sorry," he said.

For a long time she didn't say anything, but eventually she backed away from his embrace, her eyes still moist.

"One brother's enough," she said. "And stop blaming yourself. I know you blame yourself. I know my father."

A breath came out from deep in his lungs and he felt his eyes water and he couldn't speak.

"I'm sorry," he finally managed to repeat.

"Stop it," she said. "Stop the sorry. We know. We're sorry, too, and we love you, and we don't want to lose you."

She cried again. She let him hold her and when they recovered they finished the drive to her apartment.

Chapter Thirty-nine

They arrived at Sarah's a little past 4 a.m. She went straight to bed while he took a hot shower and stuffed his ill-fitting clothes into the washing machine. In the morning with less than two hours sleep, she left in her brown UPS uniform while Ed remained wearing her maroon plush bathrobe, his jeans and shirt tumbling in the dryer. He called Nancy's cellphone, not surprised when it led to her voice mail.

"I hope you'll call me," he said.

She probably had her phone turned off. They'd already be on shift, either still protecting structures or hoofing inaccessible terrain where engines and bulldozers could never penetrate. He had no message from her. Did she have access to the news? Or did she know only what she'd seen and heard at the cabin?

Next he tried Suzuki, reached him directly, thanked him for helping Sarah transport him from jail.

"They made me promise not to go looking for PUMAs," he said.

"I had them put that clause into the release."

"Why does that not surprise me? But the truth is I don't want any part of it anymore."

"I'm glad to hear that. I'd hate to see you back in jail."

"Couldn't do it if I wanted to, which I don't. Don't have any wheels."

"I heard about your truck."

"Yeah? What'd you hear?"

"It's a charred metal shell."

"Shit."

"Sorry, Mr. Kline. I thought you knew."

"I heard about a pickup, but I wasn't sure it was mine. It's on me. I put it there."

He asked Suzuki about the reporters, said he didn't want to endanger the investigation. Suzuki said the press knew only basic facts—someone had been killed, they'd arrested and released Ed, and they held two others they suspected of connections to the PUMAs, one of them named Henry Baker. Reports credited Ed with capturing them, but Suzuki didn't know how they obtained that information. The FBI and the Chelan County Sheriff's Office were collaborating to deliver a press conference later at 9 a.m.

"They know where the cabin is, heard it from the police scanners. That's how they found the name Henry Baker. For the moment, we've got the excuse of a wildfire to restrict air space but there's a whole convoy parked at the barriers waiting for fire officials to open the road."

"They were there last night when I left jail, but one of the deputies said something to them, I don't know what, and they left me alone, took pictures and video is all. Part of what the deputy told them I do know. That I'd release a statement today. I think that's one reason they didn't hound me when I left. What if I sent it to you? Could you get it to the folks at the conference?"

"I'd like to, Mr. Kline, but the FBI can't be seen as advocating your position, not while criminal charges are still pending."

"Oh. Yeah, I can see that. Don't suppose you can tell me

not to speak with reporters?"

"You're right. I can't. You have a civil right. What I can tell you is that it would be best for the investigation if you did not share particulars about what happened."

"That works for me. I've just been advised not to discuss what happened. Don't need to say who advised me. But there is something I want them to know. Nothing would have happened without Lewis. I want to clear his name. They don't know how I ended up at the cabin in the first place, do they?"

"I haven't heard anything to indicate they do. I anticipate they'll want to know, but I don't know what we're going to tell them."

"I should call the sheriff's office. Part of the agreement was that I'd stay in Kittitas County, but without wheels I'd be stuck at my place fifteen miles from the nearest store, reporters like a bee swarm."

"What about Ms. Avila?"

"Don't know if that's an option. I'll send the press something, something by e-mail. Don't want them to have my cell phone number, that's for sure. I'll look up the *Seattle Times*, and I'll send them something vanilla. I won't mention the video or codes. I won't give them shit. Just *thanks for the concern.* Look forward to justice. Can't share details yet, will let you know when I can. Sound okay?"

"Yes. And thank you for your discretion."

"Like to see you catch the rest of those bastards."

"Andrews here." But Ed already knew it was Jim Andrews, the man who fired him weeks ago. That's why he picked up the phone. Six days after his release from jail, the reporters had stopped visiting.

"Yeah."

"Saw how you took out those PUMA bastards."

"Yeah."

"So what the hell you doing on medical leave?"

"You put me on it."

"From what I heard about how you kicked those fuckers' asses, looks like you could wrestle a cyclic stick and a collective."

"Probably."

"Probably my ass. I saw that photo of Baker's face. He's a big sonuvabitch."

"I pissed off my doctor." Ed recalled Cisneros shaking her head, sending him for an examination in Yakima. He looked at the bandaging wrapped around his hand.

"Doctors are always pissed. Them and lawyers. They want you sitting in your recliner, strapped with a seatbelt. Salads only and a hundred-page manual how to eat it."

"Yeah."

"I'm putting you back to work. You okay?"

"Yeah, I'm fine. Well, maybe not all the way yet. I fucked up my hand again."

"What'd you do?"

"Baker."

"So?"

Ed rose from his chair, walked to the window, looked out over the trees into the sweltering sky. Where he wanted to be.

"Doctor says not to grip anything for a while. Says another surgery probably won't work."

"How long's a while?"

Eight weeks, the surgeon had said.

"Six weeks," said Ed.

"Puts us in...oh, end of September."

"End of fire season."

"You know damn well fire season never ends when it's supposed to anymore. What is it, 200,000 acres up near Chelan right now?"

Where Nancy was.

"Yeah."

"Down here we got 140,000 acres in the Stanislaus, another 100,000 in the Los Padres. We could bring you down here, work you through November at least."

"Don't want to go down there."

"Mark your calendar, Ed. October first, Snoqualmie Pass. That's when and where we're putting you back to work."

"I'll be ready."

"Good to have you back."

"Didn't think you wanted me anymore."

"That was never from me."

Rain—three days of it. Wearing light jackets, Ed and Nancy stood under the metal roof overhang, stared across the puddled dirt to the pad where the replacement helicopter glistened in the gray gloom. An overhauled Sikorsky S-61, she wore an ugly-ass yellow across her top and bottom, striped with white across her midsection along the passenger windows. Tomorrow he'd lift into the rain, point south, start the two-day hop to Fresno, where *Louise*—that was the new moniker for his bird—would hibernate for the winter.

What he'd come back to, he didn't know.

They'd hardly had time, he and Nancy, their lives run by the whims of the big Chelan Complex and lesser fires in the

Gifford-Pinchot and the Okanogan. Even the Olympics burned, although they hadn't joined the fight there.

And when they did have time…

He recalled Sunday a week ago, raining mist, the first time they'd ended a work week on base since before the PUMAs upended their lives. At quitting time, he lingered near the doorway out to the parking lot, the rendezvous point from which for two seasons they'd drifted to the Alpine Diner and joked and joshed. Where they'd grown close.

She stayed inside her office that day. An hour went by. Ed grew tired of waiting and he went home alone.

Now today, the end of fire season, the helitack crew and the hotshot crew had all left, even the ones who slept in the barracks. This time Nancy didn't hide in her office. They stood a hand-hold apart, water streaming a curtain off the roof a foot from their eyes. A trio of crows bounced in the mud, rose halfway up a hemlock, floated back down again.

"Meet you at the Alpine?" He kept his gaze on Louise. A light fog pronounced their breaths.

"Been meaning to tell you about my neighbor," she said.

"Yeah?"

"Hypothetical."

"Okay."

"This neighbor, he's an ornery bastard. Plays his music loud. Cusses his wife. Lets his dog crap in my yard. Police say it's not enough to do anything. Want us to talk it out but that asshole doesn't care."

She paused. He could feel dampness cling to the thighs of his jeans, cold sneak through to his toes. Odd how seasons changed so rapidly.

"If you were in my shoes, what would you do?" she asked.

"I don't know if I would trust me, either."

"No. Don't go there. Let's just talk about the neighbor."

"I know what you're saying. Am I going over there with a hatchet? Not very hypothetical, is it? Not in our case."

She did not reply.

"In your shoes you don't know me. You wonder, *what's he going to do if we have an argument?* I don't blame you for wondering. Thought I knew myself, too, but obviously I didn't."

The back of her hand brushed against his. He reached for the gaps between her fingers, and their hands entwined, a warmth in the rain. He thought if he looked at her he'd see her holding back emotions, the way he held back his own.

"I'd go to my separate corner, and I'd wait and would never say or do anything to tear you down or tear down what's between us; and when enough time went by I'd go to you, and if you'd let me I'd hold you and tell you how much I love you and I'm sorry for all the ugliness you had to see when I was trying to get my son and—"

She squeezed his fingers, enough to remind him how strong she was, and he was thankful it was his good hand.

"Let's go home," she said.

About the Author

Rick E. George writes suspense with substance. *Vengeance Burns Hot* is his debut novel Another novel, *Cooper's Loot,* is forthcoming by The Wild Rose Press. He has been a sports writer, a wildland firefighter, and an educator. He lives with his wife April in the Cascade Mountains of Washington state.

You can learn more and stay connected with Rick E. George at www.rickegeorge.com.

About The Press

Unsolicited Press is a small publishing house in Portland, Oregon specializing in fiction, poetry, and creative nonfiction.

Learn more at www.unsolicitedpress.com

CPSIA information can be obtained
at www.ICGtesting.com
Printed in the USA
FSHW021318170619
59135FS

9 781947 021914